PRAISE FOR SUE HUBBARD

'[Hubbard] has the precision, the respect for words and pain, of a poet'

John Berger

'Beautifully written and wholly knowledgeable… a triumph of literary and artistic understanding, a tour de force: masterly, moving… you are the less for not reading it'

Fay Weldon

'Lyrical, highly visual and beautifully observed'

John Burnside

'Haunting, sensuous and at times disturbingly sharp… [Hubbard's] eye – and her touch – are vividly alive to pleasures of surface, as well as to dark depths of anger and melancholy'

Marina Warner

'Generously of life and warmth and technical mastery'

Sebastian Barker

'A writer of genuine talent'

Elaine Feinstein

…ess'

Also By Sue Hubbard

FICTION

Depth of Field

Rothko's Red short stories

Girl in White

POETRY

Everything Begins with the Skin collection

Twenty poems included in *Oxford Poets*

Ghost Station collection

The Idea of Islands poems with drawings by Donald Teskey

The Forgetting and Remembering of Air Collection

ART

Adventures in Art Selected writings from 1990-2010

RAINSONGS

First published in 2018 by Duckworth Overlook

LONDON
30 Calvin Street, London E1 6NW
T: 020 7490 7300
E: info@duckworth-publishers.co.uk
www.ducknet.co.uk
For bulk and special sales please contact sales@duckworth-publishers.co.uk

British Library Cataloguing in Publication Data. A CIP record for this book can be obtained from the British Library.

Typeset by Danny Lyle
danjlyle@gmail.com

Printed and bound in Great Britain by Clays Ltd, St Ives plc

978-0-7156-5285-5

3 5 7 9 10 8 6 4 2

Sue Hubbard is an art critic, novelist and poet who has contributed regularly to a wide range of publications including the *New Statesman* and *The Independent*, and has also written for *The Sunday Times* and *Observer.* She has contributed to many arts programmes, including *Kaleidoscope* and *Night Waves.*

Twice winner of the London Writers' Award, her poems have been read on BBC Radio 3 and Radio 4 and she is well known for her poem *Eurydice* – London's largest public art poem – which stretches across Waterloo station, made possible by a grant from BFI and The Art's Council. *Rainsongs* is her third novel.

In memory of my parents

'Yes, of course, if it's fine tomorrow,' said Mrs Ramsay. 'But you'll have to be up with the lark.'
Virginia Woolf, *To The Lighthouse*

'What's past help, should be past grief,'
William Shakespeare, *A Winter's Tale*

Is beag an rud is buaine ná an duine:
The smallest of things outlives the human being.
Irish Proverb

RAINSONGS

SUE HUBBARD

Duckworth Overlook

Kerry, AD 520

Twelve men dip their oars in the waves. The sails of their curragh are full. The rowlocks slick. Ten young alders have been felled for timber and eight oxen hides soaked for days in ash-filled water. The yellow fat scraped off with knives, then dressed with sheep tallow and polished smooth with round stones. Wet wood creaks against leather. Yet despite setting out on the feast of Lughnasadh when all is ripe and benign on the land, the weather has turned. The swell is as high as a man. Their woollen cassocks are drenched. Their hands blistered with salt. In the stern the priest prays to spare the boat and save the men. As the narrow vessel plunges through the surf, they sing.

For months they have copied Sacred Gospels onto calfskin and vellum with goose quills using red ochre and green verdigris, yellow orpiment and blue from honey-smelling woad. These are the Holy texts they will live by. When they left the mainland the whole community crowded into the little church for the blessing. After the Mass their brothers filled rush baskets with soda bread and fresh-churned butter. Honey from their hives. Wrapped bees-wax candles and clods of turf in dry sacking, filled tar-stopped pitchers with new-brewed ale. Goat skins with sweet water.

The sea is their desert. None knows if this journey will end in his death or deliverance. These things are not in their hands. Ahead there is nothing but the bone-chilling ocean and, if they are blessed, the face of God. Now they must endure as He endured. May the good Lord keep them safe. Nearly there. Nearly there…

Domine, dirige nos.

Saturday 29th December 2007

1

Brendan is dead. There, she's said it. Out loud, in the empty car. Unlike his lifeless body lying in the floral hospital gown, his face pallid against the dark growth of stubble, the words make it fact. I'm sorry, the weary young doctor said just past midnight. But she hadn't believed him. Coming here forces her to accept her loss. This was always his place. She'd been here with him, of course, but not for a long time. Not since that summer. She's not sure whether she's come back to reclaim or to exorcise him. She grips the steering wheel tighter and the windscreen wipers click backwards and forwards like demented woodpeckers. It's very dark outside. On the brow of a hill she stops at the crossroads to check the map but the roads don't correspond with those on the page and there are no signposts. The locals know where they are. Ahead there's nothing but more rain and four small squares of light twinkling across the glen. Hadn't suicides once been buried at crossroads so the shape of the cross would protect the living from their restless souls? Had that been true here, too, she wonders, given that suicide was a mortal sin in the eyes of the Catholic Church?

In the distance a dog is barking.

She's been going round in circles and twice found herself heading back on the road towards Caherciveen. Squat bungalows, strung along the road, flicker beneath rain-flecked Christmas lights. A Santa plunges in his sleigh across a roof. A blue star flashes above a porch. Illuminations more suited to the end of a pier in a tawdry seaside town than a remote village on the west coast of Ireland. A few miles back she'd got stuck behind a caravan of cars and couldn't work out why there was such a traffic jam in the middle of nowhere on a wet winter's evening. Then she saw them coming out of the pub: the old men in flat tweed caps, a cigarette stub glowing between cupped thumb and forefinger, women in good black coats and gold earrings, girls holding down their short skirts against the boisterous wind. Aunts and uncles, sisters and cousins once removed. Huddled under umbrellas, their clouded breath evaporating in the cold wet air, they chatted before climbing into old vans, BMWs and 4x4s to leave the wake and return, down lanes fringed with barbed wire and deep ditches, home.

The windscreen wipers continue to tick, smearing the beads of rain on the muddy glass when, suddenly, something darts in front of the headlights and she brakes. A small white ferret stops in the middle of the road, stands on its hind legs and sniffs the air. It has bright red eyes and a rat in its mouth. She rubs the misted windscreen with the sleeve of her anorak and winds down the window. A blast of cold air, thick with the stench of fertiliser, hits her in the face. If she concentrates hard enough she might hear the sea. But the only sound is the rain drumming on the car roof. She has no option but to drive on and hope that she remembers the way. There's no one to ask. They'll all be in the pub or watching TV in their new bungalows, a pair of concrete lions guarding the front gate.

And what will she do now that she's here? There's so much to sort out. Brendan came to write. For the rest of the time he let the cottage to friends: artists or academics who needed some peace and quiet. To the few in London who'd enquired, she said she was coming over to Kerry to sort out his affairs. And the truth? Well, she's not sure. Maybe she's simply come back to make sense of all that she was unable to attend to during those thirty odd years, with their brief joys and substantial griefs that turned out to be their lives. And now, here she is, a woman in her mid-50s, driving alone along a rain-swept Irish road at the year's end because she has nothing else to do, and nowhere in particular to go. And because, like everyone else on this earth, she has to be somewhere.

She winds down the window, turns on the heater and sets off again through the driving rain, down the narrow lane, turning up the volume of the piano concerto on Lyric FM. The music fills the car as if she's in a cocoon. Separate from, yet somehow fused with the wet landscape outside. Part of her just wants to go on driving, to keep following the road wherever it leads. To become like an itinerant tinker, hanging her washing on a hawthorn bush. There's something reassuring about not choosing a destination, not having to arrive and make decisions. After another three or four miles she comes to a green phone box and turns sharp left. A patchwork of dry stone walls criss-crosses the bare hill and a bone-faced moon hangs over the headland. Two shaggy ponies stand head to tail by a blackthorn hedge. At the end of the track she stops the car, climbs out, and opens the gate. She's forgotten to bring a torch but the moon is bright enough for her to find the door. It's stopped raining. The sky has cleared. Below the steep cliff the surf pounds against the rocks and above the sky is embroidered with stars. She recognises the Plough but not the other constellations. Brendan would have known. She thinks of that trip to the planetarium. Sitting tipped in the reclining seats between him and Bruno, as if swimming through stars.

Apart from the wind and waves, it's completely quiet. The sea dark as tar and the white crests rolling into the far distance like streaks of light on a negative. This is the end of the world with nothing between her and America except the cold sea. She thinks of those medieval maps in the Vatican that she and Brendan saw in Rome. The known world was so much smaller then and at each parchment corner there'd lurked a monster warning of unimaginable dangers.

She pulls up the hood of her anorak and stands in the wind listening to the breakers. Rome. It had been a reconciliation of sorts. Brendan's book had just come out. A reappraisal of the St Ives group and its importance to Modernism. Nicholson, Hepworth and Gabo, along with the next generation of painters: Patrick Heron, Roger Hilton and Peter

Lanyon. Brendan had argued that, in their own indomitable English way, they were just as significant to the development of Abstract Expressionism as those working in their New York lofts. Just as radical as Jackson Pollock and Willem de Kooning. It took five years and was accompanied by an exhibition at the Hayward. A brave show in a climate more sympathetic to clever videos than to painting rooted in landscape and place. But it got good reviews. And it gave him a lift, a sense of purpose that she envied. He came here for weeks at a time to work on it, valuing the reclusive quiet. With its publication there were invitations to give talks at the Tate and the ICA. To contribute to the odd radio programme. Even before their lives were blown off course he never enjoyed simply being a gallerist. He relished the research, organising loans and tracking down hard-to-locate paintings, sniffing them out from obscure collections like some sort of arty Inspector Poirot. Work was his refuge. He travelled its highways and byways like an excited visitor to another country—leaving her abandoned at the border—creating an alternative reality, in ways that she was unable to do with her GCSE lesson plans and marking. Sometimes it made her angry. When he was working in his study at the top of the house in Myddleton Square, surrounded by catalogues and monographs, she longed to barge in. To ask what right he had to bury himself in all that art, all that stuff, to forget and move on. If she was going to be left clinging to the wreckage, then why shouldn't he? But of course she never did. And, probably, he never knew how she felt.

She's getting cold and feels for the key under the eaves. It's still there on its rusty nail. She opens the door, finds the fuse box, and flips the switch. Everything is just as Brendan left it. The neatly stacked peat and kindling in the willow basket by the stove. The books on Caravaggio and Aboriginal art open on the little wooden stool standing at the end of the battered leather sofa spread with the paisley rug they'd found that first summer in a second-hand shop in Killarney. On the rough wooden shelves, erected years ago from planks balanced on bricks as if he was still a student, are his books on natural history and Celtic folklore, the complete works of Shakespeare and a monograph on Jack B Yeats. A half-drunk bottle of Jameson's whiskey sits on the windowsill next to an arrangement of pebbles and driftwood, a collection of small animal skulls. In the alcove is an earthenware pot filled with stems of dried honesty. The room smells musty. As though filaments of white mycelium were already establishing themselves in the fabric of the building, penetrating the floor boards and rafters, the kitchen cupboards and drawers.

She goes to the wood basket and screws up a yellowing copy of *The Irish Times*, breaks off a fire lighter and places it inside the wigwam of kindling. It flares quickly, before dying back. Bending to blow the fragile flame, she creates a snowstorm of ash on the front of her anorak. Eventually the sparks catch the whiskery strands poking from the clods like the hairs from an old man's ears. Though the place is legally hers she still feels like an intruder. She gets up and goes to the cupboard under the stairs. The light is broken, though she can just make out a brass coal scuttle, a cardboard box full of rope and assorted fishing tackle, a straw hat and some old pots of paint. There's also a child's bucket and spade. She shuts the cupboard quickly and goes into the kitchen to put on the kettle.

On the back of the door are Brendan's battered felt hat, his muddy Burberry and a pair of binoculars in a tattered leather case. She's never seen the binoculars before. As she slips her hand inside the jacket, she realises she has no real idea what her husband did when he came here. In the breast pocket she finds a postcard of the Skelligs photographed at sunset. Its edges foxed and curled with damp.

This chapter has been a bugger. Worked all day then walked down to Cable O'Leary's for a couple of Guinness. Yesterday Eugene came over and whisked me off for a round of golf at his new place near Tralee. That man has the Midas touch. Hope your horrors are behaving and that Titania is proving a bit more co-operative and Bottom has stopped sulking. Don't forget to take the car in for service. The clutch won't last much longer. See you Tuesday week.

Brendan x

She stares at the familiar hand, taken aback by this prosaic message from the dead. There isn't a stamp on the card. Perhaps he'd forgotten to post it or thought better than to send her a picture of the Skelligs. She slips it back in the jacket and goes in search of some matches and puts the aluminium kettle on the stove. There still isn't an electric one. Brendan enjoyed the Boy Scout aspect of making do up here, of hauling in the fuel and the inconvenience of getting down to the shop. When he inherited the place there was no electricity. The first time they came they used Tilley lamps. Then it had seemed romantic. She searches the kitchen cupboards and finds a jar of mouldy Nescafé, an empty packet of Italian coffee and, in the blue and white striped jar marked TEA, some stale Earl Grey tea bags. She should have stocked up properly before she came but apart from a packet of dried pasta, some tins of tomatoes and sardines, a couple of onions and a box of eggs that she'd found in the cupboard at home and shoved in the boot of the car, she hadn't planned any of this.

She'll have to make up the bed but is too exhausted. She throws another turf in the stove, then pulls a pillow and an Aertex blanket from the pine ottoman and huddles on the sofa in her clothes to watch the glow. This will have to do. She's too tired to do anything else. Anyway, she's not sure she wants to sleep upstairs alone. She turns off the table lamp and tugs the fusty covers under her chin. A full moon floods through the small window casting shadows on the whitewashed walls. Yet despite the fire, she can't get warm. The damp seeps into her bones. Lying shivering in the dark, she feels guilty that she let Brendan come back here alone. But that's what he wanted and she was never able to face it. She wonders if he ever came with Sophie? She's glad she doesn't know.

Sophie Bawden had siren eyes. Perhaps if Martha had been a middle-aged man in the midst of a crisis she, too, might have been lured by their sea-green depths. Cliché had matched fact. Twenty years younger than Brendan, Sophie was his editor at Thames & Hudson. Young and ambitious, she'd made a bit of a name for herself with her books on women surrealists. At the height of their affair Martha knew that Brendan had considered jettisoning their marriage and setting up home with Sophie. But somehow, someone—she wasn't sure which of them it was had come to their senses, if sense it was—and Brendan had come back to her, held, no doubt, by something deeper than lust. She knew things were over between him and Sophie when he asked her to join him in Rome. It was as close to an apology as she was likely to get. So she accepted.

Each of them had dealt with grief in a different way. But it isolated rather than drew them close. She couldn't remember how she got through that time. How she coped with his late homecomings, his furtive phone calls, the distance and evasion. Looking back she was, she realises, slightly unhinged. What hurt was that he barely bothered to cover things up. Though he never crowed. It was simply that after all their years together, after all they'd been through, they were leading parallel but disconnected lives. He stayed up late working and made a point of getting up before her or taking a shower after he came home, when he always bathed in the mornings. They never had words. Brendan took out his frustration straightening pictures, switching off unnecessary lights and going round the house turning down the heating. Neither spoke of what was really going on, lurching from day to day in a miasma of denial and indecision. She got through her classes as best she could, hardly remembering at the end of the day what she'd done with her lower sixth. It was as if to have discussed what was happening would unleash some great Leviathan that would have capsized them both. Much of the time she'd no idea who this man was who lived in the same house; flossing his teeth, putting out the kitchen rubbish and sleeping on the other side of the bed. It was as if she was cohabiting with one of those wooden Russian dolls and that her real husband was lurking somewhere inside.

Another glass of wine? he'd say, opening a second bottle, slumped on the sofa in front of Jeremy Paxman on *Newsnight.* Or, have you seen yesterday's *Guardian?* Such perfunctory exchanges were all that they could manage. Yet weren't they simply tokens—proffered, as a colonial explorer might offer suspicious natives worthless glass beads—to prove that the channels of contact, however fragile, remained open?

But what could he have done? Nothing that would have made her feel any better, restored her sanity, erased the realisation when she woke into the drained light of morning from her Prozac-induced sleep that this was, now, her life. That, cry and pray to whom she liked, rail as she might against the gods, she'd have to get up each day, brush her teeth, comb her hair and face this continued, resolute absence.

The fire is dying. She's too tired and cold to sleep in this damp room surrounded by the ocean and endless night. Had she really needed to come back? To come face to face with what she thought was buried, only to find that like sheep bones submerged in the bog, revealed after heavy rain, her memories are resurfacing.

In Rome they'd stayed up by the Villa Giulia near the British School at Rome. The Villa Giulia was one of her favourite places. An ancient country house full of Etruscan artefacts. In the shuttered afternoon heat she stood in front of the glass cases of granulated gold jewellery and Roman glass, relishing the quiet, as the sun beat down outside. Brendan was attentive, like a small boy trying to get back into his parents' good books after a serious misdemeanour. They made love in the carved walnut bed of the guest house with an intensity not experienced since their early days. As if touch might somehow erase what they both wanted to forget. So intimacy amounts to this, she thought, as he rinsed shower gel from his pubic hair and she stood naked in front of the sink, cleaning her teeth. Such moments suggested they'd repaired the rent. Or, at least, patched it over. Romantic love didn't give any clues as to how to deal with things once the whirlwind had passed. But love wasn't fixed, was it? Like the skies above this Irish cottage it was in a constant state of flux.

They sat on the terrace of a small bar overlooking the Tiber drinking Prosecco, then strolled through the busy streets up to the Basilica Santi Quattro Coronati, as Rome made its *passeggiata*. Girls in short sun-dresses flaunted tanned legs, while children in carefully-ironed clothes played tag or sat on the church steps eating ice cream. When they reached the Basilica there was no one else around. Bats flitted in and out of the cloisters as the sun disappeared behind the hill and the tall cypresses turned black against a pink sky. Without a word Brendan slipped his arm through hers and she responded by laying her head on his shoulder, breathing in the scent of his newly showered skin.

It was a small enough gesture. But they both knew what it meant.

2

A beam from the lighthouse sweeps though the tiny fish-eye window, momentarily lighting up the room with ghosts. She has no idea what time it is. She pulls up the covers, wishing that she'd made up a proper bed. Wasn't tragedy supposed to bring people together? Yet even before their lives had been turned inside out like a rubber washing-up glove left on the edge of the sink, Brendan had a tendency to obfuscate. To offer explanations that he thought she wanted to hear rather than the truth. Did all lives run on compromise; on little verities that oiled the wheels? He was charming, of course, got by on his charm; had used it to get into the Courtauld, to woo her father, to build up his art world contacts. But he wore it like a suit of armour. Whether it was a form of emotional cowardice—a way of never making a deep connection, of keeping his options open—she was never sure. He was one of those men who avoided introspection, who preferred to keep things light. There wasn't any obvious reason for this. He'd had a happy enough childhood. His father, Dermot, left Kerry when he was fifteen. Took the boat across to Haverfordwest like so many of his generation. In London he found a job as a porter at the Dorchester. Good looking, with a quiff of raven hair, he had no difficulty getting on and landing an advantageous marriage.

Brendan's maternal grandparents ran a small hotel in Dorset. They were looking for a new manager when Dermot, tired of London, applied for the post and fell in love with their daughter, Rose. My English Rose, he teased her. With her freckled skin and string of seed pearls, she embodied a certain kind of Englishness he thought he wanted. When her parents retired, he and Rose took over the hotel and put in a golf course. In his Val Doonican sweaters, Dermot moved effortlessly among the guests with his soft-spoken charm. There were golf tournaments and the hotel was filled with international stars: Roberto De Vicenzo in his checked trousers and white peaked cap, Dick Mayer who'd won the US Open in 1957. Mayer loved England and came every summer with his wife and girls. Brendan and his younger brother Michael earned pocket money fetching balls from the rough and caddying. The hotel formed the backdrop to their childhood. They played crazy golf with accountants from Croydon, a dentist and his children from Surbiton. Rode their bikes up and down the laurel-fringed drive, and built camps in the sand dunes. And both boys were strong swimmers with that natural ease of children who grew up by the sea.

They also played cricket for their local team. While Rose, in her summer prints, a pastel cardigan draped over her shoulders, made sandwiches and manned the tea urn in the marquee up in the high field. It was as if she couldn't quite believe, with her freshly-permed hair and Coty-red lips, that she was grown up enough to have two big sons. Both boys were sent to Sherborne and lost their Irish accents. For Dermot being able to educate his sons privately was a source of pride. Though why he didn't chose Downside or Ampleforth, one of the old Catholic schools was, as Brendan always said, a bit of a mystery. In a boys' world of bullying and buggery, as he so graphically put it, you didn't want to sound like a Paddy.

To his surprise he got a place at the Courtauld. Art History was an unlikely subject. But a summer hitchhiking round Italy at seventeen introduced him to the Quattrocento and to Gloria, a beautiful museum curator in her thirties, to whom he lost his virginity. It was Gloria who introduced him to Uccello and Piero Della Francesca. To gnocchi and afternoon sex.

Brendan, you have to appreciate Della Francesca's calm, the utter clarity and austerity of his sentiment, she insisted in her heavily-accented vowels, as the shutters cast zebra stripes across her voluptuous body, straddled above his boyish frame. Later, he saw how Piero's geometric structures and flat earthy colours made perfect sense in terms of the modern painters he grew to love.

How different it had been from her own upbringing, she thinks, as the wind rattles the eaves. The only child of elderly parents her predominant memory of Maresfield Gardens, where the stained glass panels on the front door bled coloured light onto the black and white hall tiles, was of quiet and order. It wasn't a house for a child. The walls were covered in paintings and prints that, as a small girl, she took for granted. A Cézanne lithograph, a little Pissarro oil of an apple orchard, a Ben Nicholson constructed from white and blue cardboard squares, like a window opening onto the sea. Antique glass lamps emitted a rosy glow over her mother's discarded library book among the plump cushions on the tasselled sofa. And on the mantelpiece a black marble clock, framed by a pair of gilded fauns, ticked into the silence while, in the far corner, stood a baby-grand that nobody played. It had come from Zurich with her grandfather. A photograph of him in a feathered trilby, standing amid a meadow of wild flowers in front of the Matterhorn, sat in a silver frame on the lid next to the black and white one of her parents' wedding. Her mother in a trim war-time suit holding a bunch of freesias. Her father in his RAF uniform, looking like a boy, despite his neat moustache. She looked like her mother. Pretty, in a transparent sort of way, as if taking up too much space in the world.

But her abiding memory of that house was of the silence that descended when her mother was having 'a lie down'. The creak of the floorboards, the blue Milk of Magnesia bottle and tin of Epsom salts glimpsed on the bedside table through the half-open door as she crept across the dark landing. She tried to be quiet but sometimes her mother would call out and she'd turn on the stair to see her lying on the mahogany bed beneath the satin eiderdown, her face turned to the trellis of pink cabbage roses on the wall. Next day, everything would be back to normal. No one would mention that her mother had been indisposed. She'd find her on the phone in the kitchen talking to the grocer, or bent over the wicker laundry basket sorting her father's striped shirts.

Her mother had been born just below the equator in a country where the map was still pink. There, beyond the green gardens of The English Club, Mombasa broke into a maze of narrow streets, where hidden worlds lurked behind carved doorways. Nyerere Avenue, Haile Selassie Road. The names were a litany to her mother's mysterious colonial childhood.

She pulls the cover up under her chin. Alone on the windswept headland surrounded by miles of cold sea, the past is closing in. What if she's suddenly taken ill? Who could she call, who would she tell?

3

When Brendan was eleven, Dermot brought him and Michael back to Kerry to visit their grandfather. Despite the Kwells, both boys were sick on the ferry. For the rest of his life Brendan only had to smell that mixture of ozone and diesel to feel the bile rise in his stomach. The drive from Dublin to Killarney took hours, slowed by a shambling horse and cart, and a rickety bus belching fumes. When they reached the whitewashed cottage on the edge of the Atlantic there wasn't even an indoor lavatory.

You know, boys, Cromwell was said to have sent the rebels to Kerry as an alternative to going to hell, Dermot joked as they sat huddled in a heavy downpour behind the misted windows of their Ford Prefect, a thermos of milky tea and their fish-paste sandwiches balanced on their knees.

When I was young most of the families here still spoke Irish. But there wasn't any work. Look at me now. If I hadn't gone to England I'd never have met your mother. And then where would you two have been, he winked. I was hardly older than you when I left.

They spent the summer roaming the cliffs and helping their grandfather carry the chipped enamel pail up to the cattle on the far ridge, dug potatoes, separating the big from the small. On wet days, when the badly-drained field was full of sticky black clay, there was half an acre of mud stuck to their boots as they tramped back to the cottage.

It was Brendan who inherited the place. It wasn't much use to Michael settled in Canberra with a wife and two girls. Apart from those childhood holidays, Ireland didn't figure much in his life. At the Courtauld he became interested in the St Ives group, while writing his MA thesis, and had contacted her father to ask if he'd known the painter Peter Lanyon.

Yes, her father wrote back. They were in the RAF together. He'd also met Naum Gabo once, and Barbara and Ben Nicholson on a couple of occasions in Cornwall.

Then, one April morning, Brendan just turned up at the gallery unannounced and, by mid-afternoon, her father had offered him a job.

It's a risk, I know. But we need someone younger, someone who'll keep up with what's happening in New York. The art world's changing, he announced to her tight-lipped mother over their Dover sole. He seems a bright young man. Anyway, initially, it's only for six months.

Her father welcomed Brendan like the son Martha was sure he'd always wanted. The family gallery had been started by her grandfather in Zurich. Then, as Hitler flexed his muscles, he moved to Hampstead and opened the gallery in Cork Street. After the war her father looked after the artists and clients. Then, in the '60s, as her grandfather became crippled with arthritis, he took over completely, moving away from French and continental art to specialise in modern British painters. He'd met Peter Lanyon in flying school. They remained friends after the war and Martha can still remember, as a small girl, being driven down those winding Cornish lanes to visit him. Even then she was taken by his good looks and strange aerial paintings.

Perhaps that's why she studied drama. A tentative bid to strike out on her own. For a while she even considered the stage but never had enough confidence to stand out in the limelight. How, as a shy bookish girl, had she ever imagined becoming an actress? Friends at university thought her life bohemian.

You're so lucky, Martha, to have a father who's an art dealer. Mine's just a boring old dentist. Did he really meet Braque?

She loved her father, of course, but in that very grown-up Hampstead house, there was always a distance.

And her mother? Well, for her mother she knew that she never quite came up to scratch. She wasn't sure that her mother was even aware what she was studying at Manchester. As far as she was concerned it was neither Oxford nor Cambridge.

The first evening Brendan came to dinner with her parents he seemed, with his shoulder length hair and floral shirt, the epitome of

Carnaby Street cool. Seven years older she thought, when he asked her to accompany him to a Francis Bacon exhibition at the Marlborough Gallery, that he was just ingratiating himself with his new employer's daughter. The following week they went to see *Belle du Jour* and in the smoky darkness of the Odeon she was very aware of his long fingers resting on his worn corduroy knee just inches from hers. Then, after a drink in The French House in Dean Street, she went back to his room off Gordon Square and lost her virginity. That she'd got through university with it intact was always a bit of an embarrassment. Graham, whom she dated during her first two terms, persistently tried to relieve her of it. Why did she resist? It was 'the Summer of Love'. Her skirts were high, her hair long and the Beatles more famous than Jesus. Yet she felt weighed down, by what? Some censorious maternal voice.

Her involvement with Brendan began around the same time that she started to teach. For years she dreamt that she was standing in front of a class and had forgotten what she was talking about. There'd be giggling and whispering, the banging of desk lids. Then she'd wake, her pulse racing, fearing that she'd finally been rumbled. Of course, it never happened. But in her heart she knew it might. But as the day wore on she forgot her night-time fears and rose to the challenge of encouraging children, who'd never been inside a theatre to play Oberon and Titania.

4

Martha you can't believe how beautiful it is, Brendan enthused as he put down the phone to the solicitor. We have to go. The cottage is right on the edge of the Atlantic, as far west as you can go without falling off Europe. From the door you can see across the bay to the Béarra peninsula and, on a clear day, as far as Waterville and the MacGillicuddy's Reeks. There's nothing except gorse, rocks and sheep. It's like being on the edge of the world. And we can take a trip out to the Skelligs. They're these extraordinary rocks in the middle of the Atlantic. In the 6th century they were settled by monks. It's unbelievable that anyone should have lived there, given the weather. It's said the monks were descended from the desert fathers, you know, like that Simon-what's-his-name who sat on a pillar for thirty years near Antioch. The boats only go out for a few weeks in the summer, the currents are so strong. But it should be ok in August. The cottage is pretty basic but you'll love it. I know you will. And so will Bruno.

Brendan's death was sudden and unexpected. She wasn't prepared for it and neither was he. Maybe that's how death always happens. In the middle of an unfinished life. He was putting together his new book working, this time, with a young editor, Jonathan Chambers. Then one Sunday morning, after walking to the corner shop to buy the papers, he complained of pins and needles in his left arm.

I think we should call the doctor, she insisted, as beads of sweat broke out across his ashen face.

Don't fuss, Martha, I just need to do more exercise and lose that stone. I'm not bloody ninety.

But by the evening he was in intensive care. And by midnight she had lost him.

There were no last words. No catharsis or setting straight the ledger. He simply collapsed and didn't regain consciousness. She'd forgotten how prosaic death was as she sat in the small recovery room off the main ward, staring blankly at a Samaritans poster, preparing to go home without him.

The following weeks were spent in limbo. She stood in the middle of the living room for hours without moving, listening to the rain outside, contemplating her options—suicide, running away, taking to drink? She couldn't stay in the flat, so drove down to Brighton to be with her old friend, Lindsay. They regularly exchanged Christmas cards, always promising that *this* year they'd definitely meet up. Maybe a concert at the Festival Hall or a Chinese in Soho? When she rang, Lindsay was kind.

How terrible—Brendan was no age. Of course Martha must stay as long as she liked.

She wandered along the esplanade, watching the foreign language students sitting on the sea wall eating fish and chips. Poked around the antique shops in The Lanes and visited the Pavilion with its exotic Moorish domes, while her friend counselled the errant teenagers of the city. In the evening they drank too much Merlot, so that she was unable to sleep in the unfamiliar bed and was woken by troubling dreams. After three days she left.

Back in Myddleton Square she sorted through Brendan's study. The ash trays were still full of stale cigarette stubs. He never let the cleaner in in case she moved things. He'd endlessly promised to give up smoking and managed to confine it to his study so the place smelt like an old-fashioned pub. She went through his papers. His notes from university. The photos of his summer hitchhiking round Italy when he was seventeen. How skinny he was then, with his unruly, shoulder length hair and his arm around a voluptuous girl in white sunglasses whom, Martha presumed, must be Gloria. As she put faded pants and T-shirts in a black bin bag for Oxfam, she wondered why Brendan had so many odd socks. How did she put matching pairs in the wash only to end up with a single one at the end of a cycle? Folding the old grey cashmere he wore when writing, she buried her face in his fugitive smell and wept.

It's not bloody fair, she wailed, a string of snot gathering on her upper lip. Why do you always do this to me?

She'd taken to walking the streets rather than staying at home. Up the Euston Road towards King's Cross and York Way, past the brownfield sites, the goods yards with their obsolete rolling stock rusting in the sidings, the burger bar and the telephone boxes littered with cards offering Man2Man and Rubber Girl into Water Sports. It made her shudder to think of all those bleak encounters. In the darkening doorways drunks were already bedding down for the night and a thin reek of urine sliced the air. At the back of the station she cut through a run-down estate. Two of the blocks were boarded up where the council planned to redevelop. Discarded needles and used condoms lay in the gutters.

Another day she walked to Soho and Holborn, then down Piccadilly, across Green Park towards Kensington Gardens and watched the ducks and swans on the Serpentine, as a group of Filipino nannies in brown and white striped uniforms pushed their charges round the park in expensive buggies. Then she headed off towards the V&A and the Natural History Museum with its pink and grey striations of brick, like layered sponge cake, and wandered through the vaulted halls, across the wide mosaic floor, past the dinosaur bones, the Brontosaurus and Tyrannosaurus rex. She'd often been there with Bruno, who, like all children, was fascinated by these enormous extinct beasts. It was mid-week and the place nearly empty. With its hushed tones, its high dome and frescoed ceiling it felt like a church. In fact, she read that the architect, Alfred Waterhouse, built it in the style of an Italian Renaissance cathedral. A Victorian museum fit for the glory of God's creation. She ambled down the long dark corridors, past the mahogany cases crammed with mammals and marsupials, rodents and reptiles, then stopped, for no particular reason, in a gloomy passageway full of stuffed birds with mangy moth-eaten feathers, displayed on twigs and logs. What was it about the 19th century mind that had a passion for killing things only to rearrange them in strange dioramas that were supposed to resemble what they'd destroyed? One case contained nothing but decapitated heads and wings. Tawny owls with huge round eyes. The shiny metallic head of a starling, wings spread to show their full span. A black-backed gull next to a finch's wing. Further down the narrow gallery was a display cabinet of birds that were extinct, including a dodo from Mauritius with grimy white plumage resembling a feather duster and a billhook beak, like the one in *Alice in Wonderland.* There were several species of dodo, so the yellowing label said, and most became extinct in the mid-17th century because of their ground-living habits and the damage caused to their eggs and nests by pigs, monkeys and rats released on the island. The Reunion Island dodo was known only from pictorial records and had been reconstructed from these. How, she wondered, could we be sure it had really existed and was not simply a figment of the imagination like the unicorn? Not all just a dream?

After a couple of hours the place began to depress her and she made her way back to the tube, past the Albert Memorial. She'd often seen it from the road, but never close up. There sat Albert on his throne—Victoria's beloved husband in the middle of all that gilding and mosaic—surrounded by her subjects from the four corners of the globe. A bare-breasted Asia in fringed headdress and half-moon diadem astride a kneeling elephant, escorted by bearded moguls. Europa on a bull with her sceptre and orb. The Americas represented by a maiden with eagles' feathers threaded through her hair, mounted on a shaggy bison, accompanied by a band of Indian braves. And, finally, Africa, seated on a camel held by a Nubian slave, her hair cut in a heavy fringe like Elizabeth Taylor's in Cleopatra.

She was erased by grief. She knew she was trapped in the past but was afraid to move on into an unknown future. She'd reached a fulcrum, a point between somewhere and nowhere. Even summoning the energy to get out of bed was an effort. Her life was measured by small achievements. A trip to the bathroom to brush her teeth or wash her dirty hair. Finding clean underwear so she could get out of her pyjamas. She sat at her mother's little walnut desk staring out of the window watching the man from the council sweep the litter in the street, scooping it up with flat boards, then bagging it into green plastic bags; the illegal immigrants who couldn't read the signs on the front doors that said 'no junk mail' distributing pizza leaflets; the traffic wardens wandering up and down in the rain slapping tickets on illegally-parked cars. The next night she had a dream. In fact she dreamt of nothing. It wasn't that she didn't dream. Just that in the dream she was floating in a black void. A tiny particle of isolated matter... That's what the whole universe was made of, from the highest mountain to a grain of salt.

Just atoms.

Next day she pulled her mack over her old tracksuit and headed towards Clissold Park. It was drizzling, already late afternoon. The lights from the traffic in Green Lanes were blurred. The Turkish shopkeepers covering their pavement displays of newspapers and fruit with plastic sheets. The park was nearly empty as she cut down by the tennis courts, past a man in an anorak with a face like a brick walking his pit bull, the heavy choke chain tightening around the dog's neck so the veins stood out and spit slavered from its pink chops. She stopped at the Victorian aviary to watch the green and blue parakeets, the pairs of lovebirds on artificial branches billing and cooing, the Chinese pheasant trailing its exotic tail like a muddy ball gown. Next to the aviary stood a clutch of fallow deer sheltering in a pen under a leafless tree. There wasn't much grass and the rain had turned what there was to mud.

By the library she turned up the path past the small church on the opposite side of the road to the later redbrick Victorian one. The lintel above the heavy wooden door read: 1645. It looked like a village church. Indeed, must have been once when Stoke Newington was a rural retreat out beyond the gates of the city and the reach of the pox and the plague. Sheep must have grazed where the park was. She imagined windmills and potato fields. Green orchards and water meadows where there were now sandpits and swings. It must have been like that when Daniel Defoe lived there. Perhaps he'd walked east up the River Lea, thinking, as he passed the small farmsteads and breweries, tanneries and blacksmith's yards, of Crusoe and Man Friday. She wandered up Church Street, past the kite shop and the one that restored string instruments, to Abney Cemetery.

Death. She kept being drawn back to death.

William and Bramwell Booth were both buried beneath monumental tombstones at the entrance. She imagined the Salvationists going from pub to pub with their copies of *The War Cry*, dressed in poke bonnets and peaked caps, banging their tambourines as they preached temperance in foul-smelling snugs in a bid to get East End costermongers and pimps to sign the pledge.

The cemetery smelt of damp moss and leaf mould. A bit of fugitive country that had evaded capture by the city. Brambles and clumps of elder sprouted between Victorian gravestones. Many of the inscriptions were illegible and some of the stones had toppled over as if the earth had moved when the dead tried to push their way out of loamy graves. She wandered down the intricate maze of paths, past the family plots with their ivy-covered mausoleums, to the abandoned church in the middle. The roof had fallen in and iron grilles been erected to keep out squatters and pigeons. What went on there at night? Empty wine bottles and beer cans littered the ground scorched from countless small fires. Why had it been abandoned? Once the well-to-do Anglicans of the parish—women in black satin mourning and jet beads, men in frock coats, a silver watch chain dangling from their waistcoat pockets—must have gathered in the porch to chat with the vicar after the funerals conducted here.

She looks at the clock. 3.30 am. The rain and the endless dark are full of echoes as she lies listening to the wind chasing its tail in the chimney. Finally, as a fragile finger of light creeps across the sill, she falls into an exhausted sleep.

Sunday

1

Paddy O'Connell has been up since 5.30. That's been his habit for years. Out of bed while it's still dark, he puts on the kettle, washes under his arms and behind his ears. He pulls his work overalls over his long johns and puts on the hand-knitted jersey that his sister Nora made him three Christmases ago. Twice a week and on Sundays he shaves. He hauls in the turf, lights the stove, and folds the clean washing that's been airing on the wooden rack, before tuning his battered radio to Morning Ireland. He remembers their first wireless. A big old thing it was. The neighbours all came in for a listen. There were two sorts of battery, wet and dry. You had to take the wet battery down to Mickey O'Shea in Caherciveen to get it charged up. With the radio on he doesn't need other company. He's happy pottering about his kitchen with its ticking clock and the new calendar that hangs above the stove, next to the framed print of Our Lady that his niece brought back from a school trip to Lourdes. He throws a clod on the fire, pours a mug of strong tea that's been brewing in the brown pot and sits down at the table. He likes to keep things neat. On the wax cloth the sauce bottles and cruet huddle on the small wicker tray. His folded napkin lies rolled in its wooden ring beside the blue-striped butter dish and matching milk jug.

When he's finished his second cup he rinses his mug, pulls on his Wellingtons and goes out to fill the cattle feeders on the high ridge and to check for lambs. Many of the ewes look ready to drop. It's too early, mind, but everything's out of kilter. He can see it in the storms and high seas, the wild daffodils poking their tips up in the ditches when they have no business to be showing their faces for at least another eight weeks. Things are changing but, he hopes, it will see him out, this life. He's spent his mornings pretty much the same way for the last thirty years since he was back from Dublin. That was the only time he was away. Mickey Flynn, who was living in Hounslow then, asked him to go to England once for a visit. But he never made it. He fancied seeing Buckingham Palace, the Changing of the Guard, and the Beefeaters at the Tower of London. But, in the end, he hadn't gone. He'd heard stories of those who'd left West Kerry without a word of English. Who couldn't read the destinations on the London buses or ask directions from Holyhead. When Jimmy Reen from down the valley went to Australia it had been like a wake. But Paddy had made a bit of money in Dublin working the building sites, though that life never really suited. There were times sitting in some smoke-filled bar down by Parnell Street over a head of the black stuff with the other gangers, when something would remind him of the nutty smell of cattle feed or the view over the headland and his heart would fill fit to bursting. He'd be there in company, wiping the creamy foam from his mouth with the back of his hand and be overwhelmed by a longing to get up and go home. They called him a *culchie* with his country ways, the city boys. He wasn't cut out to be a foreman. He didn't like telling others what to do. He had digs off Cumberland Street where the poorest shopped. Those from the corporation tenements and the traveller encampments. The pavements were littered with second-hand kettles and broken clocks, odd shoes and mismatching china. In Thomas Street he went to the market to buy spuds and cabbage to cook with his bit of bacon, chatted to the stallholders and shoppers but never felt he belonged. So he came back to help his da and then, within six months, his mam had passed away. She was no age. Just fifty-two. It was the cancer. She told no one of her troubles. When they found it, it was very quick. She was gone in a matter of weeks. That was a terrible time. He held things together the best he could but his da lost the will. Then, when his da's time came, Paddy just carried on doing what he'd always done.

He has more than enough. A car if he needs to get to town and the corn merchant or to meet the lads for a pint and a bit of a blather. The wireless and TV. Most of it, mind, is a waste of the licence money. Though he likes the wildlife programmes. There was a camera crew up here last summer. A couple of young fellows in those tight rubber diving suits that made them look like seals. They were out in a small power boat to film the leatherback turtles that could still sometimes be seen off the coast. They sat on the wall eating their sandwiches and asked if he lived up here alone. One of them had dyed yellow hair on him like a girl's and an earring, though he was a great big fellow. They couldn't understand what he did all day. How could he explain there were never enough hours? That he was never lonely up here with his sheep, his few head of cattle and the changing skies. For wasn't the only time he'd ever felt like he belonged nowhere particular on God's earth been when he was living in those Dublin digs? He'd worked with good men, drunk with them, but still felt lonely in his bones.

He knew those young divers could never understand the life of bachelors like him who lived alone and worked the land. Tongue-tied and often depressed, many lead solitary lives. That some of them didn't manage very well, living out of tins, drinking too much and not changing their togs from one week to the next he knew. But he always took a pride.

There was even a girl once, in Dublin. She worked in the café in Crow Street, off Temple Bar where he was after taking his breakfast and always wore the same blue and white checked dress. Her hair was the colour of new dug turf. He felt shy when she bought him his plate of fried rashers and an egg with a yolk as yellow as the sun, which she laid in front of him without a word, on the wax table cloth.

One day he gathered his courage to ask her to go with him along Sandymount Strand on the Sunday after Mass. He got up early to boil the kettle and shave especially carefully, polishing his shoes on a sheet of newspaper and putting on his good suit. The tide was out and there was a smell of seaweed as they stood watching the children flying kites, and dogs running backwards and forwards as if on invisible threads. She had to hold down her coat and skirt against the nosey wind to stop them blowing up over her stocking tops. He bought vanilla ices and they sat under the statue of the Virgin at the far end of the promenade and, even though it was a cool day, the ices ran down the side of the cone onto her Sunday coat, so that he had to dab it clean with his folded handkerchief.

The following week he asked her to a dance. He was a good dancer. Always a willing partner for a turn with one of his sisters. Accompanying them to the dance halls in Caherciveen to keep his da sweet. There were two halls then, both funeral parlours now. Primarily he was a chaperone, hanging round the door so he wouldn't have to pay the tanner entrance fee, hoping that one of his sisters would remember to bring him out a mineral to quench his thirst. He didn't mind. He was too shy to walk up to the girls lined up against the wall with their home perms, their hand-knitted cardigans and print dresses, waiting to be picked by a fella. He was happy to loiter outside, cadging the odd fag, sipping his Nash's Lemon Soda and listening to Jimmy McCarthy's quartet through the closed door, before ushering his sisters home. His da insisted no later than 11.30. That meant leaving early to push their bikes up the hill. He remembers that May eve when the girls wanted to go into town and the Old Man wouldn't let them.

Bejesus, why do I have daughters who're such hoors that they don't know that the six-penny hops are where girls get into trouble, he shouted, bringing his fist down on the kitchen table. Didn't they realise that men on the dole lurked outside the dance halls waiting to lure innocent girls into dark alleys where they'd drop their cacks quicker than you could say a Hail Mary. That wheedling tinkers would promise iced sherbets, so that after a few sweet words off would come cardigans, stockings and brassieres and, before they knew it, they'd be fit for nothing but the Magdalene Laundry.

He'd given out something fierce. His sisters had spent the whole afternoon slapping on Pond's Cold Cream and permanent waving their hair. They cried and pleaded. But the Old Man just put on his cap and marched out to the yard to milk the cows.

It was the only time he'd held her in his arms. He felt her heart beating under her ribs like a trapped bird. Smelt the Vosene in her newly-washed hair, as he manoeuvred her across the dance floor sprinkled with Lux flakes to get up a good shine. The place throbbed with sweat and cheap perfume as they quickstepped to 'Blackboard of my Heart' and he worried about stepping on her toes. They drank ginger beer—for there was none of the hard stuff in the dance halls in those days—and had plates of circular coffee-flavoured biscuits covered in white icing. That Easter he gave her a bunch of primroses and a little palm cross. But she was the youngest. Left at home after all her brothers and sisters had upped sticks. When she wasn't serving at the café she had to help her mam who had angina. The house was small but someone had to make her daddy's tea when he came in from working the roads.

They never really said goodbye. One day he just got on a bus and headed back west with his battered suitcase. Years later he heard that soon after he left her mammy had died and she joined the Order of the Sisters of the Good Shepherd. He wonders, if he'd known, if he would have gone back and wed her, fetched her home with him here. He imagines the day she took her final vows, giving up her postulant's dress for a tunic of heavy black serge, a white linen wimple and a cincture of black leather. After that she'd have been lost to the world. A life of chastity and obedience. Corridors that smelt of silence and beeswax. He can see her slight figure, face-down on the cold stone floor. The Mother Superior covering her with a funeral pall and announcing that her old self was dead. When the cloth was removed she'd have been someone else. Married to Christ.

He hopes that she's been happy. That she's had no regrets. It might all have been different. Sometimes he imagines waking beside her in the bed where she'd born all their babbies, the smell of Lux on her. But no, he's been content enough to watch the clouds and storms sweep in from the Atlantic. To follow the patterns and dictates of the weather. He can organise his days as he pleases around his stock. It's not a bad life. It's where he belongs.

Home.

But recently there's been talk that there are those who want him gone. Who have plans for his land with its view of the Skelligs. He tries not to think about it, for what can he possibly do?

2

Martha had forgotten how much further north and west she is than London. How late it stays dark. It's already a quarter to nine. She's slept fitfully, has a crick in her neck and is freezing. She pulls on her thick jersey and huddles back under the blankets. She'll have to look for a hot water bottle. She's sure there's one in the cupboard under the stairs. Outside the sky is a fragile blue, like the washed stain of newly-laid watercolour and the little islands that in the dark looked so far away, seem almost near enough to swim to. There's not a building or tree in sight. Nothing except a vast expanse of sea, sky and the islands, so that for a moment, her heart stops at the beauty of it all.

She climbs from beneath the covers, folds up the blankets and puts them in the ottoman. She'll have to go upstairs and air the bed, make it up for tonight so she can get a decent night's sleep. She lights the stove, fumbling for firelighters and matches but doesn't bother to shower. It's too cold and anyway she forgot to switch on the immersion and there's no one to care how she smells. She brushes her teeth and, after banking up the fire, slips on Brendan's old wax jacket and makes her way up the track towards the headland. Below the waves hurl against the rocks, and the sheep, huddled for shelter in the lee of the stone wall, run off up the hill bleating as she passes, their shimmying backsides smeared in Day-Glo pink. The air is thick with salt and there's a mist coming in off the sea that's slowly erasing the view of the uninhabited islands like a coating of whitewash. In a muddy ditch a solitary black-headed crow is pecking at the carcass of a lamb. She climbs on past the scattered cottages fringing the track. The roofs have fallen in and tufts of turf sprout along the broken walls like unruly green eyebrows. Cattle graze by the collapsed hearths. Three hundred feet above the Atlantic those who once lived here have long gone, weary of huddling over a few smoky clods, wracked by hacking coughs. The crumbling walls resonate with the lost voices of those who set sail for Liverpool, Brisbane and New York.

There's no one about and the wind is full of rain. The road is steep and the stone wall boundaries marking the patchwork fields have slipped in places like displaced vertebrae along a damaged spine. Scraps of black plastic fertiliser bags flap on the barbed wire fence. Those who once farmed here were hill people. They won their small plots from the scrub and bog, leaving behind the remains of potato ridges and small circular corn fields. Potatoes, rye and oats were staples. The rye thatched houses, the potatoes and oats lined bellies.

Pulling up the collar of Brendan's jacket against the downpour she stops to gather her breath and wonders why they chose this remote spot without a harbour and with so little shelter from the elements. They must have been permanently damp. Their skin kippered from turf smoke, their lungs thick with phlegm. By twenty the women would have had a clutch of hungry, lousy children.

She remembers Brendan telling her how his father, Dermot, while on a visit to see his old man in the '50s, had been driving through some desolate glen when he passed two policemen with a donkey-cart carrying a coffin. Stopping to enquire what had happened, the fat guard told him that only days before some young fellow had been reaping down in the glen and taken a glass or two more than was good for him, then thrown off his clothes and run off into the hills. That night there was a great rain and the poor young eejit lost his way. Next morning, when Mickey Murphy was driving his flock up the mountain, he came upon the fellow's footprints in the mud, along with his half-naked body near eaten by crows.

She trudges on up the track and is beaten back by the wind. As she passes a hunched bungalow, its walls green with mould, its windows boarded up, a muddy farm dog rushes out barking and snapping at her heels. She picks up a fallen fence post to wave it off, glimpsing among the pile of tangled barbed wire, a child's rusted tricycle.

She's getting wet and remembers all those years ago, coming out of the Curzon into a tremendous shower and running for shelter to Brendan's room at the top of that shabby Bloomsbury house where he lodged. They'd stripped off their wet clothes and she hung her tights and cardigan above the rust-stained bath while, wrapped in his big plaid dressing gown, he dried her hair with a towel in front of the gas fire. There was a sagging double bed and an ugly mahogany desk piled with art books. The room looked down over a private garden off Gordon Square where an ancient medlar grew in the corner of the garden. That summer she often saw an elderly woman in a straw hat reading beneath its low branches. With her equine face she reminded her of Virginia Woolf.

She loved that room. It was there, for the first time, that she felt like an adult. She was a newly qualified teacher. She had a lover. Sundays were spent lazing in bed reading the papers and eating crumpets. On rainy afternoons they went to the manuscript room at the British Museum. And Brendan introduced her to the Sir John Soane Museum, hidden at 13 Lincoln's Inn Fields, with its casts and curiosities. A testimony to English eccentricity.

When she gets back to the cottage the stove is out and there's a note on the mat.

Dear Martha,

I should have written sooner. I heard you were over. I was truly sorry to learn about Brendan. He and I go back a long way. I do hope you'll drop by for my little New Year's Eve celebration. It's just a few friends. 7.30 for 8.00.

Eugene Riordan.

3

She's surprised. She hasn't given Eugene a second thought. She'd only met him a couple of times and, despite his thick dark hair, his imposing height and large house, didn't much care for him, had thought him arrogant and taciturn. His relationship with Brendan was a boyhood thing, based on a summer messing around on the beach. Now Eugene was one of the richest men in Ireland. A property lawyer turned developer, with a string of luxury hotels located in national beauty spots that catered for an elite clientele. He spent his days on the golf course, out shooting, or walking his Irish setters along the beach. She knows, too, that all those years ago he took an instant dislike to her. She suspects that he thought her self-consciously bookish. A stuck-up English woman in her natural linen skirts and floral scarves, with her long, girlish hair. She was too homely for his taste. Maybe she'd made him uneasy knowing that neither his person nor his wealth impressed her and that she'd never be one of his conquests. He liked trophy woman. Women with highlights in their hair, women who looked good when they walked into the golf club dinner on his arm, or sat at the other end of his long oak table when he entertained. He was one of those men who, if he ever found her on the beach engrossed in a book, would boast that he didn't have the 'time to read'. That newspapers and professional journals were all that he could manage to fit into his demanding schedule. As if reading was a sign of weakness. An indication that one didn't have a life of consequence.

She wonders if he was jealous when Brendan had turned up with a wife. Why Brendan, who was both sociable and cultured, should have put up with Eugene she has no idea. But Brendan's grandfather had been born in Ballinskelligs. Their families had old connections. Brendan could just about hit a golf ball but had no interest in shooting. He wrote books and collected art. She wasn't sure what Eugene must have made of Peter Lanyon. The walls of his house, an imposing one-time Church of Ireland rectory down on the beach, were decorated with hunting prints and oils of stags at bay. Low occasional tables sported glossy books on antiques and small bronze statues of his dogs with grouse in their mouths. He didn't have much time for 'modern' art. As to his party? Well, she's not sure she can face it. She was planning an early night with a hot water bottle, a glass of whiskey and her Edith Wharton. She wants to forget that it's New Year.

Why had Eugene asked her? A prurient interest in how she's worn after all these years? Loyalty to Brendan? And how did he even know she was here? Well, maybe she should go. After all there'll be plenty of time to spend on her own. Luckily she'd thrown a good black dress in her bag on top of her thermals.

She makes a coffee and sets about sorting Brendan's things. Even though it has to be done she feels like a spy or worse, a hyena picking over her husband's carcass. Nothing has been touched since his death. Books lie where he left them. Papers litter his desk and a graveyard of flies has gathered on the window ledge. It obviously never occurred to him to dust in here. She goes to the pine desk. Its drawers are crammed with old receipts. In the middle one she finds a series of Moleskine notebooks, the pages covered with little drawings of puffins, black-headed gulls and kittiwakes, all annotated with dates, times and locations. She'd no idea that Brendan was interested in birds, let alone that he owned a pair of binoculars until she discovered the ones on the back of the kitchen door. She wonders if he'd ever gone to the Lee Valley Marshes or up to Orford Ness with Sophie to look for some lesser-spotted-something-or-other? But huddling in a damp hide didn't quite seem Sophie's style. After their affair was over Martha thought that he'd decided to tell her everything. Yet surely a secret love of bird watching wasn't such a sin. Still it was a secret. Perhaps we never truly know those we live with. She tries to remember if she ever kept anything back from him.

She runs her fingers along the dusty book shelves, the eclectic assortment of battered spines: *The Art of Collecting Antiques,* John le Carré and Sebastian Faulks. Walter Benjamin and Theodor Adorno. There are faded volumes on the geology and archaeology of the Béarra peninsula, countless Thames & Hudson art books and rows of orange Penguin paperbacks. As she leafs through the box files she comes across a well-thumbed address book and turns, instinctively, to B to find *Sophie Bawden, Flat 3, Nightingale Lane, SW13* in Brendan's spidery script.

Why should it still distress her? Because it brings the past into the present? Because it means that what she's trying to forget is chronicled in black and white as history and fact. She flips through the yellowing pages. There are old friends from the Courtauld, some crossed through with heavy black lines after they've moved, or worse, died. Other names belong to clients, publicists, editors and press contacts. Some she's vaguely heard of, while others have long since relocated to new jobs. Their neighbours, Judy and Sam, are there. Sam and Brendan played tennis on Highbury Fields on Sunday mornings and, occasionally, they all went to the Almeida theatre together or to that Lebanese place in Upper Street.

She fills bin bags with scraps of paper and old files, as if tidiness might somehow ensure her sanity. This little address book has depressed her. As if one short existence amounted to no more than a cluster of names in a Letts notebook. How many listed here knew, or even cared, that Brendan was dead? Death changes things. This is the beginning of a new chapter but she's no idea, yet, of the plot. She's an orphan and a widow. She has no ties. She can do whatever she wants. But what does she want? The only thing she's ever wanted was impossible and she'd nearly driven herself and Brendan half-crazy with her magical thinking in attempting to bring it about. She's not religious. For her death is the end. A soundless dark beyond time and sleep. Now all she has are memories—a few letters and photos. How many stories does one person have? How many shapes can they inhabit? She shuts the drawer and opens another and finds an early draft of his St Ives book.

Perhaps that's what Brendan loved about this part of the Irish coast. Its similarity to Cornwall. The grey-greens, the yellow gorse and dry stone walls, the surf gnawing away at the rugged cliffs. She pulls the drawer out on its runners and puts it on the desk to better sort its contents. There's a collection of cuttings from *The Kerryman.* Something about a legal battle Eugene has been waging against local environmentalists. She gives them a cursory glance before tossing them in the bin bag with the taxi receipts and stray paper clips, the envelopes that've lost their glue and dried-up biros. Then as she goes to replace the drawer she notices, half-hidden beneath an old Bus Eireann timetable, a photograph, and her heart skips a beat. A small boy standing in the surf silhouetted against a dying sun, his arms raised above his white-blond head as if waving.

4

If she's going to Eugene's party then she needs to get ready. She doesn't want to stay here on her own. She feels knocked off balance, as if the cottage is closing in on her. She undresses quickly and climbs into the shower. She's not washed properly since she arrived and the hot water is like a blessing, turning her skin pink and creating a fog in the freezing bathroom. She towels herself standing under the Dimplex heater and dries her hair, hardly recognising the pale face that stares back from the medicine cabinet's clouded glass. Yet if she makes an effort she'll scrub up ok. She's taken care of herself, eating sensibly, walking rather than taking the bus. On a good day she can till pass muster. Not that she cares what Eugene thinks. But she's decided to go to his party so wants to look her best and not be pitied as the grieving widow. Anyway, most of her grieving has been done and what remains is a private affair. She dries her hair, does her makeup, puts on her black dress and a cashmere pashmina, shoves her good shoes in a plastic bag and drapes her anorak over her shoulders. Then she locks the door and hurries out to the car, letting the engine run to de-mist the windscreen. The night is cold and the sky clear as an astronomer's map. As she drives down over the hill a beam from the lighthouse flashes across the inky bay. After a couple of dark miles she turns right at the Celtic cross.

The heavy oak door is opened by a young man in black. He takes her coat and, in a cloakroom full of Penhaligon soaps and soft white towels, she changes her shoes and adjusts her makeup before being led down a hallway past an enormous Christmas tree—all tasteful pine cone decorations, clear-glass ornaments and old-gold chiffon bows—into a room with a blazing log fire. Everything is a shimmer of candles and lights. There are about thirty other guests, their faces like masks in the soft glow. The younger women are all dressed in designer wear, while the older ones, despite or perhaps because of, their hair dye and best clothes, still seem have a look of the land about them. Eugene is over the other side of the room talking to some guests and, although he's seen her, doesn't come to greet her so that she's left to introduce herself to those nearby and explain who she is. Eventually he makes his way over. Though tall, his once thick hair is thinning. He has a glass of whiskey in one hand, is wearing a grey shot silk shirt and has more of a paunch than must be good for him.

Welcome Martha, he says bending to peck her cheek, so she can smell his tobacco breath. I'm glad you could make it. It must be a while now? Have you a drink? he asks, beckoning over the young man who opened the door, who Martha presumes must be one of the many Eastern Europeans benefiting from Ireland's new prosperity.

Champagne?

Thank you Eugene, that'll do nicely. Yes, it's been some time hasn't it? It's kind of you to invite me. How did you know I was here?

News gets round, he says, without smiling. I suppose you pulled into the garage.

To buy some firelighters. Is that all it takes?

As they're chatting a young woman comes over and slips her arm proprietorially through his. Eugene doesn't introduce them. She has a brittle, horsey face, wispy blonde hair and a skirt that's a little too short and is, at least, twenty years younger than he is, though there's already a fine web of lines at the corners of her mouth and eyes. Martha has some vague recollection that he's been married twice, so isn't sure if this is a wife, a girlfriend or simply his companion for the night.

They're invited to take their seats in the dining room. A huge log fire in the grate lights up the heavy brocade drapes and table decorations, the crisp damask cloth. She wonders where the wood comes from as there are so few trees round here, then realises that Eugene probably owns the commercially-planted pine forest that runs up the side of the mountain behind the house. Branches of spruce adorn the mantelpiece and candles flicker in the silver candelabra, bleeding rings of light through the high windows into the wet herbaceous border in the dark garden. Two enormous leather sofas sit on either side of the fireplace. The place has the air of an expensive country club. Martha knows that Eugene has another house somewhere near Kinsale where he keeps a boat and goes sailing, as well as a penthouse apartment in Dublin. She's uncertain how he made all his money. Brendan once mentioned something about a multinational law firm in Chicago where he'd negotiated complex real estate deals during the '80s. But there've always been rumours about businesses in South Africa, Zaire and China which the locals, not knowing the truth, enjoy embellishing. As the evening wears on Martha recognises one or two of the guests from her previous visits. There's Sean Kennedy, the local builder, last seen halfway up a ladder replacing some guttering, who's made a fortune building holiday homes on Valentia Island. And a small man in a pink cashmere sweater, with an Ulster accent, who's a financial advisor. On the other side of the table is the director of a string of supermarkets and his heavily Botoxed wife. Next to him is the local auctioneer, his generous gut encased in a tight lilac shirt. Everyone seems to be involved with finance or property. And, at the far end of the long table, is another face she recognises. Seamus O'Sullivan, the local doctor.

But the place has changed beyond all recognition. That summer, more than twenty-five years ago, it felt as if she'd come to the ends of the earth. As far west in Europe as it was possible to go without falling into the sea. Now, with the help of EU grants the place reeks of new money. Buildings have sprung up blighting the rugged coastline. Ugly bungalows on the edge of muddy fields, complete with concrete porticos and rampant lions, like something out of the '80s TV soap, *Dallas*. Bland suburban homes, without any architectural merit, have been erected next to the carcasses of ruined cottages with their collapsed corrugated roofs. The banks are doling out money to those who've never owned anything more than a second-hand car or a rusty tractor. Developers are feeding funds into local government coffers in order to build row upon row of executive homes on the outskirts of remote villages that nobody's ever thought of commuting to or from. Who are all these ticky-tacky houses for? With a population of four million surely there aren't enough people in Ireland to fill them?

Everywhere people are dressed in brand names and designer wear, drinking champagne instead of Guinness or stout. It's as if the free Irish air would be even more desirable if it were bottled, to mark out those who can afford it from those that can't. It's like watching a lottery winner who doesn't quite know how to spend his sudden windfall. For years this country was scared by poverty and emigration. For an older generation, a new bungalow meant running water and an indoor toilet. Now this conspicuous wealth and rash of unsold holiday homes just seems uncouth, with scant regard paid to the uniqueness of what's being lost and the destruction of this savage landscape.

Sitting on Martha's left is a plastic surgeon from Dublin with a winter tan and large sapphire cufflinks at the wrists of his designer suit. He's just come back from the Seychelles, he tells her, and is planning to open another clinic in Killarney.

It's mostly boob jobs down here, he says. Or a bit of nip and tuck. On the whole Irish women don't have big noses. Nose jobs tend to come from Athens, Istanbul and Tel Aviv.

To her right is a man with chiselled features, wearing a crisp white shirt buttoned at the throat. He asks why Martha is here. She realises she's not sure and mutters something about coming over to sort out her late husband's affairs.

And you, she asks, deflecting his interest. Are you from these parts?

Sure. I'm a Kerry man born and bred. A landscape gardener. Couldn't live anywhere else. I've tried, mind. But I can't. Though I'm a fan of English gardens and those English lady gardeners. Hard as nails but magnificent in an emergency. Very practical, very sensible.

He smiles, moving in closer, to reveal a set of even white teeth.

It's something she remembers from previous visits, just how hard it is to pigeonhole people here. A gardener. Yet his conversation is peppered with references to Yeats and Joyce, the layout of Sissinghurst.

You have to admire her, that Vita Sackville-West, he continues. She may've been English but she knew how to make a garden, alright. I also play music. Just for myself, like. I learnt the balalaika in the monastery in Mongolia.

Martha isn't surprised by this exotic revelation. There's something restless about her dinner companion. She wonders what it is in the Irish spirit that seeks out this sort of extreme solitude that sent those early monks out to their rocky outcrop on the Skelligs. What demons both he and they were escaping?

As the drink flows, a woman in a sequinned cardigan launches into 'Danny Boy'. Then someone else sings 'I Dreamt I Dwelt in Marble Halls'. Some have lovely voices, while other performances are a triumph of alcohol over talent. As the evening wears on Martha becomes aware of an anti-English sentiment creeping into the proceedings. But no one seems to register her presence in their midst. Anyway, she thinks defensively, her antecedents weren't even in England at the time of The Troubles, let alone Cromwell. They were having their own problems in some Russian shtetl.

People begin to drift next door. At the far end of the room a piper and fiddler are playing and couples start to dance. Everyone seems to know the steps and tunes from childhood. As she watches, Seamus O'Sullivan makes his way across the floor towards her.

It's good to see you again after so long, Martha, he says, holding out his hand. I'm very sorry for your troubles. I liked Brendan. We occasionally shared a jar together when he was over. Put the world to rights. It made a change from babies and bunions to have a bit of culture.

Then, before she can object, Sean Kennedy grabs her round the waist and whisks her into the middle of the dancing. Despite his advancing years and ample girth, he's light on his feet and free with his big meaty hands. On the far sofa she can see Eugene with his blonde companion, sipping whiskey and smoking a large cigar. The reel finishes and, as the dancers catch their breath, the fiddler picks up his guitar. His voice is dark and raw, welling from deep within his chest. It makes her think of the wind whistling in the peat bogs and she's afraid she will cry.

Then it's midnight and everyone is kissing and embracing. Sean comes and gives her a hug. Over his shoulder she can see the wife of the pink cashmere man turn away as he reaches for her lips. How she hates New Year. What on earth is she doing here among these people she hardly knows, people who've known each other all their lives, who've grown up together, gone to school together and married each other's cousins? But where else should she more rightfully be? She doesn't want to think of the year ahead. Nor, for that matter, the one after. She wonders where the gardener has gone and goes to look for him but he's nowhere to be seen. Then, slipping off to find her coat, she leaves without saying goodbye. She'll drop Eugene a note in the morning.

As she drives back up over the hill clouds race across the face of the moon. The sky is full of stars. She unlocks the door, fills a hot water bottle and climbs into bed. And, as the waves batter against the cliffs below, tries to imagine how she's going to live the rest of her life

Monday

1

The sky is streaked pink and, across the strait, the islands rise like whales surfacing out of a tin-coloured sea. Apart from the wind catching under the eaves it's totally quiet. She sits up in bed and looks out of her little window as the light changes from peach, to oyster, to dishwater grey, and wonders what to do with her day. She should go for a walk but needs to finish sorting through Brendan's things. How little she really knew him. She can barely remember his face. She closes her eyes and tries to recall his high-domed forehead with its receding hairline, the grey eyes creased with laughter lines, his long thin fingers like a pianist's. But all she can manage is the faded memory of the man she woke beside for more than thirty years.

She picks up his sketchbook. The little drawings and watercolours with their lattice of dry stone walls and jigsaw cliffs executed in loose expressionist brush strokes. He must have climbed down onto the rocks above the swelling surf to get a better view of the islands, which is a surprise, given his fear of heights. She pictures him in his wax jacket and battered hat, gingerly making his way out over the slippery boulders with his sketch book, a tin of water colours stuffed into his pocket. Scrawled in pencil are a series of notes: *Mars black, Payne's grey, Chinese white,* and other observed details: *yellow-green lichen, blue twine on a gatepost, small weather-beaten stone cross/grey? /ochre?* It's as if he wanted to pin everything down. As though, through these observations, he could escape those moments when his feelings seemed more real than the external world, when everything turned the colour of mud and rain.

She'd always thought of Brendan as essentially urban. His natural habitat was the gallery and library, whether in London or New York. There was something grown-up about cities. They demanded panache and a thick skin. The wild, on the other hand, stripped everything away so all that was left was an essential self. Brendan loved St Ives because he loved the painters associated with it. Being in the city defined who he was. An art dealer and a writer. He relished the endless round of openings and private views. There he bumped into colleagues and exchanged professional chit-chat with curators and journalists over canapés and a glass of Chardonnay, never having to disclose anything much of himself, except an opinion on the recent auction prices achieved by Charles Saatchi as he off-loaded yet another batch of art works onto the market before moving into a new collecting phase. Brendan was never happier than when arranging to meet a friend for dinner at the Groucho or organising a trip to a gallery in New York.

Our lives are so hectic that not to be busy is considered a modern vice, evidence of inadequacy, proof that we're no longer important. Surplus to requirements. On the way down and out. A diary full of meetings and working lunches emphasises we're in demand, that we are somebody. And when all that's stripped away? What's left except a self that we hardly recognise?

Is that why Brendan came here? To sit on a clifftop and watch the ever-changing skies? To make contact with what he'd lost?

2

They'd intended that summer in the late '80s, to take a trip out to the Skelligs. For some reason those mysterious rocks had captured Bruno's imagination. Why had the monks lived in the middle of the sea? What had they eaten? Weren't they cold? They found a local history book with pictures of the beehive huts that he copied into an exercise book and carefully coloured in. On cloudy days they would stand in the high field trying to get a glimpse of the rocky crags through the mist. When the weather was clear they appeared so close.

If people can swim the Channel could someone swim out to the Skelligs?'

It's unlikely, she answered. It's too cold and rough. The currents are treacherous.

Please, please can we go?

If it's fine tomorrow. But you will have to be up with the lark.

But by the time they went down to the pier to enquire about departure times, the weather had turned.

The last few days of their stay they were trapped indoors. Bruno spent the mornings sitting by the stove cutting out old copies of *Irish Country Life*: a Lamborghini, a polo pony, a house for sale with a big blue pool in the Bahamas. She watched as he guided his scissors neatly round the shapes, then collaged them into surreal scenarios in a scrap book with the big tube of cow gum. There was no radio, let alone a television. In the evening they played cards and *Monopoly*, empire building in Pall Mall and Mayfair. Or read aloud. *The Hobbit* and 'The Pobble Who Has No Toes' were favourites. This, for some reason, she always read in an Edinburgh accent, which made Bruno laugh. How she relished those moments. Brendan, bowed over his desk as the evening chilled. Bruno at her feet while she read to him in the firelight. She wanted to hold them fossilised in that amber glow. And, as she bent and brushed Bruno's hair with her lips, telling him to put away his scissors and glue and go to do his teeth, for it was time for bed, she thought: he will never be this carefree again. Soon it will be over. He will go out into the world and make his own way.

The next day, their final day, a fog came down and settled over the headland.

No chance of the Skelligs today, Bruno, Brendan said, she thought, a little tactlessly.

So, aware of her son's disappointment, she had promised, as they packed up the car ready to head back towards Rosslare, the ferry and home, that next year they would definitely make the trip. But she knew, somewhere deep inside, that her betrayal—that they'd not gone when she had given her word—would stay with Bruno for the rest of his life.

3

Brendan never mentioned it. Yet as Martha reads through his notebooks she realises that he must have made the trip out to the Skelligs alone. He'd gone from Portmagee, the little fishing village on the other side of the headland where the first telegraphic messages were transmitted across the Atlantic to Newfoundland. In one of the notebooks he'd written:

As we chug out into the open sea there's quite a swell. We pass the squat Lemon Rock, then the small Skellig. It's as jagged as a child's drawing and almost completely white from the gannets that nest there. But our goal is Skellig Saint Michael 7 1/4 miles WNW and a 1/4 mile N in Saint Fionán's Bay that rises from the deep like a finned sea monster. When we arrive we land with some difficulty because of the swell. As I scramble onto the little pier to start the dangerous climb up the hand-carved steps I realise this place is unique. I'm scared of heights and below the slippery walkway there's a sheer drop to the Atlantic. There are no handrails and a couple of years ago an American fell to his death. But nothing could have prepared me for the clutch of beehive huts with their corbelled domes clinging to the pinnacle against a duck-egg sky. I've seen the Great Wall of China, the Blue Mosque in Istanbul and the Alhambra in Granada but this is one of the most extraordinary places I've ever visited. You don't have to be conventionally religious to be moved by this place. It's holy just because it exists. Not just on the edge of a continent, but on the edge of the human imagination. Each of us needs the chance to rediscover what's essential, to find a landscape to fit our dreams and disappointments. When there's nothing left, there's still the ocean and the sky.

Those early monks, following in the tradition of the desert fathers, believed holiness could only be achieved by withdrawing from the world. In the 6th century this rock was a bolt-hole for those descended, not from Rome, but the Copts. At the time the norm for Irish monasteries was outside the convention later established by the great continental orders such as the Benedictines and Cistercians. No Celtic community consisted of a monastery under a single roof. It was a settlement of separate buildings built around the church. There's still a tiny windswept graveyard on Skellig Michael where the monks who died are buried, the tombstones worn down to illegibility from the Atlantic storms. The terraces and three staircases from the landing stages were all built by hand. The only tools the monks had were iron hammers and chisels, a crowbar or two, a leather bag and some ropes to form a primitive pulley.

Could it really have been a simple matter of faith, a doctrinal difference between the Celtic and Roman strands of early Christianity over the date of Easter that forced them out into the middle of the Atlantic? Placing themselves in the hands of divine providence, they cast adrift, accepting their fate. The original voyage made, according to legend, by Saint Fionán and his companions, was in the great Irish tradition of 'peregrination pro Dei amore' (wandering for the love of God). The purpose was not to proselytise but, as another monk Adomnán claimed when setting sail for Iona, 'to discover a desert in the pathless sea.' This was about going into retreat to meditate on and repent of man's original sin. To embrace a life of penance, hunger and perpetual damp. It made the monks feel as if they were the true disciples of a martyred Christ. Their goal was to trample down pride through submission. To serve the Corpus Christi in the Great Chain of Being. Mediaeval communities mirrored the feudal principal of lord and serf, master and man, husband and wife, parent and child. The whole was greater than any part. This offshoot of Hebraic monotheism included the belief, virtually absent from Old Testament Judaism, of a separate, immaterial and immortal soul. Levantine Gnostic sects expressed contempt for the body. They regarded it as the dungeon of the spirit and a hothouse of vile appetites. Such views left their mark on early Christianity.

It's hard for us to understand the medieval mind. The more I read, the more I realise their world view was utterly different to our materialistic one. It was as though the ego hadn't yet been invented. And if it did make an unwelcome appearance it had to be chastised. Such trials were simply a preparation for death and the afterlife.

It's uncertain why the monks left the Skellig in the 13th century. Climactic change or the social transformation that began when the Vikings turned up raping and pillaging? Who knows? Luckily I don't have to be quite as extreme to experience a little introspection. But it's testing getting away from all the things that buoy up normal daily life. It takes you deep into the essence of yourself which, most of the time, lies shut behind a door marked 'private'. Of course, if all else fails, there's always the pub.

Martha is touched by her husband's disclosures and wishes that they'd been able to share the experience together. But Brendan seems to have needed to go out to the Skelligs alone. To survive, the monks had scaled the rocks—a noose fixed to a pole—to catch puffins and gannets, stuffing them into canvas bags strapped on their backs. They used everything: flesh, feathers, oil and quills. Every bird caught was a dice with death. She closes her eyes and tries to imagine a life of such self-induced privation with its daily diet of obedience and rank sea birds, the unaccompanied chant of male voices. She can picture them riddled with rheumatism, waking to the matins' bell, their leather sandals slapping over the rocks in the rain-lashed dark as they make their way to the freezing chapel. Half-starved and soaking, how would they have dried their heavy woollen cassocks sodden from the freezing Atlantic spray?

Perhaps the monks hadn't been so different to the lighthouse keepers who came later. Men who found sanctuary away from the demands of conventional jobs and society. Men looking for inner peace as they polished the great lamp, trimmed the wick and raked over their scrap of garden to plant a few stunted rows of kale. Were they, too, running from intimacy in order to avoid love's vulnerability? There would have been no regular letters or newspapers. Only the same waves breaking week after week against the same dreary rock. The sea birds dashed against the lamp in the fierce storms. She isn't stuck on a rock in the Atlantic but, maybe, her reasons for being here aren't so very different.

She pulls her fleece over her pyjamas and goes to brush her teeth. How opaque we are to others, she thinks, standing in front of the mirror, her mouth filled with foam. How little we're able to provide solace to each other in our moments of darkness. No other person can answer our deepest needs. Hadn't she, too, often wished to escape, maddened by Brendan's relentless upbeat tone, his refusal to talk about the one thing that hovered between them like a ghost? Then she'd slip out of the house into the anonymity of Islington, past the terraced houses with their terracotta window boxes, and make her way down to the towpath of Regent's Canal. She felt at ease among the flotsam and jetsam of the city. The alcoholics with their cans of Tennant's Extra hidden in brown paper bags. The lone fisherman bent over his rod beside a Tupperware box of sandwiches, the skateboarding boys in their back-to-front baseball caps. She'd sit on a bench by the wall covered with graffiti tags and watch the ducks dive for snails and try to get a grip. She avoided the Heath now. There were too many memories. The kites they'd flown. The hot days spent swimming in the ponds or the lido. That special tree with the low spreading branches that he'd loved to climb near the Vale of Health. She can still see him that first time he made it to the top. Triumphant as a mountaineer, waving as if he'd just conquered the world.

She breathes deeply and stretches to shrug off the night. Recently she'd joined a yoga class but is not very good. Still it quietens her racing mind as she sweats through Down Dog and the Plank, enjoying her stretching muscles. The physical endeavour replacing mental strain. As she's heating a saucepan of milk for her porridge, there's a knock on the door and a woollen hat, pulled down low over a pair of rosy cheeks, peers in, followed by a small rotund body in an outsized jumper that hangs shapelessly over a pair of old tracksuit bottoms.

It's difficult to tell whether the person in front of her is a man or a woman.

Mary Nolan's the name, the figure says, by way of introduction, holding out a calloused hand. Turf Mary they call me. I just popped by to see you've plenty of fuel. We always brought the turf up for Brendan. It's a terrible thing he's gone. Sure being in your sixties is no age now. Just you let me know if you want anything and my son Colm, will fetch it up for you. You'll not be wanting to cart round those dirty, heavy bags, yourself, she says thrusting a scrap of paper with a mobile number on the table.

That's really kind Mrs Nolan. As you can see you just caught me grabbing a bit of breakfast. I thought I'd go for a walk while it's clear.

Mrs Nolan? What sort of eejit name is that? Everyone calls me Mary.

Well, Mary, can I offer you a cup of tea?

No, I'm grand just now thanks. I hope you'll be alright on your own up here. It's a windy old place. Just you ring if you need anything. You've my number alright.

4

Eugene Riordan wakes with a thick head and a bad temper. He shouldn't have drunk so much. He hates parties, particularly his own. Why does he give these things when he never enjoys them? He didn't get to bed until three and shouldn't have had that last cigar. His throat feels like sandpaper and his tongue is huge. A sick headache is no way to start the New Year and, on balance, he'd prefer it if Siobhán wasn't lying beside him stroking his inner thigh. He doesn't want to make love or even chat. She has a large spot on her chin. The livid yellow head looks ready to burst. He just wants to be left alone to nurse his headache, then fling on some old clothes and go down to the beach with the dogs. He enjoys their mute company as they run across the wet sands retrieving the bits of driftwood he throws for them. Why does she keep coming back? She insists she's not interested in his money, just in being close to him. But he's not sure he wants to be close to anyone. She usually offers up such confessions late at night when he's mellowed by whiskey and a good dinner. She has a habit of staring into his eyes and making these declarations about which he feels nothing. And she's far too keen on telling him that he's 'in denial' and 'not in touch with his feelings'. Well that's as maybe. But she seems to want the sort of intimacy for which two failed marriages have taught him he has no real talent. He can't understand what women want, what they expect. What he's supposed to do or say. He doesn't love her. In fact he's not sure he's ever loved anyone other than his nan who died when he was five. And that might have been some other emotion entirely.

Lust. He's felt his share of lust for a variety of different women and the sense of ownership that ignites. Though these days he's not even sure that sex interests him that much. It's true that he likes a woman in his bed at night. For ever since he was a child he's disliked the dark. But such comfort in the small hours always carries the price of having to chat over breakfast or make plans for lunch the following day. He'd rather spend the morning with his accountant or out with the guns.

That reminds him, he must ring and find out what's happening with that land up past Bolus Head. His solicitor promised to hurry things along. He's trying to clear matters with the local council but the purchase is dragging on forever. The architects have already sent him the first drawings. He's impressed. There'll be uninterrupted views of the Skelligs, making it the most exclusive spa in Ireland. Actually he's quite excited. Spas. That's where the future lies. They have to be tasteful. But it's worth the investment. The architects, a young prize-winning firm from Dublin, have suggested Carrara marble, tropical hardwoods and lots of plate glass to show off the views. They want to run the minimal Zen theme throughout. An indoor waterfall flowing over natural boulders into a stream full of golden carp in the entrance. A Japanese garden. It's what the wealthy Dublin wives he wants to attract expect, as well as those from London, Paris, even the Middle East and New York. And he hopes to entice some new Russian money. All these old communists are into Armani suits and diamond-encrusted Rolex watches now. It won't just be Jacuzzis and steam rooms. But aromatherapy and hot stone treatments. Lots of thick white towels and complementary bath robes. Body wraps seem to be the latest thing, in algae and seaweed. Then there are the new exfoliating salt scrubs. He's been doing some research and found an exclusive firm that only sources salt from the Dead Sea. And he wants to serve top-class food. The best on the west coast. Locally sourced oysters, hake and lobster, but with a twist. A touch of Asian fusion along with some traditional Irish dishes presented in a new way. He's been asking around for a top chef. Maybe with a Michelin star or two. He's in touch with one who worked for Heston Blumenthal and he's also on the lookout for a sommelier. There's a young one in Dublin he's had his eye on. There'll also be a juice bar by the pool for those doing a detox—alcohol-free cocktails in any combination of fresh fruits or vegetables the client chooses—and an organic restaurant that serves a macrobiotic, wheat-and-gluten-free menu. Golden flaxseed seems to be the buzzword. And omega-3s. He's having to get up to speed on the latest nutritional advice. It's not just the wives he's after but managers away on stress-busting breaks or a company bringing its senior executives away for a weekend of male bonding. They're all up for a bit of a massage and a collagen facial after a game of golf. Pampering is no longer just for girls.

But there are obstacles. The three smallholdings on the mountain will have to be dealt with. The Kellys aren't a problem. Neither are the Keegan brothers. He can buy them out. But Paddy O'Connell in his white cottage, well, he'll prove harder to shift. His family have farmed there for generations and he's not interested in money. He also needs to speak to Martha about the access across the bottom of her field.

Siobhán's hand is becoming ever more insistent. He'll either have to get up or respond. Even though he's tried to break it off with her several times she always manages to inveigle a way back into his life, getting involved in the colour schemes for the new treatment rooms, researching plants for the Japanese garden. The idea is that it'll just be raked stones, with minimal planting, which suits this climate. And he's been thinking of building some little summer houses where the guests can lounge around in private when the weather's fine, which'll look directly out onto Skelligs.

But Siobhán has this tendency to arrive without warning, bearing endless swatches of fabric for chair covers and curtains, copies of *Homes & Gardens* and books on plants and landscaping, which she spreads all over the drawing room floor. But worst of all are the paintings that have proliferated around the house. Two have appeared on the stairs and one in the hall. She fancies herself as a bit of a collector and likes to be seen to support local artists and goes to all their private views. But he hates the sort of stuff she buys. Most of it looks as though his dogs have shaken their wet coats over the canvas. It may go down in London or New York but it does nothing for him. He's always suspected it's a case of the Emperor's New Clothes. Brendan dealt with the stuff that ended up in museums or on the walls of wealthy American collectors' condos and had tried to educate Eugene over the years. But without much success. Now everyone seems to be an artist. The whole place is awash with them setting up their galleries in every empty greengrocer's shop, encouraged by the favourable tax breaks offered to anyone who decides that they're remotely creative. Siobhán's made friends with a few of them and keeps urging him to buy their work for the spa. But it's just pretentious rubbish as far as he's concerned. Stripes and daubs. Where's the skill in that? Ask half these so-called artists to pick up a pencil and draw one of his dogs and most of them couldn't do it. He's happy to support them if they can produce something recognisable. He even commissioned one to do a painting of his house and he quite likes that. It's well done and you can see what it is. If he employs an accountant he wants one who understands taxes. If he buys a painting he wants it to be skilful. Not something that he could have knocked out in half an hour with a couple of house-painter's brushes. He wasn't best pleased when Siobhán removed it from over the fireplace in the drawing room and put up a great thing with swirls and blotches that one of her friends had done. It looked as if someone had spilt a couple of pots of builder's paint over the canvas. He insisted that she put his back and take her ridiculous canvas away with her to Dublin.

Really he'll have to end things with her once and for all. She has too much of a foothold. It was a mistake to ask her advice on alternative therapies just because she's done a six week course in Reiki. Suddenly, she's an expert on alternative medicine. On crystals and Indian ear candles. On homeopathy and acupuncture. But he's not interested in blocked energy channels, chakras or pressure points. Just in a business plan.

The trouble is he doesn't really fancy her any more. He was flattered when he first met her at the golf club dinner, where she was accompanying her father who'd recently helped him evict a troublesome tenant. Her flirtations were seductive for a while. But her boyish body with its small breasts has begun to irritate him. He's always preferred curvaceous girls. He must end it. Get the inevitable crying and shouting out of the way so he can get on with his project. What he really wants is to be on his own. The occasional fling, maybe. But he doesn't need someone around permanently. Doesn't want to have to justify himself to anyone.

He can't be bothered to get out of bed and lies staring at the ceiling trying not to respond to Siobhán's hand. Caesar is pawing at the bedroom door and whining to be let in. When Siobhán's not here the dogs sleep with him and they feel put out. They flop at the bottom of the bed and keep him warm with their dusty, livery presence. Stick their wet noses in his face to wake him and be let out. He needs to get up. But Siobhán shifts onto her elbow where, from behind a curtain of fallen hair, she moves her lips slowly up and down his semi-erect penis. He doesn't have the energy to resist, though Caesar is still scratching at the door and yowling.

He was surprised that Martha Cassidy came to his party. He'd only asked her out of curiosity. He'd heard in the garage shop, when he called in for some matches that she was up at the cottage. He never really expected to see her here again. But it's convenient. He needs to get her on board. Now Brendan's gone, he supposes she won't care too much what happens to the place. Even if she keeps the cottage, which seems unlikely, she probably won't want the field. He knew Brendan for a long time. His father knew his father, Dermot. And before him, the old man. When they were boys the two of them, and Brendan's younger brother Michael, played together on the beach, fished and built camp fires. He'd never done anything like that. It was the closest he ever came to having a real friend. Now all his so-called friends are business colleagues. He'd met Martha a few times in the '80s and she rather irritated him. There was something so English about her. So self-contained. He could never quite work out what she was thinking.

He frees himself from Siobhán's grip, intending to get up, have a bath and shave. But she reaches for his arm and pulls him back.

Don't go Eugene. How's your headache? Shall I get you some aspirin? Come on, come back to bed and I'll make it better for you. I'll give you a massage. I have some lovely geranium oil. What's the rush? It's New Year's Day. There's nothing we need do, she says, wrapping her arms around his shoulders so he can feel her small breasts with their hard little nipples pressed against his back, her slightly fetid breath on his neck. As she runs her fingers down his spine his resolve weakens. He turns, aware that he's crushing her and, with his eyes closed, empties himself quickly inside her.

5

Martha is getting ready for a walk when a red van pulls up. A tall, gangly young man in a plaid shirt and a woolly hat jumps out of the driver's seat and slams the door.

Where shall I put these? he asks, hauling two bags of turf from the back. Inside I'd say, if you've the room. No point in letting it get wet, is there?

You must be Colm.

He nods, steadying the blue plastic sack on his left shoulder, and carrying it into the cottage.

Will it suit here? He asks, not waiting for a reply, before tipping the contents into the basket, then reaching for the dustpan and brush by the fire to sweep the debris.

Crouched beside the stove in his muddy work boots, his jeans straining against his long thighs, it's his hands Martha notices. Each joint pressed against the stretched skin. The knobbly wrist-bones protruding from the frayed cuffs.

You're the fiddler, aren't you? Didn't you play at the party the other night? I didn't recognise you in that hat.

Sure, that's me, he answers, putting back the dustpan, and tucking his thick lumberjack shirt back into his belt. This should see you right for a couple of days.

Thank you. That's an enormous help. Can I get you a cup of tea? I was about to go for a walk but as you can see, she says, it's started to tip down.

He pulls off his hat and runs his fingers through his messed hair.

If it's no bother, I wouldn't say no. Been on the go all morning.

I've no biscuits, I'm afraid and only some rather old Earl Grey. I still haven't done a proper shop.

He takes the offered mug and sniffs it suspiciously.

I enjoyed your singing the other night, she says. Is that what you do when you're not delivering peat?

Sort of...

Sorry?

No need to be sorry. I mean I just play with my friend Niall. He's the one on the flute. And I write a bit. Not professionally, mind. Not yet. Though we hope to make a demo CD soon. And I help my mam. That's Mary who you met. Those are our sheep up past Bolus. There's only me here, now. Kathleen—that's my sister—she's away in Dublin. She's a midwife and not much interested in sheep. So you like this windy old place then, do you?

Well it's a long time since I've been here. It was summer then and the place has rather complicated memories for me. But it's incredibly beautiful. I love being right on the edge of the ocean. After London it feels very remote. But it probably feels different if you live here all the time.

Yeah, kind of. But sure, it's beautiful alright. Well it looks as though the rain's stopping if you fancy your walk. It changes very quickly up here. I'll be on my way then, he says, leaving his undrunk tea on the draining board. Just give us a ring if you need anything else. Then, hitching up his jeans, he turns for the door and adds:

I was sorry to hear about Brendan.

You knew him?

Yes, he says pulling on his hat. We used to chat about this and that.

By the way, she says, you haven't told me what I owe you for the turf.

It's €5 a bag.

And delivery?

Ah, I was passing, he replies. €10 cash will be grand.

She fetches her purse and fishes out a note. He shoves it into the back pocket of his jeans, swings himself up into the van, then slams the door, starts the engine and drives off down the track, Catherine wheels of mud spraying from the tyres. As she turns to go back inside the heavy bank of cloud parts to reveal a sliver of blue.

6

There's a strong wind and the waves boom against the rocks as she makes her way up the cliff path towards Bolus Head. The track is steep and she has to slow down to catch her breath. Her calf muscles ache. She thought she was fitter than this. At the curve in the track she stops at a pink cottage. Despite the dusty bottles of washing up liquid in the window it looks empty. Floral curtains sag with neglect. She goes to the gate. Above the doorway is inscribed: National School 1899. She imagines children from the scattering of mostly derelict cottages making their way up here, barefoot and hungry in the mist, to snatch a few hours practising their letters, having first fed the backyard pig or clutch of scrawny hens. Every child had to bring a sod of turf to school. Though few saw the benefit as the teacher's backside hogged the fire. Poverty and politics, the Church and superstition dominated the lives of those scratching a living up here.

Brendan's cottage, for she still thinks of it as his, was rebuilt in the '20s when the villagers left the old hamlet further up the mountain. Presumably they got tired of waking to find their roofs ripped off, blown across the fields like confetti. That they built up there in the first place, so open to the elements, seems incredible. Brendan's grandfather farmed about five acres. Fields and tillage plots of potatoes, rye and oats. He also had a herd of sheep and a few head of cattle. What must it have been like bringing up a family with no running water or electricity in a place where it always rained? They'd have been permanently wet—for where was there to dry their clothes? And smelt. A rich mix of peat smoke, damp wool and sweat.

Before this schoolhouse the children had to steal what education they could in one of the hedge schools set up in response to the 18th century Penal Laws that stated: 'no person of the popish religion shall publicly or in private houses teach, school, or instruct youth in learning within this realm...' In dry ditches, beneath blackthorn hedges or in the nook in a stone wall, Gaelic brehons secretly taught Irish literature, music and poetry, arithmetic and a smattering of the classics. The erosion of their native language was as powerful as any gun in the suppression of small communities. It had happened in Wales and the Basque country, too. This sweeping away of the vernacular and, with it, the grammar of memories that defined who you were. Peasant families bartered a flitch of bacon or a pat of butter for a bit of learning in their native tongue.

How little she really knows about Irish history. Cromwell and William of Orange had, in school, always been yoked to the 'the Irish problem'. She knows about the potato famine and the Easter Rising. Had read Yeats at university. Knew something of the Abbey Theatre in Dublin. About Synge and Tyrone Guthrie and the Irish Americans such as Eugene O'Neill. But her knowledge is little more than a list of names: Maud Gonne, Lady Gregory, Joyce, Beckett, the Black and Tans, Michael Collins, de Valera, and Sinn Féin. She remembers Bill Clinton and John Major's peace efforts north of the border. The absurdity of the BBC banning Gerry Adams's voice and dubbing it with an actor. But it was the London bombings that really brought Irish politics home. She and Brendan were in bed when the bomb exploded at the Baltic Exchange. The blast carried for miles shaking the windows of their Islington house. And around Christmas time she'd always felt nervous in Oxford Street in case the IRA should take advantage of the seasonal crowds. Then there was that time when a load of Semtex was discovered just up the road, hidden in a reservoir in Stoke Newington. Life infiltrates even when one's minding one's own business.

But things move on. Truth is only ever partial. Every picture a distortion in some way or another. Facts not entirely what they seem. Since the attack on the Twin Towers, the IRA seems like ancient history. She remembers how Brendan phoned from the gallery to tell her to switch on the television. How she stood alone, transfixed in the middle of the sitting room watching the growing horror unfold, her gaze focused on a lone man tumbling like a deep sea diver through the New York morning sky. She imagined him having coffee and cornflakes earlier somewhere in Tribeca. Kissing his wife and child goodbye before catching the subway to work, with no notion that this would be his last day on earth.

She doesn't know who owns the pink cottage. When it was a school it would have consisted of one room. The small children at one end learning by rote. The older ones practising their sums on slates at the other. And then, without meaning to, she remembers that day, a life time ago, when Bruno slipped his hand nervously from hers and ran in through the school gate to join the other children. How she stood with a lump in her throat, because she knew as she walked back to the car that something had changed. That he'd moved off into his own trajectory. That this was the beginning of his pulling away. She worried all morning that he'd forget to ask for the lavatory. Imagined him among the alphabet posters and number charts, the pictures of farm animals, negotiating his place in the world.

She sets off again up the hill, past the lichen-covered stone walls. There are no trees except for a spinney of pines planted as a windbreak above the squat bungalow where a white goose is screeching at a tethered dog.

7

The pages of the old photograph album are foxed and faded. Images peel from the transparent cellophane corners that hold them flimsily to the page between sheets of yellowing tissue paper. She remembers taking some of the snaps—the ones on the beach—on her old box Brownie. But those in Waterville? Who was holding the camera? It can't have been Brendan because he's standing beside her. Was it Bruno? Her memories are so unreliable. She stares at the photos as if her concentration might enable her to explain some elusive mystery. But they are phantoms. Mechanical ghosts.

They spent most of that summer down on the beach or taking trips in the car on the odd hazy day. But usually they woke to a blue sky and the bay still as a millpond. Then they trekked with their striped windbreak and rugs, their sun hats, bathing costumes and suntan lotion, down the lane lined with purple and scarlet fuchsia, along the gorse-edged path, to set up camp at the far end of the bay. Brendan took a small aluminium framed deckchair so he could sit and read. She can still see him in his old khaki shorts and battered denim hat, his legs white after a winter in the city, rubbed bald around the ankles from his socks. His feet self-conscious in their unfamiliar sandals, as if his toes didn't quite belong to him. She lay on her towel soaking up the unexpected Irish sun, her head resting on her arms, squinting through her fingers to keep a watchful eye on the small figure leaping like a salmon through the waves.

Watch me. You're not watching.

On the green towel beside her were his sand shoes. His T-shirt with the palm tree embroidered on the front, his checked shorts rolled into a ball. She looks out across the silver bay. And, for a moment, can feel his presence so keenly that she can smell the crusted salt on his skin. But that was another life. She was someone else then. She came here to wind up her husband's affairs, little thinking how these other banished ghosts would surface to haunt her. If she'd considered it at all, she would never have come. It was here that she'd last felt wholly and unconsciously herself. She's almost forgotten what that was like. Like an amputee she's got used to her loss. Only occasionally having the fantasy that what was once so essentially a part of her is still with her. To survive these last two decades has meant placing her feelings in a box and firmly shutting the lid.

Suddenly she feels very tired. She'd intended to walk up to Paddy O'Connell's white cottage but doesn't have the strength. Maybe tomorrow, if it's fine, she'll climb to the Napoleonic tower and look out across St Fionán's Bay to the Skelligs. Why do those strange rocks hold such a magnetic allure? She thinks of Mrs Ramsay in that dilapidated house on an island in the Hebrides. Her young son James cutting out pictures from an old Army and Navy catalogue and sticking them in a scrap book. Of their long planned trip out to the lighthouse. How Mrs Ramsay had cherished her time with James, had recoiled at the thought of him growing into adulthood. It was strange that Virginia Woolf, who never had children, should have understood.

But the mist is closing in. She needs to get back. To sit down with a cup of tea and take stock. To assess what she has left.

8

The wind is full of sleet. A night light burns on the sill of her sleeping loft, casting shadows under the eaves. Her dreams are dark and chaotic. Strauss's 'Four Last Songs' drift through her sleep on all-night Lyric FM. She tries not to think of those early hours when Bruno woke with mumps or a nightmare and she climbed into his narrow bed, under the Batman duvet, to comfort him. Or those endless nights when she lay awake beside Brendan's sleeping back, a sliver of light seeping beneath the curtains from the street lamp below, knowing that the city's derelicts were huddled in doorways and on park benches, crouched beneath a bush in a local cemetery. Soothed by the barely audible tones of 'Sailing By', kept low so as not to wake Brendan, she'd listened to the shipping forecast in the safety of her bed like a member of some secret fraternity of insomniacs, following each point around the coast from Tyne to Dogger, from Fisher to German Bight, on to the Thames and the Bay of Biscay.

Cyclonic 4 or 5, becoming west to northwest 6 to gale 8, perhaps severe gale 9 later. Moderate or rough, occasionally very rough later. Showers, fog patches. Moderate, occasionally very poor.

Then 'Lillibulero' and Radio 4 would shut down and switch to the *World Service.*

She sits up in bed and presses her face to the freezing window. The dark seems infinite, a friend of oblivion. But the disadvantage of sleep is that she must always wake from it, that the curtain edges will eventually bleed with morning light. She knows that all is not right with her world.

She manages by day but at night there's no escaping that she's utterly alone. She tries to imagine a life, not even punctuated by the demands of teaching, as retirement looms. She isn't artistic and has no desire to try her hand at writing a novel or amateur watercolours. She's been surrounded by good books and art and has no wish to add her indifferent endeavours to the pile.

What, then, can she do? A little charity work? Join the Ramblers, take up bridge? Good God! It all sounds impossibly worthy. At least Brendan hadn't suffered that gradual seepage and decline. He'd gone into hospital one afternoon, lost consciousness and been dead by the evening. There was no slowing of the intellect, no mewling or puking for him, thank god. He went at the height of his powers. Anyway he was always a hopeless patient, taking to his bed with the slightest snuffle, demanding whiskey with hot lemon and honey, and generally behaving as if he had some terminal illness. How ironic then that when he did, he chose to ignore it. Maybe he knew he was staring death in the face and was too scared to do anything. She feels guilty that she didn't get him to hospital sooner. But he was adamant that he didn't want a fuss. She feels a sudden surge of pity and wishes she could hold her frightened husband. Stroke his hair and tell him not to be afraid. But he'd never have coped with a protracted illness. Would have hated the enforced gratitude required of an invalid. The slowing of body and mind. No, if he had to go, then better this way.

It's no metaphor to say that death is close at hand. It seeps from the pores of the collapsed cottages like mineral salts from rock. It's there in the fallen stone walls and the wind-blasted crosses lying upturned in the fields she passes when out walking. She's not the only one to have suffered. She feels close to those women with their broken teeth and calloused hands who had to lift their rain-sodden skirts to piss and shit in a ditch whatever the weather. The walls of their abandoned homes are imprinted with memories: the births of children, the death of a grandfather, the fetid odour of cow dung and peat smoke. For in winter the crofters lived with their animals. And on the hearth, a loaf of soda bread would sit proving in a tin as the dog, its head on its paws, snored, and a clutch of grimy children played knucklebones.

Hearth. How close the word is to *heart*. A letter away.

Grief requires time but how much? It remains embedded like a virus to be triggered by some small external event. Last night she was woken by the storm and sat watching the lighthouse beam arching across the sky.

A lighthouse. A pharos. A beacon in the darkness warning of rocks to passing ships. Each sweep indicating the passing of another thirty seconds like the pulse on a heart monitor.

Blip, blip. Blip, blip.

The difference between life and death. Grandchildren. She'll never have any grandchildren. Her genetic imprint stops here.

Tuesday

1

White horses run between the islands as she pegs out her washing. It may be January but after the previous night's gales it feels almost like spring. It's the first time it's been dry enough to hang anything outside. Her knickers and socks snap in the wind. Up on the hill Colm is carrying bales of hay to the cattle. At least she presumes it must be Colm because his red van is parked nearby. It stands out against the brown hillside like a toy truck. She waves but he doesn't see her. She needs to decide what to do with her day. There are still papers to sort but the weather is too nice to stay indoors. She's tempted to go to the beach but isn't ready for that.

She goes back in and cleans up the kitchen, boils the kettle and does the washing up. She rinses the suds off the mugs and pans, leaving them sparkling on the draining board, then washes the bracelet of bubbles from her wrist under the cold tap. Something about the morning sun streaming through her little kitchen window with its blue and white gingham curtains makes her want to leave everything gleaming. She wipes down the table and goes outside to look for something to pick but not much is in bloom. She finds some snowdrops in a ditch and takes them back inside to arrange in a glass on the table.

Up in the bedroom she sorts through the rest of Brendan's clothes. She can't believe how many he has. He must have brought things from London over the years and forgotten about them, never throwing anything away. She pulls out a pair of battered walking boots from the bottom of the cupboard, some tartan slippers and a pair of mouldy tennis shoes. There are faded corduroy jackets and shirts with missing buttons. A moth-eaten Aran jumper and assorted woolly hats. As she takes them from the drawers and hangers she's thrown by his smell. His sudden unexpected resurrection. As she's sorting everything into piles, deciding what to keep and what to take to the charity shop in Caherciveen, she hears a noise downstairs. But before she can investigate, the bedroom door is flung open.

Martha what are you doing on your hands and knees?

Eugene is standing in the doorway under the low eaves in a wax jacket and mustard cashmere scarf.

I came to see if I can take you to lunch but you look as if you're otherwise engaged.

Lunch? Oh good morning Eugene, what time is it? I'd no idea it was so late. Now why would you want to take me to lunch? she asks, getting up and smoothing her rumpled hair, conscious that she's covered in dust and fluff.

Curiosity and an excuse for a chat. I didn't see much of you the other night. I hope you enjoyed the party. I hate them myself. Don't tell me you don't eat lunch. I'm sure you haven't got anything in. I know the garage shop doesn't sell much beyond cut-price baked beans and processed cheese like lard.

Well if you insist but you'll have to wait while I have a shower. I can hardly go like this, she says, catching her reflection in the bedroom mirror. There's a black smut on her cheek. Give me ten minutes and I'll be with you.

His Range Rover is parked outside. The dogs curled up in the back behind a grill. As Martha climbs in beside Eugene she wonders, as he speeds down the lanes in a flurry of mud, why on earth she's agreed to this. They stop at a small quayside inn and he lets the dogs out to stretch their legs. They come bounding out of the boot like bullets from a rifle, running up and down the harbour front barking at the gulls.

That's it, fellas. Come on now, Brutus, Caesar. Heel, heel. Back with you into the car, come on that's it, he says, pouring a bottle of mineral water into a plastic dog bowl and placing it in the boot. The dogs jump up obediently, furiously lapping with their spam-like tongues, spraying water all over the rug. Martha wonders whether Eugene has enough learning to know what Brutus did to Caesar.

In the bar they are shown to a table near an inglenook. A peat fire is smouldering in the grate. There are horse brasses and antique fire tongs. All the things that define a pub as having 'character'. Eugene orders a bottle of Chablis and they sit chatting about nothing much, polite but weary, as the waiter pours the wine and they wait for their grilled hake.

The walls are covered with sepia photographs: huge waves pounding the quay in the storm of '69, fishermen repairing nets, women in aprons and shawls tied in an X across their breasts as they sit gutting piles of fish beside large wicker baskets like Molly Malone. The place is crowded and Martha wonders who all these people are. What they do. Presumably they're local solicitors and business men out on expense account lunches. Not long ago the clientele would have consisted of a few glum farmers in flat caps and dung-smeared overalls staring morosely into their Guinness and discussing the outbreak of foot rot or the price of cattle pellets. Pubs like that still exist. No matter what time of day you go in there are always a couple of old fellows sitting by the bar in their Wellingtons over a dark pint. Last time she was in Caherciveen she'd gone into Mick Murts where they sold rope and rat poison at one end of the counter. Guinness and whiskey at the other.

She has no idea why Eugene wants to see her.

It was sudden then, Brendan's going? he asks.

Yes, she answers. He came back from the shop one Sunday morning after buying the newspapers and complained of pins and needles in his arm. But I couldn't get him to go to the doctor. You know what he was like, stubborn. Still it was a shock. You never expect it do you? But the doctor told me that even if I'd got him to A&E sooner it probably wouldn't have made any difference, which makes me feel a bit better. It was a massive heart attack and had probably been waiting to happen for years. Apparently he had a genetic weakness that no one knew about. Thank God it was all over quickly.

Well, I'm sorry Martha. I'll miss him and there aren't that many people I can say that about. And I'm sorry for your other troubles too.

She looks away, kneading her bread roll into grey pellets, not wanting to display her discomfort at the commiserations of this man she's never much liked. His nose is flecked with broken veins and the whites of his eyes have a slight eggy tinge. Outside in the little harbour fishing boats bob on the winter tide. The sky, the sea and the far distant mountains are grey. Why is she here? She should be at the cottage sorting out Brendan's stuff and getting on with what she came here to do.

This place was special for Brendan, Eugene, she says. That summer you spent with him and Michael as children was important to him too. He was ten wasn't he? That's sort of a magical age, don't you think? Still a child, still innocent but beginning to question the world. …

Why is she talking like this? What does Eugene care? Ten years. Everything can be divided into decades. Three of Brendan. One of Bruno. How many more did she have before her time was up? Two perhaps, three if she's lucky? Measured like this how short it all is. We spend most of the first half of our lives getting used to it. Learning the ropes, making mistakes and preparing for what lies ahead. And, for a moment, there's a feeling that it all finally makes sense, that we've arrived and understood something about the world. Then, before we know it, it's all over. The tide coming in and washing away our footprints to leave an unmarked beach.

She's getting maudlin. The lunchtime wine must be going to her head.

And you Eugene, what have you been doing since I was last here?

He lifts the bottle from its plastic cooler and pours her another glass. She doesn't refuse. What the hell. There's nothing else to do now that she's stuck here with him except drink and listen.

He begins the long narrative about his divorce from Bridget, complaining that she's 'taken him to the cleaners' and is still fighting for the Kinsale house. Why do all stories of marital failure follow the same script?

And your son? You've a young son haven't you?

Rory? Yes, he's mostly with his mother when he's not away at school. This time it's Eugene who looks away.

He's not an easy boy, you know. Though I'm told that's quite normal. Just how teenagers are these days. He comes to stay sometimes. Sits and plays computer games and loud music. I don't see him much. We each do our own thing. He's not interested in golf or shooting and I'm very busy. That's partly why I wanted this chat, Martha, he says, relieved to be on what he seems to consider safer ground. I've a few plans up on Bolus Head. A spa. It's going to be the best in Ireland. Very exclusive, I hope. And it'll bring much needed work to the area, he adds, as if throwing a dog a bone. But it's not straightforward. I own some of the land up there already, but not enough to make sure no one else can build or to guarantee the necessary rights of way and access. There're a couple of small farmers up there. Some are only tenants and most of the others are happy to be bought out. But there's one crucial place I need for the thing to go through and I think I'll have a problem with that. And then, he adds slowly, there's your field and without that and your man Paddy O' Connell's land the whole project will grind to a halt. I've got the fellows down in my office on the case. But it's not easy, even for a property lawyer, he smiles wryly. But I'm hoping that you and I can come to a friendly arrangement. In your case it's only the strip at the bottom of your field that connects to Paddy's land. So you'll not be missing it. By the way, I presume you don't have any other plans for the place? Dessert? They do a very good sticky toffee pudding here. Or maybe an Irish coffee?

She can't bear to listen to him. There is something lost about him. A man, who despite his millions, has no idea what's important. She thinks of his son, Rory, sitting in front of endless computer games, instead of playing cricket with his father on the beach. Of Paddy O'Connell up in the high fields in the early mist, his Wellingtons caked with mud, content with his own company. He is the last vestige of an old Ireland, connected to land and cattle, Church and family. For earlier generations there was much less emphasis on personal fulfilment. Marriage, yes, and producing children. But after that you just got on with it. Making a living, caring for a family and stock left little time for the subtleties of personal growth. The Church set down the rules. Relationships with husbands and wives, children and neighbours may, at times, have been strained but Belief provided the framework. People like Paddy O'Connell, the monks and lighthouse keepers, defied the modern assumption that material advancement and emotional intimacy were essential to happiness. That not to have these things was to be deficient. When she sees Paddy carrying hay up to his cows, dressed in his neat overalls, his eyes reflecting back the colour of the sea, he doesn't seem like a disappointed man to her.

At Eugene's party all people talked about were property prices. From one of the poorest and most backward countries in Europe, Ireland is now one of the richest. Its current legacy not new poets or story tellers but a blight of vulgar bungalows scarring this dramatic landscape.

I don't know yet, Eugene, what I'm going to do. I've only been here a couple of days. It's too soon to decide, she says.

They finish the Chablis, making small talk and he pays the bill, then drives her back to the cottage. They don't speak much. Then, just as she's opening the car door he leans forward, his mouth, with its wine-soaked breath, brushing not just her cheek but her lips. She pulls back. Pats him maternally on the arm, then manoeuvres herself out of the car.

I'll pretend you didn't do that.

2

Cable O'Leary's is packed. Girls in short jogging tops, white midriffs exposed above skinny jeans, stand around drinking Bacardi and Cokes. Middle-aged men, the belts of their stonewashed jeans pulled tight over ample stomachs, talk loudly above the music, while their wives sip sweet white wine, laugh and mostly ignore them. A Guinness toucan and row of little plastic harps nestle on the shelf above the bar among the Baileys and the Jameson. Martha takes her glass of wine and manages to find a free seat by the Ladies. It's a moment or two before she realises that the fiddler on the small stage is Colm. There's also a bearded man playing a flute whom, she presumes, must be Niall. And a girl with spiky red hair accompanying them on a *bodhran*.

Now this next song, the bearded man announces coming to the front of the stage, is written by my friend, Colm here, he says nodding in his direction. He's a poet but too much of a shy eejit to introduce it himself.

The *bodhran* and flute begin slowly, counterpointed by Colm's husky voice. There's something timeless about it that captures the spirit of this harsh place. The history of the megalithic stones scattered over the headland. The collapsed walls and abandoned dwellings where the occupants were forced to leave, after another failed crop, for the tin mines of Colorado or a sheep farm in New South Wales. When the set finishes the musicians down their instruments and gather at the bar. They seem more ordinary than on stage. Just three young people having a drink and a good time. She wonders, as they collect up their pints and head outside for a smoke, if either Colm or Niall is the boyfriend of the girl with the spiky hair. She imagines them climbing into his battered VW van. Taking off to gigs in Waterville, Caherdaniel or Portmagee. Bedding down in the back in their sleeping bags in a fug of Guinness and roll-ups after another late night session, before taking to the road again. Above the bar the poster says their band is called *Caidre.*

Apparently it means friendship.

She gets up and goes to the Ladies. When she returns to order another glass of wine, Colm is sitting on a high stool at the bar with his back towards her, talking animatedly to his friends. He's wearing a scruffy leather jacket and his ubiquitous blue woollen hat. As she waits to be served someone calls his name. He turns and notices her. Smiles. His teeth are slightly snagged like those of a ten year old in need of a brace.

Hey Shane, get your arse down this end. There's a lady waiting. Did you hear the set, Martha? Can I get you a drink now?

She can't remember telling him her name.

3

The Tate or the Courtauld might want Brendan's papers if they are collated and catalogued. She's trying to save what she can. But the more she reads, the more the Brendan she knew, the man who put on his white towelling robe each morning to go down and put the Italian percolator on the hob for his first espresso, the man who when she returned home tired after a hard day in school, opened a bottle of Pinot Grigio and laid out a dish of olives to signal the end of their time apart, seems to fade. To relive the past we start with a few known facts. Then add texture and colour, so that like a child's dot-to-dot drawing we arrive, if we're lucky, at an approximate outline. Though often it's not quite what we expect.

It was a freezing November day for Brendan's funeral. She was surprised by the turn out. Nick Serota from the Tate. Norman Rosenthal, Anthony and Sheila Caro, Sean Scully. Collectors, curators and artists that Brendan had known over the years. Some well-heeled. Others down on their luck, happy enough for an egg and cress sandwich, a cup of tea or a glass of sherry after the service. She remembers the cloying fragrance of lilies. The sea of sombre coats as she stood under a dripping umbrella, receiving those who wanted a word with her in the porch of the crematorium. At the reception a young waitress in a very short black dress served vol-au-vents from a silver salver. Brendan would have enjoyed that.

She was poised and calm but inside felt, what? Angry and abandoned. She got through it all like an automaton, as if giving a performance. There was a strange euphoria, a sense of drama at the heightened emotion of it all. Then the grey loneliness descended permeating everything. The books that sat unread in Brendan's study. His paisley dressing gown hanging limply on the back of the bedroom door. His shaving things that lay neglected in the bathroom, which took her weeks to chuck out. As if by throwing them away she was being disloyal. It was there in the footsteps of strangers echoing along the hard city pavements in the early evening. In the casual banter of drinkers spilling from Islington pubs at closing time. The couples snuggled inside each other's coats as they waited in the rain for the night bus to take them home to their shared beds. It filled the visible day and her solitary nights, reminding her that she was quite alone.

Wednesday

1

Paddy O'Connell lies in his narrow bed listening to the storm. Such nights are as familiar to him as the beating of his own heart. It's why he lives here. To be close to the wind and the sea. To watch the first light creeping across Bolus Head. This is the time he likes best when he feels as if he's the only man in the world. Yesterday he saw that Cassidy woman, Brendan's widow, out walking. That was a sorry business. A heart attack and Brendan still a young man. Pretty much the same age as himself. Brendan came here to write his books. He always seemed very English but his grandfather was from these parts. She looked a bit lost trailing up the track in her bright-green anorak. He hasn't seen her for years. Not since that summer. She's still a nice looking woman. Younger than Brendan. But until now she's never been back. He can't really blame her in the circumstances. When they met on the track she stopped to pass the time of day and ask if she could go across his field down to the black rocks to get a better view of the Skelligs.

No reason why not, he said, if she minded how she went. It was easy to slip.

I'll be careful, she smiled. You know you must live in the most beautiful place in the world.

He couldn't really disagree with that.

2

Before it's light he puts the kettle on the hob. He'll take a quick cup before going out to see to the animals. Get the warmth of it in him. While he waits for it to boil he pulls on his overalls, finds a box of matches and lights the stove, then pads in his thick socks to the little bathroom off the kitchen to shave. Swishing the lather in the soap pot with his shaving brush, he works it into a foam on his cheeks. With his head cocked under the neon glare he scrapes it off in front of the medicine cabinet mirror with his new disposable razor. Splashing his face with cold water he pats it dry with the striped towel hanging on the back of the door, then takes the tortoiseshell comb from its blue plastic mug. It's the same comb he's used since he was a boy. And he uses it to tame his mop of grey hair, flattening it with a lick of water. He remembers his first communion. How he plastered down every hair on his head with a film of Brylcreem. They rehearsed for weeks the difference between mortal and venial sins. It was confusing for a seven-year-old. Being disobedient to his parents or teachers was certainly a sin, but what about breaking a plate or forgetting to bring in the turf? His mother took him over in the donkey cart. There wasn't much of a fuss. Just a cup of tea and a sugar bun with pink icing after in the priest's house next to the church, with all that dark furniture and the pictures of the crucified Christ with his crown of thorns and wounds in his side. His sad hurt face. There were red velvet curtains hanging at the windows, the like of which he'd never seen, and a rug with swirling patterns in front of the hearth. He can still remember the smell of Jeyes fluid and mothballs. The priest's housekeeper brought tea on a tray and put it on the table in the window on top of the crocheted cloth. There was a separate jug for the milk and a china bowl with silver tongs for the sugar. He sat in silence as the priest poured and handed a cup to him and one to his mother, who was perched uncomfortably on the edge of a padded velvet chair in her Sunday coat and the hat and the gloves she kept especially for funerals and weddings. Despite the pink sugar bun, Paddy couldn't wait to leave.

But when it came to his confirmation it had been more complicated. You could be kept back if you didn't know the right prayer. Some of the less bright kiddies struggled or got nerves. They could already be long gone out working and still not confirmed. The Bishop of Kerry was a tall man then. When he put on his mitre he stood near seven foot high. They were all examined in advance and then asked a question. His was 'what are the fours signs of the true Church?' He doubts many would know the answer today. You were given a card and without that precious card you'd be making no confirmation. Be put back till the next time. And as the confirmation was only every three years, you might have a bit of a wait. It was short pants he wore, then. And a new shop-bought jersey. For a while he wondered whether he might have a vocation. But football was his passion. Playing with the other lads up in what they called the Flat Field.

And he liked to listen to his da. About the time before he was born and the Economic War, when exports from Ireland were heavily taxed going into Britain, so prices were low. He's just too young to remember the night a fleet of bombers passed over Caherciveen on their way back to Germany after a raid on the Harland and Wolff shipyard in Belfast. It was a moonlit Sunday night. Jamesy O'Sullivan from down the hill was over for a visit. He and his da were taking a pipe of tobacco when there was this tremendous roar along the coast and the house shook with the vibration. He'd never heard the like in all his days, his da said.

He's not much of a one for politics but Paddy remembers the stories of the bad old days. How the Black and Tans threatened to burn down part of the town. How everyone waited on their arrival, though most of the women and children left to find safer places, dispersing out on the moor, in sheep shelters and ditches. Some even ventured up the mountain. But, thank God, they never came. Not that night anyway, only getting as far as Maggie Sheehan's place.

This, then, is his life. It's mostly always been his life except for the time he was away in Dublin. Three generations. His grandfather farmed here. A small man of great physical strength, he built the stone walls with his own hands, digging the boulders from the ground with a spade and moving them in a hand-barrow. It was slow, backbreaking work. A lifelong smoker he always took a sod from the hearth when he left for work. In the absence of matches it was a necessity for a man addicted to his pipe. But the tobacco got him in the end. He was confined to his bed for months before he died. Paddy can still remember his da bringing the lifeless body downstairs wrapped in a blanket, with the help of a neighbour. It was the first time he'd seen a dead person. His grandfather was laid out on the bed, just off the kitchen, under the statue of the Virgin. Then shaved with a cut-throat razor and dressed in the brown habit especially purchased for the purpose years before and periodically hung outside for a good airing so it didn't get the moth. All the clocks were stopped and the mirrors turned. Two new white candles were lit and placed at his head. The clay pipes, tobacco and snuff laid on the scrubbed table. Every male caller was expected to take a puff to keep the evil spirits away.

Along with his elder brother Mikey and his younger sisters Bridie and Marie, Paddy was charged to sit with the remains. Nora was making cups of tea and cutting thick ham sandwiches with his mam in the kitchen. The weather was warm and they were to make sure the flies didn't lay eggs on his granda's face. In the small, poorly ventilated room these could hatch out quickly and cause embarrassment. They sat with their eyes peeled, relishing the seriousness of their task, swatting any insects that dared enter the room with a folded newspaper. The window was kept open and they were instructed to be careful not to stand in front of it in case they prevented their granda's soul from leaving. After two hours, when no one was looking, Mikey got up and shut it, just to make sure that his soul didn't fly back in again.

Friends and neighbours took it in turns to sit with the body through the night and recite the rosary. Paddy was scared of the coiners, the professional mourners in their black shawls. All the women joined in the keening, wailing and carrying on. But there were also games. 'Priest of the Parish'. 'Riddle-me-Ree'. And Tommy O'Flaherty from down the way dropped by with his fiddle. No doubt a stranger, unaccustomed to their ways, would have looked on all this merriment as irreverent but when he was a lad, it was an accepted part of the wake. All the next day people called to pay their respects and talk about his granda. After prayers everyone, except those sitting up all night with the body, dispersed and supper was served beneath the flickering oil lamps. Soda bread, baked ham, pies and cheese, with whiskey for the men who stayed drinking in the kitchen, while the women went to the corpse room. The following morning Paddy had to dress in his Sunday clothes and polish his boots. Then, just before the funeral procession left, the open coffin was lifted onto two chairs and he and his siblings were instructed to line up and kiss their granda goodbye. He was shocked by how small and shrunken he seemed. His cheeks had collapsed, his nose become beaky and his thin hands poked from his long sleeves like the claws of a malevolent bird. After the lid was nailed down and the coffin put onto the donkey cart, the little procession followed behind on foot, twisting down the mountain to the churchyard in the rain.

They were a big family. Between the eldest and youngest there were fifteen years. Brothers and sisters arrived regular as clockwork. The midwife usually came before the doctor and would shoo all the children upstairs. Paddy can still remember the commotion as they huddled under the faded paisley eiderdown on the big bed in the back bedroom with their sugar sandwiches, trying to make sense of the unfolding drama downstairs that signalled the new arrival. But where it had come from was anyone's guess. For all he knew it had come down the chimney like Santy. The previous night it wasn't there and now it was going to be part of the family. How innocent they were. But that's how it was then. No TV, no radio. And no way of acquiring any information, except from parents, teachers or the priest. And none of them were forthcoming. Even though he saw sheep and cows mating he never put two and two together. Nothing was ever explained. It was only after he watched his first calves being born that he began to work things out. One night he followed the yellow circle of torch light to the barn and stood among the rain-wet straw as his da approached the lowing cow. He can still remember the rain drumming on the tin roof, the puddles in the yard. He couldn't take his eyes off the calf hanging, half-born, from the red-gash between her back legs. The umbilical cord round its neck, its tongue lolling and frothed with white. His da rolled up his sleeves and slipped his arm up to the elbow inside the dark cavity to unhook the tangled feet and legs. Then something gave and the calf slipped out wet and shining. He felt sick at the sight of the bloodied puddle of jelly that followed but stood transfixed as the exhausted heifer licked her glistening calf to its knees and it began to nuzzle at her teats.

They each had their jobs. He had four enamel buckets to fill from the well each morning. In the evening, after school, he gathered furze. It was tough work. The furze had to be cut up in a big old machine and fed into the manger for the animals. And twice a day the cows were brought in off the land and turned into the stall. Sitting on a three legged stool he, or one of his sisters, would milk them till they were dry. He loved those cows. Their warm velvety coats smelling of mud and grass, their gentle lowing. Afterwards the milk was put into big, flat pans and left to sit for a few days. When there was enough they'd skim off the cream and churn it for butter. There were two types of churn, the dasher and the barrel. The dasher had a hole on top and a long handle with a flat paddle inside. He liked to listen to the cream slapping the sides as it thickened.

Everyone loved the duck eggs. They were large and green with specks on them. But you had to be up early to look for them if you wanted one. His mam hatched the hens, ducks and geese but bought in the turkeys. They came by rail at around five days old. He fed them hard-boiled eggs and potatoes. Then when they were big enough they had yellow meal from the corn merchant. And he looked after the pig. The children were fascinated by its curly tail. It ate all the kitchen waste: potato peelings and turnip tops, the left-over scrapings from the dinner table. They treated him like a pet, going for piggyback rides round the potato patch. His father put a ring though its nose to stop him rooting around too much. The night before the inevitable killing he had mixed emotions. They couldn't feed the pig as it had to be fasting. But there was excitement knowing that after the slaughter they'd get the bladder for a football. The following morning they were up early and took the table from the kitchen out into the yard by the back door, checking the legs for any signs of weakness as they had to withstand the weight of a struggling pig. Then the timber barrel was made ready. His mam was busy all morning boiling water in a three legged pot that hung from the crane above the open fire. This was stored in creamery cans and used for the scalding. Gradually the men who'd be holding down the pig arrived. His uncle Mick from Dún Géagáin. Jamsey O'Sullivan from down the hill and Pats Sheehan and Daniel, their cousins, from over Waterville way. His da greeted each of them with a bottle of stout. But most important of all was Ned Reilly, the butcher, who came puffing up the hill pushing his bicycle just as the pig, a rope knotted around its top jaw, was brought out squealing into the yard. Immediately the men surrounded it, each catching a leg and hoisted it onto the table, holding it down with their combined weight. The squeaking and the crying was something awful. His mam was supposed to hold the pan to collect the blood but began to feel queasy and asked Paddy to do it instead. He remembers the mix of pride and revulsion. Would he be big and brave enough when the men called 'hold him tight now' and Ned Reilly took hold of the rope on the pig's snout, to position himself at its throat and not flinch? He couldn't watch as Ned pulled the long butcher's knife from the inside of his coat pocket and thrust the blade deep into the pig's neck in the direction of her heart. The squealing and kicking was terrible. But as the blood started to flow, it slowly faded and the struggle was over. Afterwards he took three or four pints of warm blood inside to his mam, with not a little pride. He can still remember the warm rusty smell as he carried in the metal basin. Though she reprimanded him for getting his clothes splattered, he didn't mind. He felt like a man.

After the killing, a barrel was placed at the end of the table, half-filled with boiling water from the creamery cans and his da climbed up to lower the pig in, head first, and remove the bristles. All the children stood around gawping, amazed that this inert carcass had once been the pet they'd tickled behind the ear and ridden on. Then the pig was turned and its rear end plunged into the steaming water. When it was brought out and placed on the table his da and Ned shaved it, before dragging the table under the two iron hooks attached to the ceiling joists, where a skewer was run through its hind legs. After the table was removed, the intestines were cut out and placed in a galvanised bath. The liver, kidneys, heart and tongue put in a bowl and the lights fried for the dog. He can still recall the terrible smell of the innards as they searched for the bladder, which their da blew up with a goose quill. Later they took it up to the Flat Field to kick it around until it deflated and began to stink. Back in the kitchen his mam stirred oatmeal, onions and seasoning into the warm blood. For days after they would be eating nothing but black pudding for breakfast.

Going up the mountain to cut the turf was another big occasion. It was a fair old climb through the bog and gorse. Upwards of a hundred people might be working there at any one time. He was twelve or thirteen the first time he went. The children messed around pegging sods at each other, helping the *Sleán* Man and the Pike Man lay them down side by side in neat rows. There was even dancing at dinner time when someone got out a melodeon. And always there was a fire to boil the kettle. The tea a smoky mix of peat and earth. His mam would give them each a hunk of cold bacon and bread. No one had a watch. But they knew, alright, when their bellies were back as far as their backbones, when it was time to eat.

Christmas and *Nollaig na mBan*—the women's Christmas on the 6th January when the men did all the household chores—were special. They whitewashed the parlour and kitchen and his mam and da went down in the donkey cart to bring back the tea chest full of goodies. A big seed loaf, a barmbrack, and a pot of jam in an earthenware jar. And there was always a ling fish. So salty you'd be drinking for days. Then they'd fetch up the Guinness in a big brown jar. There was no Christmas tree in those days and no tinsel. Just little mottos sent from a cousin in America they hung round the walls that said God Bless Our House and Merry Christmas. On Twelfth Night they were carefully rolled up and put back in the cardboard shoe box till the following year.

Around eight o'clock on Christmas Eve the whole family would set out for Midnight Mass. The half-hour journey down the mountain could take several hours because of the stopping to chat with every man, woman and child they met on the way. When they reached the chapel the usher directed them to their seats and the queue for communion. Paddy loved that time. The smell of incense. The special Christmas candles that lit up the colours of the stained glass windows. Some of the fellows would roll in after the pubs shut a bit worse for wear. One year 'The Rose of Tralee' was heard ringing out across the aisle. But his teacher, Miss O'Shea, soon put a stop to that and your man was shown the door. But even the Mass has changed. He can well remember being told never to touch the host with his fingers, even if it got stuck on the roof of his mouth. Now people receive it in their hands. And the communion rails and curtains have all gone. So, too, has the Latin.

Now he's the only one left. Mikey is long away to Newcastle in Australia, where he's the manager of a supermarket and his wife a school secretary. He's sent Paddy photographs of the nieces he's never seen. Two little blonde, blue-eyed girls in sun hats, dangling their legs in a turquoise swimming pool. His sister Nora is a teacher in Cork. Marie's married with four children and lives in Sneem. And Jo was ordained. He works in Chile, teaching children in knitted hats, who live in the high mountains, how to read. And Bridie? Well, poor Bridie hadn't made it. The meningitis got her at sixteen.

He finishes his tea, pulls on his waterproof, his tweed cap and Wellingtons and makes his way out in the lashing rain. The ground is pock-marked with hoof holes and the cattle under the blackthorn low as he approaches them with an armful of hay, their swollen udders swinging as they push against each other. As they crowd round the concrete feeder, a damp warmth rising from their muddy flanks, a young heifer lifts a stringy tail and releases a river of warm excrement that gives off a cloud of steam as it hits the cold ground.

Paddy checks their ear tags, talking to each animal by name, scratching their woolly fringes that remind him of the ladies of a certain age coming out of Julie's hair salon with tightly crimped perms on market days. When he's seen to the cows he goes up to check on the sheep and see if any more lambs have been born in the night. High between the outcrops of rock the spongy bog is too rough for cattle. As he squelches across the field he notices a dead rabbit, its eye sockets wriggling with white maggots. Further up the headland are the small stone shelters built by the anchorites waiting to go out to the Skelligs. And beyond them, the Atlantic, as far as the eye can see.

He wonders what the Cassidy woman will do with Brendan's place now he's gone. He was no age and a pleasant enough fellow. Always had the time of day. Paddy often passed him on the track with his little sketch book and paint brushes. They'd stop and exchange civilities, chat about the weather. He couldn't see her keeping the place on and coming here on her own. It must be a hard thing for her to come back after that summer.

He finishes up with the animals and trudges down the mountain, glad to be getting out of the rain. Hangs his waterproof and overalls on the back of the kitchen chair, then gets out the old black frying pan, opens the fridge and cuts a lump of lard from the basin of dripping. While the eggs and rashers are sizzling he turns on the radio. He likes a little company while he eats. After he's finished his breakfast he clears everything away, wipes the table and puts his plate in the pink plastic bowl in the sink. Just as he's doing the washing up there's a thud on the mat and he hears the postman's van drive off down the track. There are two envelopes. An electricity bill and a white one that he can't immediately identify. He reaches for his spectacles in their old brown case, cleans them with the buff cloth resting inside the lid, then pours another mug of tea before sitting down to open the letter.

He has to read it twice. €100,000. That's a lot of money. Eugene Riordan must want his place really badly to come up with a figure like that. He breathes deeply, folds the letter along the creases and puts it back in the envelope, then goes to the dresser and slips it behind the souvenir plate from the Aran Islands.

This is his home. His mother worked in this kitchen to feed her family, cooking over the open turf fire, serving them at this same big table he's seated at. The planks were scrubbed white and on the two long benches his brothers and sisters sat waiting hungrily for a slice of the new-baked bread cooling on the window ledge, away from the dog. There were quarrels and disagreements, of course. But nothing that the odd clip round the ear couldn't sort out. It was a hard life. But he wouldn't have changed it.

3

Eugene is on the beach with the dogs. At least they don't argue or make a scene. He's wearing his wax jacket, flat tweed cap and a plaid woollen scarf. He hasn't had breakfast, showered or shaved. Just grabbed the clothes he left lying on the chair last night and slipped silently out of the house leaving Siobhán to sleep. His tongue feels furred, his skin like putty. He calls the dogs and they come bounding down the sandy path that leads to the strand. He's been up half the night and had more than enough tears and door slamming. Jesus, Mary and Joseph hadn't he simply said he didn't want her bringing any more interior design magazines or paint swatches when she came for the weekend. That he didn't need or want her advice when he was paying for a designer. It had all escalated out of control when she realised he'd been speaking to Niamh. Niamh ran a small firm of interior decorators in Dublin and worked as a contractor for the architects. Somehow it had reached Siobhán's ears that Niamh had been down for couple of days to discuss the décor for the new treatment rooms and that he'd taken her out to dinner. Siobhán had screamed and sulked, calling Niamh a scheming bitch. Surely Eugene had watched her working the party scene in Dublin and must realise she was only where she was because her father put up the money for her business and she had big tits, which she flaunted at every opportunity. And her designs? Well she had no taste, no style. Leave it to Niamh, Siobhán, screamed, and the place would look like a feckin' bordello.

He wonders if it's worth all the bother. He could just settle for a quiet life. But he needs a project, something to occupy his mind. He stands in the wind watching the dogs run backwards and forwards clutching bits of driftwood between their frilled chops, which they come and drop at his feet. He loves the way they chase across the sand barking. Their ears flapping, their coats matted with salt spray. It's a grey, drizzly morning. The sea stretches out in front of him like a sheet of corrugated iron. Two white seagulls wheel and mew overhead as the waves split on the rocks. There's no one around. Just the way he likes it. It was here that he played with Brendan as a boy. He'd never had a proper friend before but Brendan had an innate confidence that was infectious. For that summer, at least, some of it rubbed off on him. Brendan was always initiating things—fishing from the far rocks, building camp fires. As a child Eugene was crippled by shyness, tongue-tied when he had to talk to anyone he didn't know. When he considers, which he rarely does, what it means to be happy, it's that summer he remembers.

The fine rain is cool against his face. He needs the air and exercise. For last night, after the decorating fiasco, in a period of comparative calm and rapprochement, Siobhán announced that she wanted to move in with him. They had sex and he was just drifting off to sleep, the last whiskey working itself through his veins, when she leant over and asked if he was awake. He tried to ignore her as he felt the pull towards oblivion and pretended to be asleep. But she went on poking and prodding, stroking his bald patch, which always irritated him, so in the end he was forced to fling off the covers and, exasperated, sit up and take notice.

Can't a man even get a night's sleep in his own bed? And since she was asking, no, she couldn't come and live with him. It was out of the question. He didn't want to live with anyone ever again.

She shouted, cried and demanded. What were her words? That he stop dangling her on a string and make a commitment to their relationship. But what relationship was that, he wondered? As far as he's concerned the terms are clear. She can come and enjoy the house; sleep with him if that's what she wants. Though he never asks her to, even if it's true that he generally does nothing to dissuade her when she rings to say she's on the Friday train to Killarney. And he's happy to help out financially from time to time. But he's tired of her lectures about the need to 'get in touch with his real feelings'. He is as he is. He doesn't want to share his homes with anyone or let anybody get too close to him again. Hasn't he only just got rid of Bridget—and look what a mess that was? No, he doesn't need another woman to move in and lay claim. Certainly not one who keeps him awake in the middle of the night asking every five minutes if he loves her. Why do people always want things from him? Why can't they just leave him alone?

He's exhausted. He drank too much again last night, smoked too many cigars. His mouth feels like the bottom of a parrot's cage. He throws a stick to Brutus who goes bounding after it. He needs to call into the office and find out if there's been any developments with the land up by Bolus Head. It's all taking too long. Why won't your man just take the money? It's more than Paddy O'Connell will see in a lifetime. He needs to get on with things. The bank's waiting, the architect's waiting, and the builders are waiting. All they need is the go ahead from him. He's been doing some research on spas in Scandinavia and come up with a few novel ideas. He fancies the idea of a birch-twig sauna with a cold plunge pool, and a Turkish steam room for which he's seen some very attractive lapis lazuli tiles imported from Istanbul. There'll be a gym with a number of highly-qualified personal trainers and massage rooms with different scented aromatherapy oils and candles. In fact, that's a good idea. He'll call each room by a fragrance: lavender, rose, sage and decorate them in those colours so that the guests can have the relevant treatments—calming, invigorating or simply relaxing. There'll be a discount for the first hundred people that sign up for a year's membership. Six months' free for anyone who buys five years and special privileges for Life Members: VIP events, private changing rooms with their names on the door. He's planning a big opening. Lots of seafood and champagne. That's what he likes best. Making things happen, being in control.

He should call in and see Martha. She's probably still on her hands and knees sorting out Brendan's stuff but he could do with some sensible adult company. He'd be better off with a woman like that, a mature woman nearer his own age. But that's never been his style. He knows where he is with younger women and he's always felt a bit judged by her silent, English middle-class reserve. He should have gone over for the funeral. He regrets that. But he wouldn't have known anyone there and couldn't believe that Martha would really have been pleased to see him standing in the crematorium while she was saying goodbye to her husband. Still Brendan was his friend and he feels bad. He wonders what she'll do. Whether she'll marry again. She's still an attractive woman. He could do worse than her. An involvement would mean that he could get her on board. She's had her own career. A teacher, if he remembers right. She might have some sensible ideas. It would be good not to work on his own, to have someone to bounce his decisions off, to help him entertain, as well as share his bed. No, he must be mad. It would never work. She's too opinionated, too independent, too English. He wonders what she made of his offer to buy her out. She surely can't want to keep the cottage?

4

There's a stash of Sophie's letters in a box file on the top of the bookcase. The paper has yellowed. How times have changed, Martha thinks, as she unfolds the brittle sheets, many written with a fountain pen in thick black ink. Nowadays there'd be no such physical evidence. Any affair would be digital, all texts and furtive emails. She's surprised that Brendan kept the letters, carefully arranged in date order, all these years. The first ones are typed and mostly about the book. Ideas for chapter sequences and discussions about permissions sought from museums and collections for the necessary reproductions. There are suggestions for, and confirmations of, lunch dates to discuss the layout and cover. But slowly the language becomes more intimate and the notes handwritten in Sophie's cursive italic script. The letters are all on Thames & Hudson headed paper and the envelopes addressed to the gallery in Cork Street where Brendan had his office. In one she describes a day out in Whitstable: *Darling, oysters, champagne and a glorious sunset. What could have been more perfect except a long, long night together?*

How had they managed it? What had Martha been doing that she hadn't noticed? Presumably she'd been at school trying to instil a love of theatre into children who only ever watched TV and thought that Andrew Lloyd Webber was a great dramatist. Sophie and Brendan had, apparently, strolled along the front by the coloured beach huts, watching the wading birds scavenging in the mud and the working boats hauling their blue nylon nets onto the quay. They had lunch in a whitewashed pub on the beach. It was early November and they walked out onto the spit of shingle that appears at low tide to watch the display of fireworks over the little Kent town. She imagines Brendan standing behind Sophie, his arms wrapped round her, his chin resting on her thick red hair caught up in its tortoiseshell clip, as rockets exploded across the darkening sky. Other letters describe lunchtime assignations or snatched drinks in Soho after work when, presumably, they didn't manage to have sex because Brendan had promised Martha he'd be back for her sixth form production of *Cat on a Hot Tin Roof* or dinner with the Evans.

She was surprised when Sophie turned up at the crematorium. She should have been angry. But she wasn't. It must have taken a degree of courage. They didn't speak but Martha noticed her standing on the edge of the proceedings in a black wool coat, her thick curls loosely held at the nape of her neck with a big copper slide. She looked genuinely upset but was discreet, hanging back until everyone left for the hotel, and then quietly slipping away without joining the reception. As she reads through the letters she can only guess whether the impetus for the affair came from Sophie or Brendan. She'd lived with him for more than thirty years, borne his child and yet still there was so much she didn't know about him. Perhaps everything we do is simply an imperfect version of what we think we're actually doing. What had he and Sophie talked about? On one level they had more in common than she and he had done. Both of them were involved in the art world and Sophie must have seemed fresh, untrammelled and free.

But what had Sophie seen in Brendan, a middle-aged man with a bit of a paunch? He didn't look particularly young, dressed fairly conservatively: corduroy trousers, checked shirts from Marks & Spencer. In the winter, a lamb's wool sweater with a Harris Tweed jacket. Sophie must have had plenty of admirers her own age. No doubt she was attracted by the same thing that Martha, herself almost a decade younger, had been. His natural Celtic-tinged charm. She'd always convinced herself that Brendan's time with Sophie was a sort of interregnum in the real business of their marriage, a hiatus, an aberration. Yet a part of her can understand his need for a port in a storm. The storm that had descended, nearly wrecking them on the rocks. She wanted to believe that his behaviour had simply been that of a middle-aged man trying to hold onto his youth. That what happened hadn't really been important.

But now she can't be so certain. Maybe it was a sacrifice to give Sophie up and come back to her. Was it love or simply guilt for cheating on her, for leaving her alone to cope? Or maybe he just decided, in a way that would seem old-fashioned to many, to do the right thing. For hadn't that been what he'd promised? For better for worse, till death…

She finds some photos taken at a private view at the Tate. Sophie is holding a glass of wine and talking to Antony Gormley, raising a glass and smiling directly into the camera. Brendan must have been on the other side of the lens. Another, taken on a glowing autumn afternoon in the middle of Hampton Court Maze shows her looking windswept in a navy anorak and a big, knotted tartan scarf. She's not only young but very pretty. It would have been surprising if Brendan hadn't fallen in love with her. This is a part of his life he lived without any reference to her. Had she, in her turn, ever been tempted to have an affair? Not really. There was a lukewarm flirtation with Stuart, who taught history at her school before moving on to become head of a large comprehensive in Peckham. But that never amounted to more than the odd drink after work and a bunch of rather tacky garage carnations on her birthday.

She remembers her wedding. She wasn't really that young but had felt, for the first time, as if she was on the threshold of adulthood. A marquee was erected on the back lawn of Maresfield Gardens and a champagne buffet served beneath the blue and white striped awning. She wore an Empire line dress, carried a spray of forget-me-nots and blue hyacinths. On the whole it was a happy day and she tried to forget that her mother didn't think Brendan was really good enough.

Their honeymoon in Florence was the first of many trips to Italy. When they returned, London was in bloom. For a time they lived in a small flat, two rooms really, in Notting Hill Gate, before moving to the house in Islington. There they lay naked on a blanket in the empty drawing room with the high ceiling—they didn't yet own anything other than a mattress, two stools and a kitchen table—the windows thrown open onto the dusty summer heat, the curtains billowing in the warm air as they listened to Leonard Cohen. In those days Islington was run-down, full of Irish navvies in rooming houses. In the basement flat opposite was an elderly German Jewish refugee with a sweet smile and wiry grey hair. Whatever the weather she wore the same overcoat as if perpetually prepared for a quick getaway.

Brendan divided his time between the gallery, the Courtauld and the British Library where he was researching his first book. There were dinners, and parties at the Chelsea Arts Club. She knew enough about art not to put her foot in it. People tended to be impressed, which she hated, when they found out that her father had been the original director of the gallery. Maybe they thought that's why Brendan had married her. Once, after too much to drink, she suggested as much. But he just laughed and told her not to be so ridiculous.

Thursday

1

An El Greco sky. Shafts of sunlight pierce the clouds. When artists painted skies like this, Martha had always thought they were an exaggeration. Not something that occurred in nature but a symbol in praise of the glory of God. All those angels in Italian churches sitting on cottonwool clouds surrounded by rays of celestial light. Looking out of her little window at the sun-washed islands, she can understand how people believed in heaven. How could anything this beautiful be mere accident? It would be a comfort to have faith, wouldn't it? How many times in the last twenty years had she pleaded with God, promising that if he gave her back the one thing she most wanted that she'd believe in him unconditionally? She knew it was nonsense, of course. A measure of her desperation. And when it hadn't worked she understood that no God would get involved in anything as tawdry as a plea bargain. God was, if he was anything at all, not some venture capitalist who struck deals. Yesterday she walked down to the ruined abbey on Ballinskelligs beach with its windswept graveyard and worn Celtic crosses, its glass bubbles like upturned goldfish bowls containing faded plaster Virgins and cheap plastic roses. Was faith, then, simply a matter of habit and custom or something you decided upon, like the decision to dive off the high board into the swimming pool in front of you? Perhaps all you needed to do was shut your eyes, jump and believe you wouldn't hit concrete or drown. Wispy clouds hang over the far mountains. The sky is clear blue. She imagines swimming through it, floating up and up into its saturated blue depths.

She goes to the bookcase in Brendan's study to look for a Bible. As a Catholic, even a very dilute one, he must have one somewhere. She finds a battered copy among the dictionaries on the top shelf. The flyleaf says that it was awarded for the best Latin translation in the Lower VIth. She's touched by the thought of the young boy, who one day would become her husband, diligently translating Horace. A silk ribbon marks the passage: *The meek shall inherit the earth.*

Will they? There doesn't seem to be much evidence. She closes her eyes and tries to imagine that these are the direct words of God. But can't. She's taken to reading her horoscope and started to meditate, sitting cross-legged on the Turkish rug in her Islington bedroom, eyes closed, concentrating on her breathing and listening to whatever sounds occur. The postman pushing letters through the flap. The rev of a motorbike in the street outside. Birdsong. All that would normally blur into the white noise of morning. She knows that she's being pulled further and further into a world of chance and superstition and that death, whether she likes it or not, is irrevocable and eternal and nothing, nothing, she can do will ever change that. Everything seems to be dissolving and slipping away. Her life, her memories and all that they contain. And, with it, any sense of who she is. A gap is opening between her and the world and she's not sure how she's going to bridge it.

When Brendan turned his back on Catholicism at school he closed the door on anything to do with formal religion. The only religion for him after that was art. He argued that there was more spirituality in a Mark Rothko or Jackson Pollock than in any church. Their paintings were proof of the life force. The struggle to articulate the divine within a secular world. No, he insisted, you didn't need God to be spiritual. Artists managed to achieve spirituality and none of them had ever killed anyone in the name of religion. No genocides had been committed for the sake of art. For a painting to be spiritual it didn't have to invoke God. Feeling was meaning. A painting could suggest a new way of being in the world. All the viewer had to do was be open to the experience of looking. To give a work their undivided attention in order for the self to shrink and boundaries to dissolve.

She misses her husband. His bulky presence, his solidity, his sense of balance and the fact that he was the only other person in the world who could understand the gaping hole in her life.

She gets out of bed, washes her face and brushes her teeth but doesn't bother to shower. She wants to get out for her walk before she changes her mind, while the weather is still good. She knows if she thinks about it for too long she won't go. She ties back her hair and slips on a fleece. It's not going to rain.

The last time she'd walked along this track it had been high summer. Butterflies flitted in and out of the brambles and the lanes were aflame with wild fuchsia. There were foxgloves in the ditches and the cliffs were fringed with yellow gorse. In the small fields the hay had already been cut and gathered into beehive ricks. It was hot. The sort of heat more associated with the Mediterranean than with the west coast of Ireland. The sea a deep ultramarine. She always thought how like Greece Ireland looked, or at least like Greece would have looked, or like Greece would have looked if it had a rope slung round it and was pulled further west and north, where it rained a good deal more.

She turns down the track and a village dog follows snapping at her heels. In the middle of the path, she spots a hare. She freezes, but it's caught sight of her and sits stock still, its ears twitching. They stay like that for a long time, she and the hare. Watchful and alert. Then, as she moves slowly forwards, it springs away over the wall and disappears into a tussock of reeds. She's read that in Kerry there used to be a superstition that hares were bewitched old women. Locals were warned to walk at night with a stick to protect them against the *pooka* and other malevolent spirits.

Eventually the track opens out onto a small bay surrounded by a windbreak of pines. On the far shore there's a lone fisherman's cottage and a concrete slipway where a wooden boat has been pulled out of the water. Since she was last here someone has built a bungalow on the previously empty headland. Beside it, in the next field, is a notice tied to the fence with blue twine. She clambers over to read it. It's a planning application for another bungalow 'with sea views'. With another bungalow will come bungalow taste: concrete lions and box hedging. No doubt they'll also put in an asphalt drive and wrought iron gates to mark the boundary between what they've tamed and the wilderness beyond. It seems, that at all costs, the anarchy of the wild Irish landscape must be disciplined and kept at bay, suburbanised by plastic tubs and garden gnomes.

Behind the beach is a boggy area of reeds that grows down as far as the shingle. It is littered with debris. A broken flip-flop, an asthma inhaler, some shredded blue nylon netting, along with fragments of a smashed packing case from a wreck, all lie washed up by the storms. The strand is empty except for an old fellow in a baseball cap, his trousers held up with string and stuck into his Wellingtons. He is trying to unscramble a knot of buoys, driftwood and plastic fishing net. She calls hello and he nods, looking at her strangely, as if he doesn't understand her. He has hardly any teeth.

That long-ago summer when they came to this beach they'd set up their striped windbreak at the far end of the bay. She'd brought sandwiches in a wicker basket; cheddar and chutney for her and Brendan, peanut butter for Bruno. As she stands on the shore in the wind she can see him waving to her from the edge of the surf, his new adult teeth slightly too big for his mouth, his brown skin encrusted with salt.

They'd searched for shells in the rock pools, collecting them in a red plastic bucket so they could identify them later in his *Collins Shell Guide*. And he'd swum. For hours until his skin was wrinkled and blue. She had to call him out of the sea and wrap his shivering little body in a big towel. They'd stayed on the beach as long as possible, playing cricket into the early evening. She can still see him running across the sands, silhouetted against the low white sun—her golden boy.

Making their way back up to the cottage in the fading evening light, their skin tingling with salt, they'd climbed up on a rock to look at the stone shelters where the monks had waited for good weather before setting out for the Skelligs. Brendan had gone on ahead with the deckchairs, while she and Bruno sat on the cliff edge looking out to sea.

But why should anyone want to live on a rock in the middle of the ocean, Mum? Weren't the monks lonely?

She thought, she said, that was the point. That all those centuries ago people believed that if they lived in extreme places they'd, somehow, be closer to God. It was their souls that mattered, she explained, not their bodies. They thought that if they denied their physical needs they'd become more holy. God was a real presence in their lives in a way that it was hard for modern people to understand. They believed they were born sinful and spent their days in prayer and meditation trying to achieve redemption. Life on the rock was dictated by the weather and, in the winter months, by the short dark days. They'd had to be self-sufficient, growing cabbages and a few potatoes on their little stony plot, making tallow candles with the fat and feathers of sea birds. Nothing was wasted. There was virtually no fuel so they'd have been wet and freezing most of the time. It's almost impossible for us with our warm beds and full fridges, she said, to imagine what that must have been like. And talking of warm beds and fridges, it's supper time.

As they'd made their way back up to the cottage he'd asked, again, if they could take a boat out to the mysterious rocks. And she'd promised that before they left they would try. In those days the cottage still had no electricity or mains drainage. Meals had been simple affairs. Yet there was something magical about the three of them eating in the glow of the Tilley lamps. Even in summer they'd had to light the peat stove against the damp evening chill. Then, when they woke the following morning after nearly three weeks of sun, the weather had broken. A mist had come down and a gale was blowing. It had been impossible to go out to the Skelligs.

2

She turns up the beach, empty except for two gannets mewing and wheeling overhead. Apart from the new bungalow, everything is the same as it had been that summer. How cavalier nature is as it carries on regardless. For some reason she's always had an inner sense of foreboding that she couldn't explain. Some would say her fears were morbid. Her worries that those she loved would be involved in a car crash or suddenly taken ill, irrational. Life simply wasn't tenable if you considered the myriad possibilities of things that might go wrong. Everything is random. Yet we generally assume that tomorrow will be the same as today; that our children will lose their milk teeth, sit their exams, fall in love, grow up and flourish.

He was to go off directly they got back from Ireland for the last week of the school holidays. It was his first trip alone away from home. He was nervous but the thought of meeting up with his friends somewhat made up for the disappointment of not going out to the Skelligs. Back home she laid out his newly-ironed Cub-Scout uniform, his scarf and green jersey covered with badges for swimming and tracking. She baked a carrot cake, which she put in a tin in his rucksack. And before he went to sleep they sat together on his bed underneath the darkening skylight and he asked: Mum, where do the stars go when it's light?

They don't go anywhere, darling. They're always there. It's just that you can't see them in the day.

The next morning she dropped him off at school to catch the coach to Exmoor. He was excited, torn between kissing her goodbye and not wanting to appear babyish in front of his friends. There was quite a little gang of them. They played football together on Sunday mornings, rode their bikes together, went to each other's birthday parties and had sleepovers in one another's houses. She delayed the moment of separation by reminding him to put his ground sheet under his sleeping bag and brush his teeth. Telling him that there was clean underwear in the inside zipped pocket of his rucksack and several pairs of socks, as he was bound to get wet. And then she turned, climbed back into the car and waved goodbye as he stood in his green and yellow T-shirt and a hat a size too big for him, chatting with the other boys.

He phoned a few days later from a pay phone full of it. The midnight feasts and songs round the camp fire. The marshmallows roasted on sticks and the soaking they'd got on a moorland walk. And he'd made a new friend, James, a member of another pack who had loads of badges and was nearly eleven.

And tomorrow, Mum, we're going canoeing.

3

Brendan took the call. There'd been heavy rain and the river was swollen. The canoe had tipped up in the fast moving flow and Bruno hit his head on a rock. There was no blood, no gash but he lost consciousness as his lungs filled with water. One of the teachers had waded into the torrent and managed to pull him onto the bank and give him mouth-to-mouth resuscitation. But when the air sea rescue helicopter finally arrived he wasn't breathing properly. And by the time they got him to the local hospital, he was dead.

She vaguely remembers Brendan trying to catch her flailing arms as she screamed in his face: it's not true, it's not true. I spoke to him yesterday. He phoned me. You're lying. What do you mean you fucking idiot, dead? Healthy ten-year-old boys don't just die.

Poor Brendan. She hadn't meant to attack him but she punched, spat and kicked as if killing the messenger would kill the message. He took it badly but she was out of her mind. When they arrived at the hospital to identify the body, still tanned from their holiday and perfect except for the bruise on his left temple, she climbed onto the bed and held his small frame in her arms, just as she'd done when he had mumps or had been unable to sleep, willing him to get warm. But he no longer smelt of Bruno. Just the chemist's lab. She remembers the venetian blinds drawn against the warm September afternoon. Outside she could hear people laughing in the visitors' car park. A car door slamming and the wail of ambulance sirens bringing emergencies to A&E. Eventually, the ward sister came in to ask her if she needed more time. She shook her head but requested a pair of scissors. Then she cut off a lock of his hair, kissed him goodbye and walked out of the door.

4

Brendan hadn't particularly wanted children. They weren't part of his life's plan. He was good at selling paintings and writing books but not certain that he had it in him to be a father. She agreed at first because she wanted what he wanted but then, slowly, the desire grew until it became a physical ache and each month, when her period arrived, she felt a deep sense of loss. She never cheated, never stopped using contraception. Yet, somehow, five years into their marriage she found herself pregnant. Cliché though it was, she bloomed. And Brendan had, in fact, been delighted as though she'd just presented him with a surprise present that he didn't know he really wanted. As she grew larger and the child became more real, he lay in bed, his head on her distended stomach, listening to its heartbeat. She thought he might be turned off by her expanding girth, her swollen breasts with their dark, prune-like nipples. But he was protective and kind, bringing her breakfast in bed, holding her head over the toilet as she threw up, and taking time off to come with her for her check-ups, even though he loathed hospitals.

It was a difficult birth. A forceps delivery in the early hours of a November morning. Brendan was with her throughout. From the moment Bruno was laid on her stomach in the delivery ward and she held his tiny fingers in hers, all the pain of labour dissolved. As the first light broke through the venetian blinds, she knew that this was her life's greatest achievement. And Brendan? Well, he was thrilled to have a son. They called him Bruno after her father.

Bruno the bear. Her little blond bear.

5

For weeks after the accident she didn't go out. She had compassionate leave from school but when, finally, she went back she was struck by the world's indifference. Its relentless normality. Why didn't the sky turn black or the sun go out? Her child was dead. Yet still her pupils misbehaved, didn't do their homework and ignored her in class. People continued to push trolleys around Sainsbury's, go to the cinema, argue and make love. When she first lost Bruno she thought she would die. The ache, the longing, was like a wound. She could hardly breathe and found herself gulping for air like someone drowning, as if her lungs were unwilling to take in sufficient oxygen to go on functioning and just wanted to shut down. She was swathed in migraines that clamped her head like a metal vice, her body mimicking her mental anguish. She could barely see, her vision disturbed by the slightest light. All she could do was lie in the dark with her head under a pillow until she was violently sick then lie curled on her bed, limp as an old dish cloth.

Again and again, drifting between dreaming and sleep, she tried to imagine his last moments. The canoe overbalancing, the collision with the rock, the icy water filling his nostrils and lungs. It was as if she was watching a film in slow motion. She tried to call out to him but no sound emerged. Had he known what was happening? Been afraid? She can't bear to think about it. She goes over the last things she said to him. Don't forget to clean your teeth. Don't stay up all night talking. And under her breath, so he wouldn't be embarrassed, I love you, before heading back to the car.

For days after she came home from the hospital without him she lay on his bed under the skylight looking up at the phosphorescent glow-in the-dark stars stuck to the ceiling, which they'd bought at the planetarium, his Arsenal posters and judo certificates, willing it to be a mistake, willing herself to wake up and find that it was all some grotesque dream. But, even then, she knew that it wasn't. Eventually she climbed out of bed and sat for hours in her dirty pyjamas, her hair lank and greasy, as she watched endless daytime television: gardening and game shows, cookery programmes, American chat shows. She drifted through re-runs of *Brief Encounter, The Sound of Music* and *Dallas*. It was as if she was trapped in a goldfish bowl and that the real world was somewhere on the other side of the glass.

Finally she forced herself to go to the supermarket where she bumped into people she knew who gave her a wan smile and a wide berth. Acquaintances avoided her or, worse, waylaid her in the butcher's or the greengrocer, grasping her hand, their eyes filling with tears, so she felt the need to comfort them. It went on for days. The cards, the flowers, the phone calls. Each well-meant but like another thorn in her flesh reminding her that her loss was an inescapable reality.

Brendan wasn't able to comfort her and she didn't let him. She didn't want to be consoled, didn't want to do anything other than grieve. It was then that he must have turned to Sophie. He was working hard, finishing the book, getting together the plates, still chasing up museums and private collections that hadn't got back to him to give permission. It kept him afloat and Sophie was full of enthusiasm. Often he came home late and climbed into bed, smelling, Martha realises, of another woman, as though he hardly had enough strength to conceal the fact. They lay side by side unable to reach across the gap between them. Poor Brendan. He loved Bruno, too. Had coped in his own way. Then one evening, while standing in the middle of the living room during the Six o'clock News, he took her in his arms and, without a word, buried his head in her neck, his whole body convulsed with dry sobs. She stood there holding him, then took his hand and gently led him upstairs, where she helped him onto bed and covered him with the duvet, before lying down beside him. They lay like that, fully dressed, clinging to each other as the light faded and the room gradually grew cold.

6

The weather for January is glorious. The clouds above the two uninhabited little islands of Scariff and Deenish, that are normally shrouded in halos of mist like those mountains in Japanese prints, have lifted. Rain and blustery storms have given way to sunshine. The bay is shimmering. In the pine tree behind the cottage a blackbird is singing, fooled into thinking it's spring.

When Martha gets back from the beach she decides to walk up to Paddy O'Connell's cottage in the hope that she'll bump into him. But he isn't about, though his car is parked by the turf reek. He must be out on the mountain. She's wanted to have a word with him ever since she had lunch with Eugene and he told her of his plans. She may have softened towards Eugene but she can't bear to think of Paddy being pressurised to give up his way of life. Anyway, she doubts that he'll accept Eugene's offer. He doesn't seem like someone who'd be unduly influenced by cash. She knows Eugene has his legal team looking for any loopholes where he might take advantage. He isn't going to let his multimillion-euro scheme be scuppered by one small hill farmer. Apart from being a very lucrative business opportunity it seems to be a way of re-establishing autonomy from Bridget and Siobhán. But he needs the bottom of her field to get in the heavy machinery that his builders require. She wants to tell Paddy that he's not on his own.

She takes a shortcut up the back lane past the turkey shed, a long wooden building without any natural light that emits a continuous low hum and a noxious smell, past a battered caravan parked in the lay-by where the sails of a child's beach windmill turn in the breeze and red plastic roses sprout from a row of cracked white tubs beside a broken picnic table. The caravan windows are held together with string and masking tape and behind one, in pride of place, is a stuffed peacock. It's so incongruous that she stops to look.

You likes my Percy then?

Martha turns to find the question coming from behind a pair of thick pebble glasses. Their owner is dressed in a filthy sweater, his stained trousers tucked into a pair of shit-spattered Wellingtons. Clamped on each ear is a hearing aid attached to the thick blades of his spectacles. He's wearing a baseball cap and holding a stick, having just shut the gate on the cows in the field.

It didn't register when she saw him down on the beach trying to unravel the knotted fishing net that it's Donald-Four-Eyes. The boy who limped round the village in his outsized Wellingtons and shorts three sizes too big for him during those summers they spent here more than twenty years ago. Everyone knew him. Largely because it was so unnerving to find him heading your way, his head bobbing like a puppet's on a string, his yellow teeth forming a rictus grin like the smile in a Halloween turnip. Lame, deaf, and a bit simple, she remembers passing him in the lane after a group of local children had pulled down his trousers and left him snivelling as they ran off across the field shouting: Donald-Four-Eye's got skid marks in his pants. She can still see his scrawny white backside stuck in the air as he tried to pull his mucky pants up over his little twisted legs. She feels guilty that she hadn't gone to his rescue.

Yes, he's certainly fine, she answers. What happened to him?

He lived up in the big house. It were raining. All his feathers gets wet and he drowns. Drowns dead. Eugene stuffed him. But he got the moth and Eugene gave him me. He lives with me now, he says, with pride, white spittle gathering at the corners of his mouth.

Martha wonders if Donald is making the story up or has just got things muddled. Though she does remember that years ago Eugene did have a pair of peacocks that used to sit on the dog's kennel uttering blood-curdling cries. It seems as though Donald does odd jobs for Eugene. Stacking peat, washing his Range Rover, herding cows and clearing ditches. Generally lending a hand roundabout to whoever needs it.

7

It's a wet, cold evening. How could she have be so stupid? She's run out of turf and the cottage is freezing. The light is fading and the mist so thick that the islands have disappeared. What an idiot not to plan ahead. There's only one shop within a fifteen-minute drive where she can buy turf briquettes and that's closed. This isn't London where she can just pop out for whatever she wants round the clock. She puts on her jacket and begins to look for the scrap of paper Turf Mary left with her mobile number. She hasn't a clue where she put it. Everything is in chaos since she started to tackle Brendan's papers. Notes on Anselm Kiefer and the YBAs, essays on Agnes Martin and Chris Ofili collated for the book Brendan had just started on 'the end of painting', lie scattered over the floor. There'd been talk of a show at the Royal Academy that might also have gone on to the Netherlands and New York. She doesn't know what to do with all the files and papers. She can't just throw them away. But what use is an unfinished project to anyone else? So much effort and so many hours wasted. Eventually she finds the scrap of paper with Mary's number in a pot on the dresser among a collection of old stamps, and rusty nails.

She dials and Colm answers.

Oh, I thought this was Mary's phone. I'm so sorry to bother you. This is Martha, you know from Brendan's cottage. I realise it's late but I've stupidly run out of turf and it's freezing. Is there any chance that you might bring me up a load? I'm really sorry to be such a nuisance.

Sure 'tis no problem. Are you up there now? I'm after finishing the cows. Then I'll be right over. Is it two or three bags you'll be wanting?

I guess three to be on the safe side.

By the time Colm arrives the light has gone as if a black curtain has been pulled across the bay. A gale is blowing and the rain cascading in a river down the track. Colm parks his red van and unloads the bags as the doors bang on their hinges in the wind. Bowed against the heavy rain he balances the bags on his shoulder and carries them into the kitchen, leaving a trail of boot-shaped prints on the flags. Crouched in front of the stove he stuffs twists of paper and kindling into its mouth, then strikes a match. As it flares he adds clods of dry peat. Watching from the other side of the room, wrapped in her big coat, Martha notices that his anorak has risen up over the top of his jeans to expose a patch of dark hair in the small of his back.

That should do nicely now. The secret is to mix in a little coal. It gives more heat. I'll bring you over a bag tomorrow if you like, he says, standing and pulling up his jeans.

That's really kind of you. As you can see I'm a bit of a townie. Look, I was just going to have a warm up with a whiskey—can I offer you one? I don't normally drink the stuff but Brendan left half a bottle and it's such a filthy night. Though maybe you have to get off?

A whiskey would be grand.

So you often met up with Brendan, then? she asks, passing him a glass and settling herself on the arm of the sofa, realising that now that she's invited him for a drink she'll have to talk to him.

We occasionally met for a pint. More by accident than design. He was trying to educate me about painting and he seemed to like my songs. And he was interested in Irish poetry. Not just the usual Yeats and Heaney. He'd read Derek Mahon and Kavanagh's 'The Great Hunger'. It was like he was looking for his Irish roots. But I'm sure you know all about that, he says, pulling off his woollen hat and mussing up his hair.

Actually she didn't. She didn't know anything of Brendan's interest in either Patrick Kavanagh or Derek Mahon. This was something else she'd just discovered about the man she'd lived with for thirty-odd years. In all the time they'd been together he had never shown much interest in his Irish side. He'd grown up and gone to school in England, and an English boarding school at that. His relationship with Ireland amounted to little more than a few childhood holidays. Slowly hidden bits of him keep emerging like the secret writing children do in lemon juice, which only becomes visible when held over a flame.

He always asked after my work, Colm continues. He was on at me to send out my poems to poetry magazines and get a critical response. He said it wasn't enough to write for myself or the band. That wanting to be a writer wasn't the same thing as being one. That lots of people have ideas and claim they have a book in them. But that's just baloney. It's sitting down and beginning, then keeping going that's hard. And he was dead right about that.

So you write poetry?

Yep. But mostly just for me and Niall to sing. Though Brendan was after encouraging me to put together a collection. He suggested I give it him to read. But it's exposing showing your work to others. While it's private you can always pretend you're a feckin' genius. Singing to your mates is one thing. Literature? Well that's something else. You know I did three terms at University College, Dublin, but my mam couldn't manage the land after my father died. I suppose she could have sold up and gone to live in Caherciveen, got a job in Supervalu. But they've always had sheep and cattle and I was brought up here. So I came back. There's plenty of time to write in your head when you're feeding animals. Ted Hughes kept sheep. So I'm in good company.

Well I'm not a poet, or even a writer, Colm. But I am a teacher and love reading. So if you think it might be any help I'd be happy to take a look at your poems.

His thanks are noncommittal as he picks up his woollen hat, pulls it down over his ears and drains the dregs of his whiskey before making to leave.

Has she embarrassed him? Why on earth did she say that? Hasn't she enough to contend with? His cheeks are dark with stubble. He can't have shaved for days.

I'll be off then, he says. It's pretty mucky out there. I'll drop by with that bag of coal tomorrow. If you're not here I'll leave it on the step.

Friday

1

Her chest is tight as a drum. Her nose blocked. Everything aches, her head, her back, and her limbs. She'd intended to finish sorting Brendan's study but feels too weak. This isn't the time or place to get flu. Outside it's blowing a gale. She goes to the bathroom to look for something to take. There's a half bottle of Listerine, a packet of old razors and a rusty can of shaving foam in the cupboard. She finds some out-of-date aspirin and dissolves three in a tumbler of water, then gargles. There's also a half-empty pot of Vicks. She scrapes out the remains of the sticky menthol salve with a teaspoon, puts it in a bowl and covers it with boiling water, then sits down at the kitchen table with a tea-towel over her head and inhales. She can feel the steamy eucalyptus penetrating her blocked tubes and congested nasal passages. She's always been prone to chesty colds ever since she was a child when her mother insisted on inhalations of foul-smelling Friars' Balsam and a Wright's Coal Tar burner in the bedroom. Sickness has always been associated with these smells. She was off school for weeks, wheezing and coughing. She got behind and missed nearly all of Macbeth. In the end her mother had to call out Dr Simpson who came with his black bag and cold stethoscope, which he placed against her rattling little chest.

She searches for a hot water bottle and then drags herself back to bed with a cup of tea. It's too wet to go out, though she only has a tin of sardines and a can of tomato soup in the cupboard. Still, she's not hungry. The only thing she wants to do is sleep but just as she's dozing off there's a knock at the door. Irritated she reaches for her fleece, half expecting it to be Eugene again about her field. But it's Colm with the coal.

Looks as though I've come at a bad time. Was just passing so thought I'd stop by with this, he says, dropping the heavy bag. You don't look too grand if you don't mind me saying so.

No, I'm not too bright. In fact, I feel pretty awful. I can't seem to get warm. I think I must have the flu. Not really very convenient up here.

Do you have anything for it? A hot toddy, whiskey with honey and lemon, that usually does the trick.

I did take some rather out-of-date aspirin I found in the cupboard. But there's no whiskey left. I think we drank the last drop the other night and I certainly don't have honey and lemon. It's not quite the land of plenty up here, she says, trying to make light but ending up spluttering.

Well I've a couple more things to do. Some deliveries to make and then I'm off down to Caherciveen. I'm going anyway, so it'll be no bother to get you a drop of the hard stuff and some honey and lemon. Even if it doesn't make you any better it'll cheer you up. Is there anything else you need while I'm in there?

She's asleep when he lets himself in. Suddenly he's standing at the end of her bed with a mug of hot whiskey.

How you feeling? Get this down you and you'll be grand in no time.

She must look dreadful with her lank hair and red nose as she hauls herself from under the duvet. It feels odd having him in her bedroom. Not because he's a young man and she hardly knows him but because her sleeping loft, with its tiny window, is so small. There's just enough room for a double bed under the eaves, a chair, and a small chest of drawers. Colm's big hands and feet fill the space like a giant's in a Wendy house.

It's kind of you to take pity on me but there's really no need, she says sitting up and taking the mug.

Sure there's no need, I know that. But I'm devious, Martha. You see there's always a price, he grins a snag-toothed smile.

And what might that be? she asks, blowing her nose into a balled Kleenex.

Well you may have forgotten, Martha, but I haven't. And you may not have meant it but I took you as being a woman of your word. I'd like you to look at my poems. I know you heard me sing the other night. Well that's all fine and dandy like, and I love the *craic*, but my real work, well that's my poetry. I really regret that I didn't show my poems to Brendan. He was a good guy your husband. I learnt a lot talking to him. After he told me to send my stuff out I won a couple of small prizes in competitions and published in some magazines. One here and one in England. It's not much but I'd really like to pull all that work into a collection. I've no idea whether the poems work together or if the prize—it wasn't that much, so I won't be running off to the Bahamas just yet—and the publications were just luck. I'd really appreciate your opinion. I don't want you to be nice, mind. None of that Yeats' bollocks about treading softly on my dreams. I want you to tell me what you really think. If I've got a chance of getting published.

Colm, I'm flattered that you think my opinion is worth having. Look I'm not a professional writer, she says brushing back her greasy hair. And although Brendan wasn't a poet he was an accomplished critic. I'm just a teacher. But I do read a good deal, so if you think it might be helpful I'd be honoured to look.

Thanks a million, Martha. That's really grand. I'll drop them in when I'm next passing. And ring if you need anything. Anything at all.

2

She's in her pyjamas heating up one of the tins of soup that Colm brought up, when Eugene calls her mobile. He wants her to join him for dinner. He is on his own and needs company. She tells him she's not well and that she can't. That at this very moment she's standing in her pyjamas and fleece heating up a can of soup.

I'll come up and see you then. Bring you some smoked salmon or something.

Honestly, Eugene I rather you didn't. I look a wreck and feel lousy.

She puts down the phone and goes next door, banks up the fire and has just settled down with her soup and a piece of toast when there's a knock on the door. She throws off the tartan rug spread over her knees and goes to answer. Eugene is standing in the rain with a packet of smoked salmon in one hand, and a bottle of champagne in the other.

Goodness Eugene. That was quick. I only put the phone down to you ten minutes ago. It's like Clapham Junction here. I'm not well and no sooner has one person called than another is banging on my door. And I thought this was the middle of nowhere. Anyway as you can see I'm hardly at my elegant best, she says wiping her raw nose with a tissue. Well now you're here you'd better come in but don't blame me if you catch something. You can't say I didn't warn you. I know what you litigious lawyers are like. You'll be suing me for giving you flu before I know it.

He smiles weakly and shuts the door behind him, then takes the smoked salmon and champagne into the kitchen uncertain what to do with them.

And fix yourself a whiskey if you intend to stay, she calls after him. There's some on the side. I've just had a new bottle delivered for medicinal purposes but I'm not up to doing anything for anybody so you'll have to pour your own.

She can hear him opening and closing the cupboards looking for a glass before coming back into the sitting room with a large measure.

Sit down Eugene if you must. What's so urgent all of a sudden that you have to come over on an evening like this and see me?

It's a bigger question than she'd anticipated. He settles himself in the wing chair by the stove and sets about answering it. His life isn't his own any more. The divorce from Bridget has been protracted. She's fought over everything. His business assets, the house in Kinsale, even demanding to have the dogs.

And she doesn't like them, Martha. If they ever came into our room and slept on the bed she went mad.

As he talks it seems, despite the gruff bravado, that what terrifies him most is being on his own, which is how Siobhán seems to have wheedled her way into his life. He needs someone to have dinner with him at the end of the day. To drink the other half of a bottle of Beaujolais and share his bed.

You know Martha, you're the sort of woman I should get involved with, he says without irony. Attractive, sensible, mature.

She's not sure whether or not she's being insulted. She doesn't feel very attractive with her running nose and blotchy skin. As to mature and sensible?

I'm not young enough for you Eugene. You'd be bored in two minutes and besides you'd drive me mad. I'd end up wanting to kill you, she says sneezing.

He smiles uncertain how to respond to her wry English humour. Not knowing whether she's being serious or teasing him. As he sips his whiskey she can see, despite the weight he carries, something of the handsome man he once was. He is tall and before the good living and cigars took their toll was regarded as something of a catch. But his voice is without inflection, his sentences monotone, as if the whole process of making connection with another person is quite beyond him. She wonders whether he is autistic in some way for there appears to be a connective element missing in his makeup. She feels sorry for this wealthy man who seems to have no one else to talk to other than an English widow with flu, whom he barely knows and has never much liked.

She'd learnt a little about his past from Brendan. From a prosperous family of four children, he was the youngest by a number of years and the only boy. His father, a bit of a wastrel and a gambler, had an eye for the women and was seldom home to mind the family business. Most of the time he could be found in the members' enclosure on the race track at Listowel in his hallmark felt trilby. A pair of binoculars slung round his neck and a wad of cash in his back pocket. He studied the racing pages, knew the trainers and breeders and what to look for in a horse. And, it has to be said that, more often than not, he won. And when he did he was judicious enough to buy up land from his struggling neighbours. It didn't make him popular and, on the occasions he lost, he'd return home and take it out on Eugene. The boy had always been withdrawn—his mother had died from breast cancer when he was three—and his shyness irritated the older man who needed only the slightest provocation to let rip. There were times when he took his belt to him in a drunken rage but the more Eugene cried, the more vicious his father became. As for Eugene's sisters, they could do no wrong. His father got on better with women and all his sisters were pretty, which was what he expected of girls. They knew how to handle him. Flattered and cajoled him, twisting him round their little fingers. Eugene learnt to stay out of his way. His happiest times were spent at the family corn merchant where they also sold basic veterinary supplies. He liked to help the foreman, Patrick. He enjoyed the grassy smell of the cattle cake, the feel of the meal in the deep wooden bins, which he dug out with the big metal scoop. By the time he was eight he knew which liniment to suggest for horse sprains and the correct worming powder for farm dogs.

Brendan and Eugene had met on the beach below his family house. At first, Eugene was hostile when he discovered Brendan and Michael playing there, telling them that it was his beach and that they weren't allowed on it. But they took no notice. Brendan said it was silly, that no one could own a beach. Every day Eugene would show up and sit on the rocks to watch them play. At first he was moody and morose but slowly he started to chat. Then one afternoon he ran across the sands to retrieve a ball that Michael had just bowled to Brendan, before it was swept out to sea. For the rest of the holidays they played cricket together, collected bait in the rock pools, fished for mackerel and made fires in a circular hearth of stones to cook their catch.

He and Brendan were both ten.

After that they met only rarely. But when Brendan inherited the cottage he dropped Eugene a note to say he was in Ballinskelligs and that it would be good to catch up after all these years. He received a reply by return. Eugene insisting that he come and play a round of golf at his new hotel. Eugene, it seemed, had spent a decade in the States working for a big company and done pretty well for himself. As a young corporate lawyer he'd kept up his father's old habit of buying parcels of land with any savings he amassed. Now he was back in Ireland for good, he told Brendan. Using his legal know-how in the property business. He'd bought the house by the pier which he'd extended and renovated, building a glass house with a vine, a conservatory, and a semi-tropical garden that ran down to the sea. He'd planted rare palms and orchids which, because it was sheltered, seemed to thrive. He had also acquired three hotels. Two with beautiful golf courses in outstanding beauty spots. And recently had invested heavily in the redevelopment of the Dublin docks.

He was also, Brendan told Martha, as they drove from the ferry, on his second wife. A classic Irish beauty, with raven hair and milky skin, she had a passion for breeding horses which Eugene indulged. Feisty and wild, it seemed, she also had a passion for the grooms and stable boys. There were shouting matches, followed by long frosty silences in which Rory was banished to his room, crying at the chaos breaking out around him. He was too old, Eugene told Brendan, by the time he met Bridget, to have a child. He didn't understand children. He never knew what to say. Whether to be strict or indulgent. In the end he felt humiliated by her increasingly erratic behaviour, her flagrant infidelities and threw her out. But she was determined not to go without a fuss. It cost him a fortune.

It's sad, Brendan said. I don't think Eugene has ever been happy. He's really a man of simple tastes but there's something driven about him. As if he's still trying to prove himself to his father.

3

I owe you an apology, Martha, Eugene announces, now well into his second glass of whiskey, and I'm not good at those. So please hear me out.

She fears she's in for a long evening. She just wants to go to bed.

I should have come over for Brendan's funeral, he continues. Sure I had a business meeting that day, but that was only an excuse. I didn't feel comfortable. That's the honest to God truth and that's why I didn't come. But I should have. I haven't loved many people in my life, Martha, but I loved Brendan. He did something few others have done before or since. He made me feel I belonged. What's more when we were boys he wanted to be my friend. We went fishing, played on the beach. I'd never done anything like that before. I'd always been on my own. Even though I had sisters. I was so much younger, just the runt at the end of the litter. Brendan gave me time. He never wanted anything in return. When he came back it would always be the same. A bit of *craic*, a round of golf. He may have sold pictures that looked like the scrapings of a builder's yard but he knew what he was talking about, even if I wasn't a very responsive pupil. And he never shoved it down my throat. I should have come to say goodbye. To pay my respects. He was my friend and I'm sorry for that.

She's uncertain how to respond but is touched that this gauche man should struggle to express his feelings for her husband.

I'm sure he wouldn't have held it against you, Eugene, I'm sure Brendan knew that you would have come if you could.

That's as maybe. But I should have been there.

Saturday

1

When she opens the front door to go and get in her washing she finds a plastic carrier bag on her step. There's a scrawled note shoved inside.

> *Didn't like to disturb you. Thought you might be sleeping. Hope you're on the mend. Here's the manuscript. Please take your time and let me know what you think. Honestly!*
>
> *Colm.*

She doesn't read it immediately but goes into Brendan's study and digs out the photo of Bruno she found a couple of days ago taken on the beach in the light of a dying sun. The corners have curled and there's a scratch across the surface. Yet it has an alchemy of sorts, turning a single moment on an August evening all those years ago into something tangible. This is her saint's bone. Her section of the True Cross. Bruno will stay forever young. Always her lovely boy. He'll never get acne, never fail his exams or get arrested like her north London friends' teenage sons for smoking dope or for coming out of the pub on a Saturday night and throwing up on the pavement. Never have an unsuitable girlfriend or forget to phone on her birthday or lie about where he's been. Had this been Brendan's private *memento mori* hidden at the bottom of his drawer? She remembers when she took the photo. She'd just called Bruno to get out of the sea and dress as they were leaving. Brendan was already folding the wet towels and rolling up the windbreak and Bruno had shouted: *Just ten more minutes Mum.* She'd been about to put her camera away but had turned to see him waving from the surf, his arms raised above his head in front of the low white sun like some feral boy.

Some years ago, on a trip to Colorado, her friend Lindsay visited a Native American reserve and brought her back a dream catcher. Made of twigs and feathers the dream webs were woven by grandparents for their new-born grandchildren and hung above their cradles in order to give them peaceful dreams. Good dreams knew their way to the dreamer and made their way down through the feathers. The slightest movement indicated the passage of yet another benevolent dream. Bad dreams, however, got confused and trapped, evaporating at sunrise. If only the same was true of memories. If only she could hold on to what was good and let all the rest dissolve with the early morning mist.

2

When Paddy O'Connell returned from Dublin he'd been away for three Pucks. That's how he measured it, by the number of fairs he'd missed. Dublin was strange to him at first. The Custom House, the Four Courts, the Old Parliament House and Rotunda. The complicated bus routes and up and down escalators. Even the food. It had been hard to leave home. He missed his brothers and sisters. When he picked up his battered suitcase to walk to Caherciveen and catch the bus, his da had stood in the bend of the road watching.

Go on, Paddy, son, go. And write when you can.

All the time he was away he sent part of his wages home.

It was August when he finally returned just in time for the fair. A party was laid on. An accordion and fiddle player found and a small barrel of Guinness purchased. It wasn't properly tapped so those nearby got a good soaking of black stuff. The table and chairs were pushed back against the kitchen walls and the dancing lasted till the early hours when the paraffin lamp was turned off and the exhausted neighbours went their separate ways, knowing there was work to be done in the morning.

Despite being the worse for wear, he was up early next day to help his da round up the cattle for the fair. Two or three broke free and forced their way back over the fence to join those that weren't going. So he had to start all over again.

Ask for more than you expect, son, his father said, as they pushed their bicycles along beside the cows, the fifty miles to Killorgan, past the makeshift creamery at the crossroads where the dairymen with their donkey wagon sold milk straight from the churn.

The roads were alive with cattle, pigs and horses. His da reckoned that before breakfast at least £800 worth of bacon would rush squealing into town. As they approached the lanes, rows of painted barrel wagons were encamped along the verges, a ribbon of smoke curling from their stove chimneys. Already the horses were unharnessed, hobbled and grazing on the banks. The washing strung up on the hawthorn bushes and the fires lit to cook the evening meal. The tinkers made regular forays into town to drink, bargain and beg, causing quarrels with the settled folk.

The place was full to bursting. Men jostling with cows as they tried to reach the pub, cows jostling with men as the animals snatched a mouthful of grass poking from an old stone wall. The streets were ankle deep in dung.

Muck and money.

And on every corner there was some sleight-of-hand merchant. John Joe Collopy with his 'Six-a-Pick' card game and a monkey on his shoulder to draw the crowds to the tombola machine that everyone soon realised never stopped on certain numbers. There were barefoot fortune-tellers—a grubby child anchored with a tartan shawl to a swayed hip—who forecast 'passing over water' or 'coming into money' as they thrust sprigs of heather from dirt engrained hands into the faces of passers-by.

Long before midday the final touches were made to the platform in the square where the Puck goat was to be hoisted. Orange, white and green flags fluttered from the wooden scaffolding. Frank Houligan, your man in charge of catching the goat up on the mountain, had been up since the crack and was now parading the furious animal through the streets on his rickety lorry, followed by the local pipe band. Schoolgirls in their Sunday best were tying green ribbons in their hair, getting ready to perform their *céilí* dances to 'The Walls of Limerick' or 'The Haymaker's Jig'. When the goat was finally crowned with the copper crown by that year's young queen in her homemade regal robes, the tinker lads went wild. Sporting paper hats, their faces blackened with soot, they rode bareback through the town, scattering women, children, and guards in all directions.

That year he and his da had a good fair and finished the day, over a couple of pints, with a few bob in their pockets. Others were less lucky.

They felt sorry for the fellas trekking home with tired beasts and empty purses. But he has other things on his mind. The letter from Eugene Riordan is still sitting behind the Aran plate on his dresser and he's uncertain what to do.

3

Martha is learning to be alone. There's something pure about the quality of solitude. Like crystal or ice. She can imagine being a nun. Julian of Norwich, perhaps. Her day mapped out by a series of spiritual exercises, periods of contemplation and meditation, alternating with study and work in the garden: keeping bees, hoeing radish and kale, the cultivation of medicinal herbs. Borage, feverfew and rosemary. Days uncomplicated by the loss of love and human attachment. Other cultures provided a designated period for mourning. In rural Greece bereaved women mourned for five years. They talked of visiting, not a grave, but a husband or daughter. It was understood that grieving takes time. The end of the mourning period happened only after the body was exhumed and the bones placed in a metal box to join other relations in the local ossuary. Friends and relatives wore black clothes and armbands to alert others to their plight. But her mourning has mostly taken place in the long watches of the night and in the solitary recesses of her mind.

For months she refused to move anything in Bruno's room. To unpack the rucksack of dirty clothes returned from the cub camp until it began to smell and grow mildew and she had to throw it out. When Brendan couldn't comfort her he began to avoid her. He must have been with Sophie the afternoon she crawled into Bruno's bed sobbing and clinging to his bald panda until she could cry no more. She lay for hours in his cold room, her face and eyes red and swollen, staring helplessly at the ceiling.

She took up swimming. Going to the pool early when she couldn't sleep. She slipped into her old black costume, bundled her things into a locker and tiptoed out avoiding the muddy puddles between the duck boards. At 6.30 the place was usually fairly empty apart from a cleaner mopping the tiled floor and the same old man in goggles plodding up and down the slow lane as water ran off his walrus moustache and skinny arms. Standing with her toes curled over the edge of the pool, ignoring the No Diving signs, she plunged into the chlorinated water, a stream of bubbles floating like a soda stream up behind her as she pushed on, length after mindless length, the muscles in her chest and shoulders flexing and expanding against the glass wall of water, her heart pounding as physical exertion stilled her unquiet mind.

She walked to the pool. Or, if it was raining, caught the bus with the early-morning office workers, sitting squashed on the top deck between the Eastern European office cleaners or the broad-hipped African woman who always sat in the same seat, her cheeks engraved with cicatrices, a wicker shopping basket on her lap, her broad feet splayed in gold sandals whatever the weather. Martha was fascinated by her hair woven into intricate braids like the threads that held together the fragile fabric of the city.

Recently she'd read a disturbing story in the *Islington Gazette* about an old couple that lived on the nearby Peabody estate. The man had worked for the Post Office for over 40 years. After he retired he rarely went out. Occasionally he was seen shuffling to the corner shop in his slippers. He'd nod to the Turkish proprietor, pick up the *Daily Mirror*, a carton of milk, a pack of Senior Service and two cans of baked beans. Neighbours often saw him on the stairs struggling with heavy black bin bags. There were reports of a strange smell coming from the top flat. Tenants phoned the council. A health inspector was sent round but unable to get in. People began to leave notes. But the stench just got worse. There were sightings of vermin. Then, one morning, the young Bangladeshi woman from the floor below heard a scream. She dashed upstairs and found the old lady bent over a heap of rags on the top landing. It was her husband. He'd had a stroke. An ambulance was called. But the old woman wouldn't let them take him away unless she went too. They'd never spent a day apart in fifty years she told the paramedics, visibly upset. While they were at the hospital the workmen, putting up scaffolding at the back of the building, broke into the flat.

Every room was packed with putrefying bin bags. The bedroom, the kitchen, even the bath. The old man had been bringing back all the refuse left out in the street. How had it started? What had motivated him to drag that filth up four flights? Had their lives been so colourless, so drab that they felt compelled to recycle the detritus of other people in order to feel they existed?

4

Yesterday afternoon Martha had walked up past Bolus Head to the Napoleonic tower on the headland. The day was dying and the light already fading, diluted by immense diaphanous shadows. The impassive stones and rocks seemed to reverberate with memories. As she stood in the squally wind, looking out across the darkening bay, she suddenly felt very insignificant. As if merged with the rough brown scrub dotted with megalithic stones and sheep, the grey mountains and vista of metallic sea. Was this how Caspar David Friedrich felt as he looked out from his crag into the hazy distance? Or stout Cortez when, eagle-eyed on his peak in Darien, he gazed over the Pacific Ocean? Freud dismissed such feelings as being akin to faith. But they didn't have to be specifically religious did they? Weren't they simply a measure of human consciousness? A desire for transcendence beyond the humdrum? The need to give meaning to what so often felt meaningless? Underneath the hubbub and razzmatazz, the rush of crowded streets, wasn't there a single pure note for which we all yearned? Her feelings might be similar to those of religious mystics but that didn't mean there was no other way they could be understood. Wasn't it a love of sorts that connected her to her late husband and child? To the histories of all those who'd lived and suffered in this wild place?

5

She takes Colm's manuscript from the carrier bag, opens a bottle of red wine and settles herself by the fire. She doesn't know what to expect. For some reason he's typed the poems on an old typewriter so the 'e's and 'a's are slightly higher than the rest of the letters. She reads slowly at first, trying to find her way through the imagery. It's a while since she's read any poetry and, at first, she finds it tricky to get to grips with the rhythms and syntax. There are passages that swell like the incoming tide. Others that seem intentionally dissonant, staccato as the rain beating on a shed roof. Some of the poems are obviously set on the wild cliffs and beaches of Kerry. Others appear to have been written in Dublin. But it's a lost Dublin. A Georgian city of crumbling 18th century houses and haunted souls inhabiting dark rooms filled with shadows, the scent of beeswax and sexual repression. Houses full of musty perfumes, crowded with unspoken memories. Where others such as Heaney celebrate the warmth of Irish life, Colm attempts to reveal what is taboo. The harshness of the Church. The repression of women. The power of the priests and their sexual misdemeanours. And throughout all the poems there's the presence of some ethereal other. Martha isn't sure whether it's male or female, a lover or a mirrored self. It appears fleetingly as a reflection in a smeared glass and the corner of a dusty pub window or on a lonely windswept beach.

She's surprised. This isn't what she'd expected from this young man with the blue woollen hat. She imagined something more traditional. She wonders about his life. What he did in Dublin, whether he's ever been abroad, if he has a girl friend? She doesn't even know how old he is.

6

Colm has never belonged to a political party. To the Greens or Fianna Fáil. He thought of joining an environmental group in Dublin but joined a band instead. That's not because he doesn't care. He hates this Celtic Tiger bollocks that means everyone is on the gravy train. Those that can doing, those that can't just getting by or lolling at home on benefits. Europe! The eejits are behaving as though their rich aunty was giving handouts to all the family. There's money flowing in as if it's just been invented. Suddenly everyone with a field to sell is a millionaire. Driving round in a 4x4, drinking champagne when a Guinness or stout would do just as well. All round the Dublin docks developers are building apartments the size of shoe boxes to fleece anyone stupid enough to buy them. Everyone is in finance or insurance. Even Kerry is turning into a tourist trap. Killarney and Tralee flaunting their big hotels and golf courses. Out for the Americans who drive round the Ring in their air conditioned buses, little shamrock badges stuck to the lapels of their rainproof jackets. Don't they realise they're part of the problem with their Hollywood versions of Irish history, looking for the beach where *Ryan's Daughter* was filmed. All along the coast bungalows are springing up blighting this wild place he loves. Kerry people are decent enough. But a breath ago they were peasants taking their milk to market on a donkey cart, believing in fairies and original sin, in immaculate conception and weeping statues. Now they're all would-be property dealers.

He wonders what Martha will make of his poems. She seems nice enough. Not a bad looking woman for her age. There's something vulnerable beneath the surface. He's heard talk about her young son. But Brendan never spoke of him.

Sunday

1

There's hardly anything left in the cupboards except half a packet of dried pasta, some stock cubes and a few tea bags. She's been existing on scraps. Cooking doesn't interest her any more. But she needs some basic supplies and they're not so easy to come by on a Sunday. She gets into the car and drives down the mountain. It's a beautiful morning and hard to believe that for the last few days the weather has been so wild and unpredictable. As she heads towards the bay, the sea is calm, the surf white as a wedding dress, the brown mountains behind Waterville soft and undulating. It might almost be spring.

She turns off the main road. If she waits to go for a walk until after she's been to town the sun might have gone. She parks on a grassy verge and walks to the ruined priory on the beach. A stonemason doing something to the walls wishes her good morning and asks, perhaps because she doesn't look like a local, if she's an artist. The tide is out and there's a strong smell of ozone and seaweed. Groups of black and white wading birds paddle in the shallows searching for shellfish. She's not sure what they are. Presumably Brendan would have known.

She makes her way through the gate to the churchyard. The religious community established here in the 12th century was small, according to the information on the municipal plaque. After a winter of bad storms the monks on the Skelligs ran out of fresh water and food. Half-starved, and suffering, no doubt, from scurvy and pneumonia, they abandoned their rocky retreat. Here they adopted the Augustinian rule. Moving away from the extreme asceticism endured on their Atlantic eyrie. A notice in both Irish and English says the place is dedicated to St Michael. She wonders who St Michael is and if he's the same as the angel Gabriel? Much of the monastery is eroded and the roof collapsed. The church and the domestic buildings were arranged around a grath or yard surrounded by covered walkways where the monks worked and prayed. Now only a section of the hall and tower remains. The monks' cells, the workshops, infirmaries, kitchens, refectories and the guest houses have all gone. Six hundred years ago the matins' bell would have called the community to early morning prayer. Its ghostly reverberations carrying across the bay in the mist to Horse Island.

All the headstones look out to sea. Some are inscribed in Gaelic. Others worn down like broken teeth from the salt wind. The more recent graves are marked by black marble slabs with machine-etched crucifixions and lachrymose Virgin Marys. Presumably that's how they come from the undertakers or whoever it is that supplies headstones. You pay your money and take your pick from the catalogue. A cherub for Auntie Maeve. A cross with ivy garlands for Uncle Sean. Many of the stones have been ripped up and smashed in recent storms when the waves breached the church wall. Plastic roses and Christmas wreaths lie tossed and sodden. A string of rosary beads hangs from the broken finger of a concrete angel.

The same names occur again and again. Sugrue. O'Sullivan. O' Connor. Murphy. A large granite stone was erected in 1973 to John P Shea and his wife Kathleen by their grandchildren in the USA. Why had they left Ballinskelligs? What had made them pack up their beds and blankets, their clocks and china and ship them all the way to New York? Martha imagines their offspring with their American accents and white American teeth, watching the Pittsburgh Pirates or the Detroit Tigers, cheering on their favourite pitcher at the Saturday afternoon match, before returning to their lives as lawyers, plumbers or doormen, with Ireland little more than a quaint memory. She walks on past a plaster cherub and a headless saint kneeling on either side of a white concrete heart.

In memory of baby Mary Josephine O'Connell, died 5th December 1963. RIP. Erected by her parents.

2

She turns away quickly and heads back to the car but just as she's pulling out onto the main road an old man flags her down. She stops to give him a lift. As he opens the door and climbs in beside her, she realises he reeks. But it's too late. There's nothing for it but to drive him to where he wants to go. She can hardly make out his thick Kerry accent but understands that he's on his way to the garage to place his weekly order. It's the only shop for miles around that apart from selling petrol and diesel also stocks turf briquettes and bundles of kindling, aged carrots, shrivelled apples, biscuits and tea. She drops him in the forecourt and, as he staggers out clutching his string bag, winds down the window to let in some fresh air.

It's fifteen miles to Caherciveen across the moors. The mostly 19th century buildings in Market Street are painted yellow and blue, blue and red, red and green. Many sport Republican flags. There's an abundance of charity and Celtic crafts shops and, for a small town, pubs. There's Kelly's Bar, the Shebeen, the Kerry Coast Inn, the Townhouse Lounge, The Harp Bar, The Anchor Bar, Craineen's, The Corner House, Cha Healy's, Tom's Tavern, The Skellig Rock, The Fertha Bar and Mike Murts, its windows thick with grime and crammed with what appears to be the entire contents of someone's attic. Rusty Oxo tins, an old fashioned soda siphon, packets of Player's No 6, a ball of string, a green and white tin of Castrol Grease. A ship in a bottle, a wooden plaque that says: *Love thy neighbour—but don't get caught,* a collection of horse shoes, a stone hot water bottle and a red tobacco tin of Maltan Rich Dark Flake. Several cut throat razors, a scythe, a tap and an old felt hat.

Halfway down the street is O'Shea's the undertaker, and a wool shop crammed with knitting patterns and boxes of buttons. Next to this is an amusement arcade that seems to be permanently shut and a hardware store that sells garden gnomes as well as plaster saints. A faded floral curtain sags across the empty window of McCrohan's.

She wanders into the church named after the town's most famous son, Daniel O'Connell, who established civic freedom for Irish Catholics in 1829. A painted board charts the growth of the restoration fund for the sagging roof, though the heavy 19th century architecture is without much merit. Pushing open the heavy wooden doors she feels as if she's suddenly in France or some Italian village. A large mahogany confessional stands beside a rack of burning candles. Up near the altar two women in headscarves sit with their heads bowed. A gloomy wooden tableaux of the Stations of the Cross runs around the walls and there's a fragrance of stale incense. Martha considers lighting a candle but decides against it. On either side of the altar a pair of blue banners urge visitors to: *Repent and believe in the gospel* and *Return to the Lord your God.* She picks up a leaflet that claims the average weekly attendance is around two thousand souls. Could that be true or just wishful thinking in the light of recent Catholic scandals? She thought people were leaving the Church in droves.

In a side chapel, Blu-tacked to a pillar on a sheet of lined paper, is a hand-written prayer:

> *Dear Saint Anthony. You are the patron saint of the poor and the helper of all who seek lost articles. Help me find the object I have lost so that I will be able to make use of the time I will gain for God's greater honour and glory. Grant your gracious aid to all people who seek what they have lost—especially those who seek to regain God's grace.*

She's impressed by the nifty logic. The shift from lost objects to lost souls. Outside she stops in the porch. There are posters for prayer meetings and a forthcoming discussion on domestic violence. On WaterAid and classes to prepare for Catholic marriage. Two recycled Coca-Cola bottles, wrapped in slips of hand-written paper secured with elastic bands, sit on an oak table beside a dish of coins.

Every Catholic home should have in a supply of Holy Water. Remits Venial Sins. Untold spiritual wealth is contained in a tiny drop of this blessed water.

Outside, the churchyard is covered over with grass and concrete, though her leaflet informs her that Daniel O'Connell is buried here somewhere but she can't see any graves. So, too, she reads, is Monsignor Hugh O'Flaherty. The Scarlet Pimpernel of the Vatican. O'Flaherty was, it seems, no lover of the British and supported the IRA. His mother came from local farming stock and his father, a policeman, was a golf pro. The young O'Flaherty appears to have been something of a charmer. A boxer and a golfer who did a spot of caddying at his father's club and had a scratch handicap. Yet despite his athletic talents he had a calling to be ordained. After time in Egypt, the Caribbean and Czechoslovakia in the '30s, he was sent to Rome. Many there found him rough-edged. Despite his rise through the Vatican he raised a few eyebrows when he became an amateur golf champion. By 1942 the Germans and Italians were cracking down on Jews and anti-fascists. O'Flaherty was friends with many of these people and had played golf with them before the war. He hid them in convents and monasteries, even in his own residence, playing cat and mouse with the Gestapo. Despite his previous antipathy to the British he began to help British POWs escape. He'd take the evening air on the porch of Saint Peter's, in the neutral territory of the Vatican City, in plain view of both the German soldiers across the piazza and the windows of the Pope's apartments. There escaped prisoners of war and Jews would find their way to him. Disguised in the robes of a monsignor or the uniform of the Swiss Guard he smuggled them through the German Cemetery to his old college. One evening a whey-faced young Jew slipped out of the shadows, drew him aside and unwound a heavy gold chain from his waist. He and his wife, he whispered, expected to be arrested at any moment. They'd be taken to Germany where they would almost certainly perish in a Nazi gas chamber. They had a young son. He was only seven. Would the Monsignor consider taking both the chain and the boy? Each link would keep him alive for a month. O'Flaherty agreed, somehow managing to procure false papers for the parents. When the war was over he was able to return both the boy and the chain.

And, all the while Rome's Gestapo chief, Herbert Kappler, was setting traps. While dining with Prince Filippo Doria Pamphili, the man who funded O'Flaherty's operation, the SS surrounded the palace. O'Flaherty managed to escape through the basement and make a getaway in a coal truck. Of the 9,700 Roman Jews, nearly 2,000 were shipped off to Auschwitz with the connivance of the Church. Others were saved by the bravery of individual priests and nuns. After the war Kappler was sentenced to life in Gaeta prison, where his only visitor was O'Flaherty, who converted the man who'd sent thousands to their deaths to Catholicism.

Martha had been deeply affected by her visit to the Jewish ghetto in Rome, now a bohemian quarter full of bars and little restaurants. When she visited with Brendan there was still a Yiddish bread shop on the corner of the narrow street, tucked beneath lintels carved with Hebraic script that must have dated back to Roman times. It sold plaited poppy-seed loaves and delicious cheesecake. Then, as she'd wandered into a little square, she noticed a small plaque on a wall that marked the spot where Rome's Jews were rounded onto trucks and transported to the death camps. She thought of her grandfather leaving Zurich for London. Switzerland may have been neutral but still it hadn't felt safe.

Parting and exile. Remembering and forgetting. The Jews and the Irish have a lot in common. James Joyce knew what he was doing when he made Leopold Bloom a Jew. At first glance they seem so different. But look harder and they begin to seem like brothers separated at birth. Two ancient peoples destined to wander the world as outsiders subject to suspicion and derision. No blacks. No dogs. No Irish (and, probably, they'd have added No Yids if they'd thought about it) announced the notices on slammed lodging house doors in 1950s London. She'd read that some even speculated the Irish were one of the 'lost tribes' of Israel. What was it Brendan Behan said? 'Others have a nationality. The Irish and the Jews have a psychosis.'

Is this what so attracts her to this little country? The passion. The lack of reserve. The warmth and raw emotions? Is this why she feels so at home? She puts the leaflet back on the porch table and, as she leaves, it starts to rain.

3

It was Breda McKenna who turned Colm on to literature. He can still remember the shiver that ran along his spine as she read about a 'beast slouching towards Bethlehem.' He was thirteen and, suddenly, felt excited by the power of language. Breda had spent years teaching in rough London schools before coming back home to Kerry. Thin, plain and tough, with hair scraped back from her face in a childish hairband, she had a formidable intelligence and a gift of empathy for those she taught. She insisted it was Colm's duty to work. That there was another life out there beyond sheep, cattle and the pub, beyond marrying the first girl you kissed, and that it was yours for the taking if only you read, if only you were inquisitive about the world, asked questions and did not accept that because things had always been a certain way they always would be.

He was never sure about University College but loved Dublin. The music scene, the museums, the squares with their 18th century houses, their green doors and polished brass knockers. Quite probably he'd have stayed if things had been different. And what then? What would he be doing now if he'd finished his degree? Teaching at the university, working for a publisher, running a bookshop? The first term they'd studied Irish poetry from Yeats to Ciaran Carson. He'd always read poetry but it had been a private thing. Now he enjoyed the analysis. Breaking down the imagery with the precision of a lab technician carrying out a dissection. He read Eavan Boland and Paul Muldoon. The experimental prose of Paul Auster and Italo Calvino, as well as English writers like Martin Amis and Ian McEwan. He knew that the more he read, the more it would feed into his own work.

Like all Kerrymen he grew up with music in the house. His father was a mean fiddler and his mother, Mary, still had a sweet voice. When he came back from Dublin he loved to listen to the old fellows in the pub. Eavesdrop, as they set the world to rights, blathering on about cattle and politics, their hernias and overdrafts, football and racing. They were great talkers. Every one of them a philosopher.

Being in Dublin gave him the chance to develop his music. At school he wasn't much interested in the Celtic stuff his parents played. It was U2 and House. For a while he fancied himself a drummer and was part of a five-man rock band that played student gigs. But studying Irish poetry took him back to his roots. He wasn't interested in all that pseudo-Celtic, New Age mysticism shite. He wanted the real thing. He developed an interest in *sean-nós*, the old-style unaccompanied songs that grew out of the oral tradition. He started to write his own to be sung, just as they'd originally been at weddings and wakes. Like the older Christy Moore from County Kildare, with his tongue-twisting rush of garrulous monologues that told of growing up in Catholic Ireland in the 1950s, Colm used his voice to explore the harsh landscape and sing about the people he'd been raised among.

And singing attracted women. It didn't take him long to suss that out. Being in a band meant you never had to go home alone. That's how he met Sinéad. She just followed him into the bar after a session and stood beside him in her black leather jacket and Doc Martens while he bought a pint. Then she asked if he'd buy her one too. He liked her nerve. So he did. It took him a while to realise that he was attractive. Perhaps he was just slow on the uptake. He didn't think he had a snowball's chance in hell of going with her. There'd been the odd girl at school. He wasn't a virgin by the time he was sixteen. But still he never clocked that women actually fancied him.

Sinéad was older. Just back from university in England where she was studying textiles and set design. Her room was full of strange knitted webs of raw wool strung from the ceiling and bits of bark woven through muslin. She was working in a swanky new coffee place off St Stephen's Green—all blond wood and minimal cool—while she decided on her next move. The night she asked him to buy her a drink, she sat in her short black skirt and ripped fishnets, perched on a stool at the bar, sipping her Guinness, chatting about this and that till closing time. Then she invited him back to her place. Straight out. He'd have been an eejit not to go. She had a tiny blue stone pierced through her belly button and her skin was soft, her mouth wet, as she pinned him to the bed, tying his arms on the bedpost with a velvet scarf so he couldn't move. But she was completely crazy. She'd say she was going to go to some interview for a job with a film company or a gallery and then forget or disappear for days, once spending a week in Bruges for no reason he could ever fathom, only to turn up at his digs in the middle of the night as he was finishing an essay, demanding a night of drink and lust. But when he told her his father had died, that he had to go back to Kerry, she stopped coming round or answering his texts. The day before he left for the funeral he saw her in the pub with an American from his faculty. Everyone knew that a bigger bollox never put his arm through a coat. But though the guy was as thick as shite, he was rich. Sinéad waved as if there'd never been anything between them. Then she went on talking to her new date. He wasn't going to beg.

Anyway he admires women who knew their own minds like Breda and his mam, who'd taken over the herd after his father died and was as good as any man. He enjoys their company. Particularly if they don't take any bullshit. He hates girlie girls, into fashion, spray tans and New Age therapies. He likes women who think as well as fuck.

He first met Brendan a few years ago, one winter evening in the small pub at the far end of the village, where the local musicians hung out. It was a regular Sunday night gig and Colm was trying out a few new songs. A heavy mist had come down over the moors so that apart from a clutch of local stalwarts gathered round the peat fire, the pub was fairly empty. After their set Brendan came over and offered him a pint. He sounded English and lived in London but was, he told Colm, half-Irish, and had inherited the old cottage up on Bolus Head. An art dealer and critic, he was working on a book up there.

They met on a number of occasions after that. Brendan always insisting that he buy the drinks. It was, he said, good to get out and have a bit of stimulating conversation. Colm was doing him a favour. Brendan talked about art and his passion for Abstract Expressionism. For Rothko and Cy Twombly. In return Colm lent Brendan books of contemporary Irish poetry. If he wanted to reacquaint himself with his Celtic heritage then no better way than to read the poets. And Brendan took an interest in Colm's work. He knew a couple of editors of English literary magazines. If Colm wanted to show him some of his poems he might be able to recommend where to send them. But, for some reason, they never got round to it.

Martha was out when he left his manuscript in a plastic bag beneath a stone on her doorstep. He wonders if she'll read it.

4

Time has become elastic. Collapsing and expanding in ways that have little to do with reality. Her classroom feels a world away. If she never went back, would anyone even notice? Normally she'd be preparing for the next term but has taken extra leave until Easter. Now she's having to familiarise herself with her own rhythms. She should be organising a trip for her GCSE students to the Globe and another, later in the year, to Stratford. Often it's a waste of time and the kids just see it as a chance to miss a day's school. But, occasionally, someone becomes struck and one or two have gone on to study drama at university or got into RADA. And that's made her proud. Particularly Alex, who lived on a crime-infested council estate in King's Cross. His mother surviving on antidepressants and never showing the slightest interest in anything her son did. An absent father in and out of prison, he'd plenty of opportunities to get in with the wrong crowd. But Martha had taken a chance and cast him as Brick in the end of year production of *Cat on a Hot Tin Roof*. For one so young, he was electric, finding some deep connection with the character once he got on stage. Martha badgered and cajoled him through his exams. Sorted out his grant applications and helped him apply for a scholarship to the Central School. Recently she had seen him in the Almeida production of *The Winslow Boy*. She was touched that he bothered to send her a ticket. Afterwards, as they chatted in the bar, he still occasionally forgetting and calling her Miss instead of Martha, people came up to congratulate him and she wondered if they might think this gangly young man was her son. He could have been. And she'd have been proud.

5

She hopes that everything is alright at home. Françoise, the French PhD student who rents her top room said she'd keep an eye. A serious girl from a big family in Limoges, she's studying international relations. Although they live quite separate lives, occasionally she comes down to the kitchen for a glass of wine or to share a spaghetti bolognese and they chat about her plans to work for UNESCO. Such brief exchanges force Martha to stay connected. Prevent the house from being inhabited solely by ghosts.

She and Brendan had, like many of their generation, bought the place as a wreck in the '70s. It was divided into rooms for Irish navvies working on the motorways. There were cracked basins with a single cold tap in each bedroom, stained lavatories on the landings and mottled linoleum on the communal stairs. The deposit came from her father who didn't think they should squander money on rent and felt, once Brendan was working at the gallery, that they should have a place of their own. She remembers the day they got the keys. The wallpaper was black with damp and a rusty geyser in the bathroom, just off the kitchen, dripped brown water into the stained tub. Slowly they pulled the place apart, sanding floors and pine shutters, fixing the wiring and revealing Victorian fireplaces hidden behind plasterboard, decorating the rooms to create the home she still has today. They bought old furniture from Bermondsey and Portobello markets early in the morning for a few pounds. A pine and marble washstand with blue and white Art Nouveau tiles. A tallboy for the hall and a Victorian spoon-back chair, when such things could still be had for a song. Carting them back strapped to the roof of their old green *deux chevaux*. The walls of her sitting room are still covered in the paintings Brendan collected over the years by the artists he showed. A Sean Scully with subtle taupe and grey rectangles. A Hughie O'Donoghue diver. A Tony Bevan head. She also still has the piano her grandfather brought from Zurich. She always hoped Bruno would learn. But he never practiced willingly and, rather than create a rift, she reluctantly allowed him to give up.

6

She takes the low road that sweeps down to St Finéan's Bay and then up over the mountain but hasn't reckoned on the fog. When she left the cottage the weather was quite clear but as she climbs up onto the moors the road suddenly disappears in a swirling white mist. She switches on the headlights but that just makes it worse. She can't see a thing. The edge of the road, the ditch or the way ahead. She changes down into second gear and creeps along but the gradient is so steep the car stalls. She pulls on the hand break and revs the engine hoping that she'll manage to follow the curve of the steep bend and not come off the road or, worse, fall over the cliff. On one side there's a sheer drop down to the sea. On the other a wide expanse of boggy moorland. She can't see either. There isn't a house in sight or a single other car out on the road. It must still be another ten miles to Portmagee. She could be stuck for hours. No one knows she's here so she has no choice but to drive on. Suddenly she feels scared as she edges along the road, trying to follow the left hand verge, telling herself that if she drives slowly nothing much can happen. It's like being smothered by a great white blanket and she nearly hits a disorientated sheep, which runs off bleating into the fog. Eventually she makes it to the top of the moor where the cloud lifts, and turns down into the little fishing port where she parks outside the pub. It's taken her more than an hour to do a half-hour journey. Piles of nets and lobster creels sit stacked along the slipway and, ahead, is the new concrete bridge that joins the mainland to Valentia Island. Old fishermen's cottages, now mostly B&Bs, nestle between gift shops and the two village pubs. Parked on the quay, watching the fishing boats bob in the darkness, she realises how anxious she's been. She climbs out of the car and makes her way to the first of the pubs. There's a fire in the grate and a group of men, women and children are standing around a flat-screen TV watching the end of a rugby match. All are dressed in green, white and orange T-shirts. She goes to the bar and orders a glass of white wine and wonders why in Ireland it always comes in little bottles. She can't see Colm anywhere.

As the match finishes, the television is turned off and a crowd gathers round the accordion player on a small stage. He's joined by a big fellow with a ponytail on the uilleann pipes. These are not so much held as worn. Balanced against a leather strap on the piper's thigh as he squeezes the air from the bag tucked under his elbow. A couple of whey-faced children in green tracksuits, who've been tucking into bowls of chips, get up and dance. Arms pinned to their sides, their feet flick and kick beneath their stiff little bodies. The adults clap approvingly.

As Martha is watching, the door bursts open and in come Colm and Niall, accompanied by the girl with spiky red hair, carrying their instruments. They're bundled up in hats and scarves against the damp. Martha hasn't seen Colm for a while. It was just chance that she noticed the poster in the post office advertising their gig when she was sending back some of Brendan's more valuable books to London, worried that they'd deteriorate in the damp. Then, struggling with her own company she decided, on a whim, to drive over to Portmagee.

The girl with spiky hair is wearing jeans and a short crochet top. She and Colm josh and joke as they get ready for their set. Martha wonders how long they've been together. Colm is handsome in a scruffy sort of way. He must have lots of girlfriends. Over the last few days she's been reading his poems and some of his images have come back to her when she's been out walking. There's a muscularity to his writing. A world-weary cynicism balanced by a tender humanity. When the fellow on the pipes finishes Colm climbs onto the stage, still in his blue woollen hat, settles himself on the stool and starts to sing. A hush falls over the bar. Again there's that frailty, tempered by toughness, she first heard on New Year's Eve. As he is taking the applause she picks up her things intending to slip quietly away. But just as she's putting on her jacket he calls her over.

Hey Martha. That's grand you're here. I was wondering if you found the package I left on your doorstep. I haven't been up to your place to check. Don't want to be seen pestering the critics, he jokes. And this, he says, putting his arm round the girl with spiky hair, is Kathleen. My greatest fan! She's left the sick and ailing of Dublin for the holidays to come and play with her big brother. Now, won't you join us? What can I get you to drink?

7

The last clods are glowing in the grate. The clock above the glass-fronted dresser containing his mother's rose-pattern china, her statue of the Virgin and the school photographs of his nephews and nieces, ticks into the silence of his kitchen. Paddy O'Connell makes a pot of tea and settles himself at the table. He finds the Basildon Bond pad of blue-lined writing paper, his glasses and a decent pen, then arranges them neatly on the flowered oilskin. He takes his time. He is not one for writing. He removes the letter, with its printed letterhead, from the long white envelope and reads it again. Then unscrews the lid of his pen and writes to Eugene Riordan to tell him that his house is not for sale. When he's finished he reads what he has written, folds it carefully, puts it in an envelope, licks the flap and props it on the dresser. In the morning he'll go down the mountain to the post office and get a stamp from Maggie O'Shea. He empties the brown teapot into the compost bucket under the sink, washes his mug and leaves it in the wooden rack on the draining board, then banks up the fire, turns out the light and makes his way up the steep flight of stairs to his narrow bed.

Monday

1

Dawn the colour of rain.

It's twelve weeks since Brendan died. For more than thirty years she shared her bed with him, comfortable with his thickening girth, she with the crows' feet beginning to appear at the corners of her eyes. She realises she can't be sure he never brought Sophie here, that they hadn't made love in the bed she's sleeping in now. She'll never know. Looking back there's so much they didn't talk about, so much that she didn't ask him. She wishes that she'd known him better, her husband. That they'd been able to support each other's grief. She misses him. His stolid balance, his reassuring bulk in her bed and wonders if her fingers will ever smell of sex again. She is fifty-six. Nearly old. Maybe on a good day she doesn't look it but if she pinches the skin on the back of her hand it no longer springs back like firm elastic. She has pains in her shoulder and, despite the yoga, sciatica in her right leg. Recently she broke a tooth and had to spend a fortune having it capped. There is, she thinks, nothing dignified about getting older. How does it happen? It's easy to believe that ageing is what happens to other people. Being young is what she's used to and then, suddenly, without warning, it all changed. She woke up one morning and there was more life behind her than ahead.

She has lost her child and her husband. She's forgotten who she is and what her life is for. Sometimes her recollections are clear and vivid but other days she can barely remember anything that's happened and her existence seems full of dead purpose and thwarted desires. A sense of anguish about the hours and minutes she can't recall washes over her. She thinks of that poem about the road not taken and wonders how else she might have lived, what other decisions she might have made. For the last twenty years her days have been full of 'what ifs'. What if the sea had been too choppy and the boat from Rosslare delayed after their holiday? What if they'd stayed another week? If she had packed Bruno better and different clothes, made him a chocolate instead of a carrot cake? Or the weather on Exmoor had been bad so that they'd been unable to go canoeing at all? What if they'd gone out to the Skelligs before they left as she'd promised? Would that, in some way, have safeguarded him? Would any of these things have changed the alignment of the stars, tilted the earth in a different configuration? She was his mother. Surely she must have been able to do something to protect him?

She's been over and over it with her grief counsellor. It was normal for those left behind to blame themselves. But, he told her patiently, pushing his half-moon glasses up on the top of his balding head and looking at her directly: we are not that powerful. We can't change the orbit of the planets. Events are random. A chain of actions set off by a butterfly flapping its wings in the Amazonian rain forest. Not something we can control. Not something for which in some mysterious or magical way she's responsible or that she should spend the rest of her life punishing herself for.

2

The touch of skin on skin? Could she ever make herself vulnerable again, undress in front of someone new, let them see her stretch marks, her less than youthful thighs? Brendan knew her when she was young. At her best. They'd grown older together. He'd watched her body change over the years, with the birth of their child and the onset of middle age, as she had his. After the affair with Sophie it was a long time before they were intimate again. Then in Rome, in that big mahogany bed, he'd leant over and kissed her with a tenderness that always made her open up to him. For a mad moment she wonders if she might have made a silly mistake and left him in London and that, even now, he's on his way to the ferry to join her at the cottage. All his things are here. Maybe she's throwing everything out only for him to turn up and be furious with her for tampering.

She wishes that they'd had another child. But Brendan had made it clear that although he loved Bruno, he didn't want any more. For a while she'd tried to persuade him, cajole him with arguments about playmates and someone to share the burden when they got old. But he was happy with their little trinity. For him the balance was right. There was just enough time left over from his books and running the gallery to spend with her and take an interest in what Bruno was reading or go with him to the British Museum to see the Egyptian mummies. She wonders if she'd had a daughter, if it would have been a comfort. Someone to share the loss of Brendan and Bruno. Her two Bs.

3

It's market day in Caherciveen or some sort of fair. All along the library railings horses are tied up with bits of rope and blue twine, stamping their big feathered feet. Their tails and manes mangled and their coats caked in mud. There are skewbalds and piebalds. A mare and her foal with tiny hooves. Horse droppings steam on the pavements. There's nowhere to park and makeshift stalls everywhere. One man sells reproduction antiques, another net curtains, pots and pans. There's a goose in a pen with four ducks and some baby chicks. And a litter of yapping puppies in a cage. A chubby little girl in a pink frilled dress and muddy anorak is crying and carrying on because she's been told that No, she can't have one. And across the road the MegaBites van is doing a roaring trade in chicken nuggets and cups of strong brown tea. Men in flat caps and woolly hats stand around chatting. Their faces are ruddy, their shoes black and their trousers Dralon. Some have big Rolex watches and gold-sovereign rings. Others are unshaven and wear trousers that are too short, hitched up over large stomachs with wide leather belts. A few have cigarettes cupped in their hands and appear to be doing a deal over the bay in the horsebox. A Heath Robinson contraption cobbled together from sheets of corrugated metal attached to the back of a battered car. Further down the road a woman and her assorted children sit perched on kitchen stools in a trailer that's being towed into town behind a rusty tractor.

You'd think the Irish were put on this earth for others to feel sentimental about, wouldn't you?

Martha starts to find Colm standing behind her, smiling.

We're adept at turning other people's dewy-eyed fantasies into myths.

But be warned, he continues, anyone round here found wearing an Aran gansey or singing 'Danny Boy' is unlikely to be a native. May I enquire if you would do me the honour of a drink? I've a real throat on me.

Goodness, Colm, I didn't see you. Where did you spring from?

Oh I'm just in town like everyone else for a bit of the *craic*.

She's not sure why he's asked her for a drink but follows his blue woollen hat into the crowded bar. The place is packed, even though it's only mid-morning. There are market traders, cattle merchants in Wellingtons and women in their best clothes fresh from the hairdressers. There's hardly room to move.

You grab that table over there, Martha, while I do battle at the bar. So how've you been doing then? I haven't seen you for a bit, he says arriving back with two dark pints, which he sets down in front of her trying not to spill them in the crush. She hates Guinness.

Did you read my manuscript?

I did.

Ah, that's grand, and what, may I ask, did you think? No, don't tell me now. Maybe I can pop by sometime and have a chat. It's a bit noisy in here for a literary seminar. So what you think to all this, then? he asks, casting an eye round the crowded bar.

It's very colourful.

It's that alright. Even though we're what Joyce called the 'afterthought of Europe,' he says, taking a slug of stout, 'haunted by a history that's dead but just won't lie down'. That's because we don't really know who we are, Martha. We've told ourselves so many stories that we can't see the wood for the proverbial trees. Believe me, quite a lot of what seems indigenous here is an invention. But you're likely to be labelled a heretic if you say so. Irish stew, now, well that was concocted for Irish navvies working on the roads in Britain. Irish coffee was cooked up by a chef at Foynes airport in the early days of air travel to keep the pilots from freezing to death. And Dublin? Well, at the beginning of the last century it was a slum that would make even Calcutta seem cosy, rather than the chosen destination for Ryanair stag nights. And Dublin isn't just St Stephen's Green and a few nice Georgian houses, you know. Not that long ago the streets were full of barefoot children, toothless women, and priests with polished shoes who spoke of hell but cuddled up in the four poster with their housekeepers, before taking confession. Mean little shops sold everything from bacon to coal. You could buy just enough fuel for a single night's firing. Tea and sugar were sold by the pinch and it was five Woodbine for tuppence. It wasn't so long ago that the pawnbroker was as familiar as the priest. You could pawn your clothes on the Monday and redeem them on Saturday for Sunday Mass. Now pole dancers outnumber poets and we love it because it's so modern. Forget Beckett or Synge. Riverdance and computer call centres are our best exports now. We're not really a land of twinkly-eyed fiddlers but bent politicians, property developers, and financial cowboys. And it's a feckin' disaster, he says, pulling off his hat and taking another swig of his pint.

Surely that's a bit harsh.

Not really, Martha. It's just that people like to buy into the collective myth. Even in the '50s, just after we became a newly-proclaimed republic, for most of those living in the south, Ireland stopped at Newry. Unity was something people paid lip service too, like the restoration of the Irish language. There's always been this fantasy that Ireland was homogenous. We've been sold the story of a shared struggle by politicians and teachers. I've never much bought into the version of donkeys, boreens and harps, myself. I've always thought it a bit of an invention and it annoys me that we sell ourselves short to the world that way. School children are still sent here because it's the *Gaeltacht.* That means we're officially supposed to speak Irish. It's not true, of course. Every one speaks English, except for kids in school who're forced to learn it, some teachers and a few old people. But for me, what's really important is the vitality of Irish-English. Its Celtic roots, its old rhythms bouncing off modern idioms. That's the excitement of our language. It's alive and continually growing. That's why, for a small place, there are so many seriously good writers. We've constantly sought to retell who we are. And now? Now what matters? Well, we're not sure. We're caught between two worlds. Two ways of being and we don't know which we want more. We think we can have both but don't realise or want to see that one kills the other. We're in danger of becoming a pastiche of ourselves. But the Technicolor version pays the bills. All those American tourists looking for their Irish roots in Connemara and Cork. But basically, he laughs, so Martha's not sure whether or not he's being serious, we're just a load of feckin' brawlers with a talent for words and music that other people look down on but would secretly like to be.

But everyone's so friendly, Colm. Compared to England the place has, oh I don't know, so much more soul. People have time for each other.

He snorts. Hey Martha, don't you be seduced by that Hibernian-Disneyesque shite. 'Nothingness'. Now that's the real topic of Irish life and literature. Look at Ulysses. Bloom was grand at doing nothing. Drink, talk, humour, storytelling and sitting on the lav. All ways of escaping the oppressions of life in a small, stagnant colony going nowhere fast. That's why we're writers and drinkers. For us writing is a form of perpetual complaint. Brendan Behan once described himself as a drinker with a writing problem and you could certainly say that about quite a few I've known, he says, wiping his mouth with the back of his hand. Until recently this was one of the most Catholic countries in the world. Spain, for instance, has always had a left-wing anti-clerical strain. But not here. The Church gave people a national identity all through the Troubles. Then it demanded its pound of flesh. Piety and tedium are the traditional themes of Irish culture. The soul-killing, mind-numbing monotony of everyday life and the monolithic grip of the clergy. Religious and political piety were staples. People would sell their own mothers for a pensionable job under the state. And the price? Silence and cynicism. But, hey, we've joined the European club and, by Jaysus, it's like religion and the euro our gilded saviour. We're all so modern now. In England you had the '60s when we were still in the dark ages packing girls off to Liverpool for abortions, pretending they were going to look for a job. Have you heard of the Kerry babies case, Martha? If you want a microcosm of life in rural Ireland before the Celtic Tiger that gives you the lot. Lies, secrets, silence.

Yes, I remember vaguely reading something about it years ago.

Things had changed in Ireland by 1984, after the Second Vatican Council, he says taking a swig of his pint, but not that much. The case was about the clash of two cultures. An old repressive Ireland and the new secular one that was just beginning to emerge. You know the story, don't you? How a baby was washed up on White Strand near Caherciveen with a broken neck and stab wounds. The Garda went into overdrive. Bigwigs came down from Dublin. Speculation was rife. They got the names of local girls who might have got rid of a baby, of romances that had broken up, of pregnant women back from England. They pulled in hippies and tinkers. Priests asked for information from the pulpit. A ten-year-old reported that next door was after having a baby. Someone else that her friend's sister was getting the tablets from Dublin. Joanne Hayes came from a small farm. There was another sister, as well as two brothers. One was simple and talked of nothing but cows. The father was dead and the elderly mother struggling with the family's acres, which were in pitiful decline. Joanne already had an illegitimate daughter with a married man and was rumoured to be pregnant again. But there didn't ever seem to be a baby. God Martha, the investigation was mediaeval. Our own Salem witch hunt in 20th century Ireland. Under prolonged pressure from the Garda, Joanne finally admitted giving birth in a field, then panicking and burying the stillborn baby. But the guards, in their infinite wisdom, decided that she'd had sex not just with one man but with two; that she'd had twins and then killed them both, despite blood tests showing that it was impossible. And all the time the feckin' priests, who were preaching against contraception, were enjoying their own hanky-panky. Michael Cleary had two children with his housekeeper. Bishop holier-than-thou-Casey, despite abandoning his partner and child, confessed his sins each morning before taking confession from his parishioners. It was the dog's bollocks! Eventually an English forensics guy examined the baby's remains. And do you know what he concluded? That it hadn't been stabbed at all but probably pecked by gulls. Would you credit it? The whole thing was a ball of shite. The prejudice of the guards, the hypocrisy of Church and the judiciary. The Kerry babies case tells you everything you need to know about what rural Ireland was really like.

But you came back to Kerry, Colm. Presumably you could have stayed in Dublin or even gone abroad?

Sure I could. But I love this feckin' place. Not the diddly-diddly leprechaun or Eurotrash mentality. Language. That's our great strength. For a little nation, we punch well above our weight. All of us speak with the accents of our native place. No Irishman is judged by the way he speaks as you are in England. We're not obsessed by class or with where people come from. Though I can't be doing with all this contemporary spiritual bollocks about ley lines and standing stones. To me it all feels like some sort of weird hippy nonsense from muppets who've lost their way and given up thinking. Ireland's always been full of dysfunctional families, miserable loveless lives, illness, old age, mind-numbing religion, and rain. Our national hymns are rain songs, our pastimes boredom and drinking. One keeps the other at bay. That's the truth, Martha. My truth—and that's what I write about. That and the savage beauty of this place. The other sort of Irishness? Well, that's for tourists.

As they're talking a German woman with peroxide Heidi-plaits and a wrist wrapped in knotted leather bracelets is leaning over the bar talking animatedly to two local men. Apparently she's lived here for a long time and in her inebriated state feels that gives her the right to be frank.

The Irish, they are stupid, she says, in her accented English that has both a Hibernian lilt and a heavy German inflection. They do nothing for the environment. They are just dirty. Dirty. Drive behind them and you'll see they throw the cigarette packets out of the car window. A German would never do something like this. Ireland is the last free country in Europe, she continues, warming to her theme. Wild spaces, clean air and water, but my neighbours they would destroy it all. It makes me sad. But we Germans are bringing environmental education and good taste to Ireland. Of course, the Irish are lovely people, but ignorant.

Sure you Germans are hardworking, sure you're smart, one of her drinking companions, a young man in fisherman's gear with a lobster face, sneers. Smart enough to feckin' have voted for Hitler, he says, storming off and plonking himself, unasked, at Martha and Colm's small table.

God-give-me-strength, he says, pulling up his stool, before launching into his own drunken diatribe about how he could sort out the six counties, no trouble at all.

The Prods, now, they need a proper pasting before they come round, he slurs. You can't alter the march of history. *Ireland unfree shall never be at peace.* Did you ever hear that now? he asks, leaning a beery face into Colm's across the table.

I certainly did Colm says, pushing his unfinished pint aside and getting up slowly. It's from Patrick Pearse's oration at the graveside of the Fenian O'Donovan Rossa, 1915, you fucking eejit. Come on Martha, he says, grabbing her coat sleeve and pulling her through the crowded bar into the street. Let's leave this lot to their nonsense. They're about as bright as a lighthouse in a damp fog.

4

Eugene is driving to his solicitor in Killarney. He has Paddy O'Connell's letter in his pocket and is seething. Joe McNeil has been his lawyer since the early days. They were at school together and still regularly play golf. Joe understands Eugene's needs. He must be able to find a way round this. Eugene has just heard from the bank. They're all ready to go with the money at a good rate. It's there for the asking. He met with the architects again yesterday. There shouldn't be any problem sourcing the materials they want. He parks his Range Rover in the Church of Ireland car park and makes his way up to Joe's office.

Joe is short and balding with broad shoulders. He wears an expensive pink shirt that only just buttons round his middle, slip-on suede loafers and strong aftershave.

Good morning to you, Eugene. It's been a few days since we spoke. How's Siobhán?

Eugene ignores him and sits down in front of Joe's desk and hands him Paddy's letter.

Well, Joe says, glancing at it. That's most unfortunate. But I'm sure we can find ways and means. Whiskey?

Joe passes Eugene a heavy Waterford crystal tumbler, then takes off his reading glasses and leans back in his chair. His office is sleek and modern. Through the glass partition Eugene can see his secretary busy at her keyboard. Joe's desk is covered with files and documents. A photo of his wife, his three red-headed children and their golden retriever, sits in a silver frame.

Look, I see it like this, Eugene, Joe says, sizing up the situation. Like a cool-headed poker player. You have to plan your moves carefully. Keep a few paces ahead. Outwit the opponent. You need a long-term strategy. Now, as I thought, the Keegan brothers are happy to take the money and sit in the pub all day and I've had a word with Mike Kelly. He'll let the deal go through and move into one of those new bungalows if he can keep his grazing rights in the far field. That shouldn't affect anything in terms of the building programme and I think guests would appreciate seeing a few genuine Irish cows out of the window. It keeps things authentic, gives the place a bit of atmosphere. But this thing with your man Paddy. Well that's a bit trickier.

Eugene sighs impatiently. I know that Joe. That's why I'm here.

Well my suggestion would be to go ahead with the purchases that you can make. Crowd him out. If you get those other two properties you can at least widen the track to the edge of the Cassidy woman's field and start getting in some building equipment. Make it look as though you mean business. That it's all a done deal. No harm in a bit of bluff, is there? Any further thoughts from her, by the way? Will she sell?

Eugene shrugs. I've no idea. Who knows what goes on in the mind of a woman like that?

You can make it difficult for O'Connell, Joe continues. Disturb his stock. Make it awkward to get feed through. I'm not suggesting anything illegal mind, but the track officially runs over the Keegan boys' land. I've checked that. So it's just habit that he uses it. There's nothing in writing, nothing binding as far as I can see that gives him the right. Now, if you were to own that stretch, you can say no. It'll be your land, and you don't have to let anyone cross it if you don't want to.

But that's not going to guarantee that I can go ahead with the project, is it? Eugene asks tetchily. Not unless I have O'Connell's place. That's where the building's going to go.

Well, maybe not immediately, Joe says, scratching his ear and swivelling round and round in his black leather chair. But give it time, Eugene. It wouldn't do any harm to buy that land up there anyway. After all you aren't paying much for it by today's rates. And the bank will let you have the money for more or less nothing. Hopefully the Cassidy woman will play ball and want to be shot of her place. That would certainly help.

Then you'd have direct access and that would leave O'Connell isolated. He'll have a real problem if he can't get in feed or drive his sheep and cattle up on the mountain. Maybe then he'll see it's no longer viable to farm up there and that he'd be much better off taking up your offer and living the life of Riley, rather than struggling on. And you know a few people on the council. Arrange a few *pro bono* dinners, some rounds of golf at one of your clubs, bend a few ears. You know as well as I do how these things are done.

But that could take a while, Eugene sighs. This is ridiculous.

5

Paddy has fretted all day since he put the letter in the post. He's not sure what more he can do to stop Eugene Riordan. That he owns the title deeds to his cottage and land, he knows. They go back three generations. His granda built these walls. But wealthy men like Eugene don't just get rich by chance. They know a thing or two and have clever people working for them. Paddy has put his heart and soul into this place, keeping the corrugated iron roof in good repair, repainting the outside walls each year with lime wash, the inside with green gloss paint: dresser, window ledges, and chairs. Every week he puts out the furniture and mops the floors just as his mam used to do.

Until he was ten they hadn't the electricity. His da collected *talla* from the strand. A big yellow ball of grease that used to drift in off the boats. He made candles with it and had a special thing for threading the wick. When it was lit it would burst like a bomb. He remembers his mam sitting by the Tilly lamp knitting; the click-clack of her needles, the dog snoring by the grate. When they got the electricity they looked up at the bulb for a week. Thought 'twas blind they were getting. His mother's eyes were never good with all that knitting and mending. She bought a pair of rimless spectacles from the little Jew man in the felt hat. He came spring and autumn with his suitcase of glasses, with their buff cloths to give them a polish. When he opened his battered leather case there was all sorts: bottles of liniments for rheumatism and cough mixture guaranteed to loosen even the firmest phlegm.

His da was always suspicious of the Jew. Warned that like the dark-skinned gypsies on market day he'd cheat you soon as look at you. Furriers and jewellers were Jews. That was well known. You had to check they'd not slipped the jewels from out your watch when you took it to be mended.

The day they buried his mam, the long red curtains blew in and out of her window in the rain. She always slept with them wide open to get the benefit and no one thought to close them. Marie and Nora, his two sisters still at home, were beside themselves. They sat next to her wardrobe, their faces buried in her dresses that still had the scent of Ashes of Roses on them.

The gloom was palpable. His da moped in the kitchen, while the girls tiptoed round him, fixing his dinner, which he pushed away. He didn't seem to notice if there was food in the house or not and the girls were too frightened to ask for money. As like as not he'd get in a rage. It was the alcohol talking. Although he'd never been a drinker, now he'd drink and drink until he passed out. It wasn't that he was a violent man but he couldn't deal with the grief. He stopped going out, stopped having baths. The time the parish priest came round he just shut the door in his face.

Paddy's parents had been fixed up by a matchmaker. In those days if you saw two men with their heads together in the pub you knew a match was being made. Not all the marriages worked out but you were stuck with what you got. His parents were blessed with seven children. Though they lost one early to the scarlet fever and then poor Bridie at sixteen. After his mam was taken, his da just went downhill.

And all the while Paddy carried on feeding the cattle, laying muck and digging potatoes. Slowly his da began to take an interest again, stopped hitting the bottle and went back up the mountain with the sheep. He always liked the sheep. Getting up in the early morning mist as the sun rose over the sea. He knew every nook and cranny of the hillside. There was none better with a lamb that was breech. And although he never touched the whiskey again, he never really got back his strength. It was then that Paddy knew he wouldn't be leaving. And he's been here ever since. Minding the place, minding his business.

6

Martha is running a hot shower. She got cold in town. As she slips off her thermal vest she notices she put it on inside out. A sign of good luck. Well, she could do with a little luck right now. She's soaping her hair and enjoying the jet of hot water when a car door slams outside, followed by a knock. She can hear someone in the front room. She never locks the door.

I'm in the shower.

Irritated, she wraps herself in a towel and goes through to the main room to find Eugene standing with a bottle of whiskey in one hand and an expression on him like the back end of a sheep.

Martha, I have to talk to you, he says, not apologising for disturbing her, or making any reference to the fact that she is half-naked and dripping wet.

Does it have to be now? As you can see I was otherwise engaged.

Yes, yes it does.

Well, you'll have to wait while I put something on.

She goes back into the bathroom, pulls on a pair of jeans and one of Brendan's old sweaters, and then wraps her wet hair in a turban. Next door Eugene, is still standing in the middle of the room.

Oh for goodness sake, Eugene, do sit down. You're making me nervous.

He takes off his coat and settles himself by the stove.

Have you any glasses?

She's tempted to say that they're in the same place as they were the last time he was here but resists and goes to fetch two from the kitchen.

So what's all this about?

I need to talk to you about this place. I need to know if you'll sell, or at the very least, let me have the end of the field. It's crucial to this project. We'll be creating a lot of work up here, he says, in what sounds like a justification, if not an apology. At least ten permanent jobs.

She takes a long slow sip of the whiskey he's poured and breathes deeply.

The truth is Eugene, I haven't decided what I'm going to do with the place. It's just too soon.

But surely you won't want to come back here on any regular basis? Not now. And I'll give you a good price.

She feels such a swell of anger. As if she can just be bought off. As if the money has anything to do with it. She realises that this is the only language Eugene understands. His eyes are the colour of winter sea. She tries to make sense of what he's saying. Why does he want this so much? Why does it matter? He's a wealthy man. What's driving him? She finds it almost impossible to look him in the face and fiddles with the towel tying up her wet hair. She wants to say something but can't find the words. As he sits there waiting for her to reply, surrounded by her late husband's books, the Bible he won as a schoolboy, the catalogues on St Ives and Peter Lanyon, she realises that there can be no meeting point between her and this man, however much he once cared for her husband. Would he, she wonders, have asked this if Brendan had still been alive? What would Brendan have done? Surely he wouldn't have agreed or maybe he'd have been able to discourage Eugene before things ever reached this point, talk some sense into him. But perhaps this is just what Eugene does. Pursue things he doesn't really want or need but that will mean an inestimable loss to others, simply because he can.

She half had it in mind, when coming over on the boat from London, to put the place up for sale and be shot of it. She couldn't imagine coming back here on any regular basis after all these years, and wouldn't be here now if it wasn't for Brendan's death. It would be a drain on her resources to keep on a cottage that she never uses. She could let it for part of the year as a holiday let. But that would have its own problems. She'd need to find someone to change the sheets and clear up after the tenants left. And then in winter there'd always be problems with tiles or bits of guttering blown off by the wind, a leaking window or the electricity going down. She will have to give some serious thought to what she's going to do with the place.

7

The moon is pale as a shut eyelid.

Colm climbs from his van, slams the door, hunching inside his anorak against the rain. What does he want her to say? Perhaps he should have bought her something. A bottle of wine or chocolates for her trouble. But he's driven here in his work clothes and is later than he intended, unshaven and unwashed, after milking. He wonders how long he can sustain the herd, keep things going with so little help. His mam is not getting any younger. But he likes the earthy closeness to the animals, going to the corn merchant for feed. The smell of the place. Oats. Antiseptic. Saddle soap. But cows are demanding and leave him little time to write or play music.

Martha is the first person he's ever asked to read his work. He's not sure why he decided on her. Her relationship to Brendan, no doubt, and the fact that he hopes as an outsider she'll be objective. There's also something vulnerable about her that attracts him, something sympathetic.

Her hair is wet when she opens the door as if she's just climbed from the shower. She's wearing jeans and a man's knitted jersey. Her feet are bare. It makes her look like a girl. When he steps across the threshold the room is nearly dark except for the glow of the stove that throws shadows onto the whitewashed walls and the candles burning in a brass candelabra on the sill. He takes off his wet anorak and hangs it on the back of the chair. Then settles by the fire. She brings him a glass of wine and, uninvited, says:

They're good. Your poems, you know. Very good.

He doesn't speak but waits as she settles herself on the sofa, her legs curled beneath her like a teenager, a rug over her knees to keep out the chill.

Well, I know 'good' is a pretty feeble word, she continues. But they are. What I mean, she says leaning forward and reaching for her glass on the small table and taking a slow sip, is that they move me. Stay with me. They seem, somehow, I'm not sure if this is right, to transcend the world as it's immediately experienced. I read them slowly, each one several times. There is, if this doesn't sound too pompous or corny, something transcendental about them. Of course they deal with the everyday, with the life you know and experience around you. But still, there's something other-worldly about them. Isn't there a phrase Yeats used—you'd know better than me—about the 'foul rag-and-bone shop of the heart'? I think something like that applies to your poems. I like the merger between traditional and modern idioms. They're nostalgic but not soft. There's something uncanny and tough about them. If anything I want a little more of that. Occasionally, for you to explain less. To trust the reader.

She stops, as if aware of the sound of her own voice.

Oh dear! I sound like a teacher! I made a few notes in pencil on the text as I was reading them. Just a few suggestions. I hope that's alight. Things that you might want to consider cutting or making more emphatic. As I said, I'm no expert but it might help a little to have another point of view. But I'm impressed. I enjoyed reading them very much.

He can hear water pouring from the gutters down the side of the cottage, running along the track into the ditches and streams that cross the fields to make their way down to the beach and the sea. A halo of light from the candles bleeds through the window into the dark night. Somewhere a door is banging. And for a moment the world seems to consist of little more than this room, the endless rain, a glass of wine and a woman he barely knows talking about his poems.

His feet are propped on the small coffee table in front of him and he's still wearing his big boots. He should respond but isn't quite sure what to say. He leans forwards.

Can I ask you something?

Yes, she says, taking another sip of wine, her shoulders slumped in her big sweater.

Do you think you understand my poems better because you've

experienced loss first hand? You lost your son didn't you, before Brendan?

She gets up. And with her back towards him looks out of the window into the teeming night. Her damp, sandy-coloured hair hangs around her shoulders and he can hear her suck in her breath, as though inhaling all the air in the room, then sigh.

He shouldn't have been so direct. He's upset her but he's curious.

Yes, she says. I did. It seems that most people know most things round here. It was nearly twenty years ago and I've not been back here since. I probably wouldn't have come if Brendan hadn't died and I needed to sort out his things. But to answer your question, she says turning round and looking at him directly, I don't know if that makes me appreciate your poems more or not.

I'm sorry. I shouldn't have said that. It's none of my business. It was impertinent. Would you like me to leave?

No, she says quietly. Actually I'd rather like it if you stayed, if you don't mind. I rarely talk about Bruno but he's been with me all the time I've been here. I hadn't expected it. Though I suppose I should. I was just so caught up with Brendan's unexpected death and sorting out his affairs that it didn't occur to me.

He doesn't reply and she seems to takes this as an invitation to continue.

Bruno was ten when he died. He was just a normal little boy but for me he was special. I suppose all mothers feel that. But being an only child I think he had an old head on young shoulders. He liked to ask questions, big questions about space and the stars, about infinity and what happened before the Big Bang. He had no religious upbringing but had deep thoughts for a child. He wanted to understand why people die, what happens to them afterwards, and why there are wars. It wasn't always easy to know how to answer him. And he was fascinated by history. When he was here he badly wanted to go out to the Skelligs. The idea that people once lived on a rock in the middle of the Atlantic fascinated him. I promised to take him. But we never made it. The day after we got home that last summer we were here, he went to Cub Scout camp on Exmoor. There was an accident.

After that I couldn't clear out his room for ages. I used to go in there and sit for hours among the dinosaur posters, and the globe on his desk that lit up inside. I couldn't believe he wasn't just going to walk through the door, throw down his jacket and backpack and go to raid the fridge. I continued carrying the touch and smell of him inside me, almost as I'd done before he was born and I was pregnant. I just sat on his bed and looked up at the stars through the skylight. You can't always see them because of the light pollution in London but somehow it made it more special when it was clear and I could. I liked their unknowability, their otherness. It was as if looking at the Milky Way, with its thousands of dots of light, that I could somehow believe Bruno had become part of a web of being—the biosphere if you like—that matrix in which we're all embedded. I'm not conventionally religious but it was a comfort to realise all matter is made up of protons, neutrons and electrons. I could believe that he still exists, that he hasn't been completely obliterated that, if you like, he's simply changed form and his soul carries on. Perhaps that's as close to the idea of immortality as any modern person can sanely come.

I'm sorry, she says, as if she's forgotten he's sitting here. I'm not sure why I'm telling you all this. It's certainly not what you came to hear. So yes, thinking about it, maybe it does help me to understand your poems better.

8

Colm can't sleep but lays propped up in his childhood bed in his mother's house. He's wearing his blue woollen hat for warmth as he goes through the manuscript and the notes Martha's made in her round italic hand:

When your poetry's at its best, something of your spirit infiltrates this wild place. It's as if the landscape is capable of remembering. When you describe the bleak moorland, the cliffs and bogs, you don't, like Yeats, appear to be creating symbols but more like Hopkins to be revealing the essence of things. And that essence—or so it seems to me—is the intrinsic individuality and innate loneliness of all animate and inanimate things. There's something savage about your poems. For me that's when they're strongest, when they're most honest. The times they seem to falter are when they become more polemic and move away from a sense of place.

The act of looking and waiting corresponds with what is, in the widest sense of the word, beautiful and, even though it's a difficult word to use in contemporary culture, spiritual. It's as if, as long as we go on yearning, the beautiful can't appear. You capture that paradox. That's why, I think, in so much current artistic expression there's a contradiction; an absence, as well as a bitter nostalgia.

Many of your lines have come back to me over the last few days as I've been out walking, trying to find a sense of bearing in more ways than one. I was particularly affected by the stanzas:

how love must be a surrender,
  a letting go of that dark grieving
    lodged in marrow bone,

and how life is only this moment
at midnight: a guttering candle
and a terrible wind

howling across a strait of wide water
like something lost in the anthracite dark,
beating its way home in the battering rain.

Through your poems I've come to understand a little more about the lives of those who live here and the structures that make up Irish society. Structures that are being eroded in this new welter of prosperity. I found reading them a haunting experience and have no doubt that, with a bit of editing, you should send them out for publication.

Thank you for the privilege of letting me see them. I hope my comments are of some little help to you.

Yours,
Martha.

Tuesday

1

Outside it's still dark. That moment of stillness just before the sky whitens. The only sound is the small clock's tick. Colm folds his arms behind his head and stares at the ceiling. This is his boyhood room. His football trophies and comics are packed in plastic boxes at the back of the cupboard. But it's still recognisably the room where he discovered the secrets of puberty and poetry. Where he studied for his exams and read the tatty copy of *Hustler* that was being passed round his class. He goes over the notes from Martha again. He's touched. She's taken trouble and understood exactly what he's trying to do. Even her criticisms are spot on and sensitive. It's not really what he expected from this English woman. She is deeper than he thought and seems to have a feel for this place. He's not quite sure why she spent so much time on his poems. Perhaps reading them helped take her mind off Brendan and her boy. He tries to imagine what it must have been like for her to lose her only son. He realises he knows next to nothing about her except that she's Brendan's widow and a teacher. He's strangely attracted to her but can't quite make her out. There's something fragile, yet feisty about her. Like a strong current beneath an apparently calm river. Sometimes she seems very much younger than she must actually be. He hopes his bluntness last night didn't upset her.

He gets out of bed, pulls on his jeans that are standing stiffly inside his boots where he climbed out of them the night before, puts a couple of slices of bread in the toaster, brews a quick mug of tea, then takes his anorak from the back of the kitchen door. His ma is already out with the cows, giving him a break.

A mist is coming in off the sea as he heads up towards the Napoleonic tower on the headland, squelching through bog and bracken, careful to place his feet on firm ground. It's steep. He can feel the hill in his thighs, his breath catching in his chest, as he pushes on against the wind. Clouds of surf scoters overwintering in Ballinskelligs Bay, far from the chill of the Canadian Arctic, fill the sky with their immigrant cries, casting dark shadows over the sea. As they squawk overhead he imagines the path of their long flight. Their tiny hearts beating beneath windblown feathers as they follow the compulsion written in their DNA, to head for home.

Walking helps clear his head. Maybe it's time to take himself seriously. He doesn't want to be just another young writer milking his Celtic roots. Sure he feels loyalty to his family and tribe. But as one of his profs at university had wryly put it, it's all too easy for the Irish to be quaint. Harsh and raw. That's how Martha described his poems. That's what he wants. He's only interested in the truth. He's read all about formalism. Knows that technique is important. But for him it's simply a means to an end and not the end in itself. He wants his writing to affect his readers like a wound. A beautiful wound.

He climbs on through the wind and sleet towards the tower, though there's too much mist for him to see the Skelligs. Ahead the sky and ocean merge in a grey veil that stretches away towards America. How he loves this place. The savagery, the untamed wildness. Here on the edge of the land, the edge of Europe. He can feel it in his bones, the threads and connections running back through the centuries. It pushes him up against his own limits. It was during the last Ice Age that the corries, lakes, and valleys of the Iveragh Peninsular were created. The sandstone and siltstone washed down by rivers from the mountains to the north. Much of the mountain is still held in common. Though once it was shared by kinship groups who lived together in a *clachán*, the head dividing it between families for cultivation and grazing. But with its unclear boundaries, its absent shareholders and complex multi-ownership systems much of it has been abandoned. It's as if the land has forgotten what it's for.

Not long ago these hill farms kept a mix of livestock. Cattle browsed the vegetation too rough for sheep and trampled the bracken under hoof to keep the swards low and sweet. Scottish Blackface sheep, Wicklow Cheviots, and Kerry cows. But now the number of dairy farms has declined, accelerated by the introduction of milk quotas in the '80s. Small farms can't provide adequate returns. At first the Common Agricultural Policy helped maintain farming in this remote region and, with it, the social structures. But reforms in Brussels are beginning to take their toll.

Yet all around him people are enjoying the fruits of the so-called economic boom. New cars, holiday homes and house prices all indicate that many are doing very nicely, thank you. But while the *craic* is in full swing for some, others are finding it nearly impossible to survive. If there's supposed to be a trickle-down effect, well, as far as he's concerned, this new wealth isn't trickling in their direction. There's a hostility towards taxation. A wish for personal freedom at all costs. Brown envelopes have become the norm. Walk down the streets of any town in the Republic on a Saturday night and you can see the ugly side of modern Ireland. Flagrant wealth on the one hand, social deprivation on the other. The morning news is full of muggings and violence. There's suspicion, too, of the new immigrants. Eastern Europeans, mostly. It seems his fellow countrymen only know how to be emigrants but are uncertain how to welcome strangers into their midst. Intolerance, indifference, injustice, forced emigration, homelessness. The Irish have suffered their share of oppression and injustice. He only wishes that it had given them a greater sense of common cause. A century after the Famine, Catholic Ireland showed about as much compassion as a block of stone towards those escaping Nazi Germany. And there's little concern now for those who've been made stateless or are refugees.

It strikes him as ironic in a country that makes a big deal of the family, that more and more he sees young parents out at gigs on long drinking binges, the kids left at home with a bottle of Coke and a couple of videos.

Eccentricity, wit and humour. Those are this place's great strengths. But beneath the *craic* there's a sense of disenfranchisement among many of those he's grown up with. Why bother to work long hours to maintain the family farm if the children don't want it? If you can get a job in Spar or as a bank clerk or barman in Tralee? It depresses him. He's the fifth generation of his family to work the land. Most of his contemporaries have given up. He's a rarity. All the more so because he left, went to college and then came back. But it's a struggle. He wants to write. Wants to make music. His father was out with the dog, hail, rain or snow. He loved his sheep. They offered two-to-three-year-old wethers and cull ewes for sale. The ewe lambs were kept for breeding. The wethers for wool. But with the collapse of wool prices things have changed. Some farmers still keep back ewe lambs as replacements but the wethers are sold off to butchers and meat factories. He's thinking of giving up the flock. Just keeping a few cows. And the turf business. His mam cleans for Eugene. Then there are his gigs with Niall. They could get by. He's not sure how much longer he can keep going. It's too much pressure. His heart isn't in it.

Disease is always the main fear. He had witnessed the impact when he was nine. One dark afternoon in the dead of winter he went down to the yard with his father. There was a sheet of ice on the water trough and the slurry in the yard was frozen. It was unusual to get such a heavy frost. He can still remember the rime on the blades of grass and hedgerows, his plume of breath turning to crystals as it hit the cold air. One of the cows was having triplets. It was a big deal, a rarity. It had been a beautiful thing to watch those three calves coming into the world, knowing that back in the kitchen his mother was standing at the Aga baking scones, her apron dusted in flour.

But later that night his father told him their cattle had contracted a disease and the following morning they were taken off to be slaughtered, including the three new calves. Some of the cows in the lorry were still calving, the new borns half-hanging between their hind legs. It distressed him to think of them being born in a slaughter lorry only to be destroyed a few hours later. He'd never seen his father so upset.

But he's tired of trying to snatch time to write, balanced on the single bed in this childhood room, of not being able to afford a place of his own because local property prices have soared, of feeling trapped and unable to move on. He's torn between what he really wants to do and loyalty to his mother. The family way of life. Perhaps, he thinks wryly, we're all in recovery from childhood.

As he reaches the ridge he's surprised to find a scattering of heifers wandering among the wet gorse and heather. No one brings cows this high up. Most of the upland is unsuitable for anything other than sheep. Cattle get their legs stuck in the furze and rocky crevices. What are they doing so high on the mountain? He's not sure who they belong to. He manages to grab one and from its ear tag realises that they're Paddy's. He scans the glen to see if he is out with the dog, then retraces his steps back down to his cottage. There's a ribbon of smoke coming from the chimney but no sign of Paddy, though his car is by the turf reek. So he can't have gone into town. At the bottom of the track there's a gap in the fence where the wire has been roughly cut and the fence posts recently pulled out of the mud. He goes over to look. The ground is pitted with hoof-holes. This must be where the cows got out but who in their right mind would do something like that? Slowly he trudges back up the mountain in the rain, wondering how he's going to gather up the herd on his own and get them safely back in the field.

As he takes a short cut past the standing stones he can hear a cow lowing. It sounds agitated, though he can't quite make out where the sound is coming from. Then, as he scrambles up over the escarpment, he sees her below in the ditch. She's fallen and got stuck and, half buried under her left flank, lying face down in the mud, is Paddy. Out stone cold.

2

It takes the fire crew the whole afternoon to free the trapped animal. It's too high to bring up a tractor and lifting equipment, so they use ropes and mud mats to haul the floundering beast in like a flailing whale. The whites of her eyes roll in fear as she kicks and bellows, frothing at the mouth. Colm stays with Paddy until the air-sea rescue helicopter can winch him up and fly him to Kerry General. He has a smashed nose, two black eyes and several broken ribs. The paramedics are also concerned about his neck and lock his head in a brace. Colm wants to go with him but they assure him that he's in safe hands.

Don't you worry about a thing, Paddy, old fellow. I'll get a few of the lads and see to the milking, he reassures him. We'll have those other cows rounded up in no time. You just go and rest yourself and get yourself sorted.

There are things we all fear. Loneliness, isolation. Colm tries to imagine what it's like for Paddy with no one to rely on but himself. Day after day out in all weathers. He must be in his sixties now. He's always been a model of fitness. Wiry and agile, up and down the mountain like a ram. Colm's known him since childhood. He's his da's cousin. He used to meet him on his way to school in the lane as he was turning the herd out into the fields after early morning milking. He was always friendly. Even helping him to straighten the back wheel of his bike when, once, hurtling down the hill late for his lessons, he came off in a ditch. Paddy took him back to his white cottage, cleaned up his knee with Dettol and made him a mug of strong sweet tea. Then he'd brought the bike into the kitchen and bent the buckled wheel back into shape.

Colm knows that Paddy stayed home to mind his father but wonders if he ever had the chance of a different life. The done thing was to meet someone, marry, and have kids. Then hang on in there until the light went off for one or other of you. But things weren't always so straightforward. For some, duty and health, even fear, got in the way. And now, how will Paddy manage? His neighbours will muck in while he's in hospital. But after that? Everyone's stretched.

How the fuck did those cows get out?

3

Worn out by the day's dramas Colm takes himself off to the pub at the far end of the village. The only people in there are local. It's a male domain. Everything's familiar and strangers are rarely expected except during the summer when they're searching out live music. On damp winter evenings the same men while away rain-sodden hours playing darts. Many lack any human comfort except for pub company and alcohol. Tonight there's an old fella in from the next village. Ruddy-faced, with bad teeth, he never removes his cap and is rabbiting on to a couple of other fellows standing at the bar. Colm's seen him before but doesn't know his name.

Cattle prices will never recover, he's saying to his neighbour, who isn't listening. I may as well sell the land to the German. Sure the chances to make money are as scarce as hen's teeth.

Colm orders a pint and settles himself on a stool in the far corner on the other side by the fire, under the framed print of Jesus with a bleeding heart. He's not in the mood to be sociable and spends the evening staring at the glowing turfs.

As closing time approaches the crowd playing darts gathers round the bar eager to get in their last orders. They heave and jostle. Each determined to shove the others out of the way and squeeze through the gap to the front. These men are serious drinkers. Most have been working outside all day and are still damp from the recent downpour. The patterned linoleum is awash with their muddy footprints. There's only minutes to go, to down another pint before they are flushed out into the night.

Your man in the cap is still wittering on to no one in particular. He's been drinking all evening but the limited drinking time left won't allow him to relieve his bursting bladder—the lav is at the end of the unlit yard—as well as finish the two pints and the short he's just ordered. His dress is the same as most of the other men in the bar. A flat tweed cap, never removed except in church, bed or at the doctor's. A dark jacket and trousers tucked into large green Wellingtons. A tieless shirt frayed and incorrectly buttoned. Haphazardly tucked into his leather belt.

Everybody is talking and no one listening. Like their pints, these men's stories need to be finished before closing time. They crowd round the counter pushing and shoving, packed together in a huddle of animal warmth like heifers at the cattle market. Suddenly Colm is aware of a pungent smell mingling with the beer fumes and unwashed bodies as your-man-in-the-cap, still on to no one in particular about the Galway v Mayo match, casually reaches for his new pint. But his dilemma appears to have been solved and his oversized Wellingtons put to good use. The other drinkers pull back. Their vague sense of propriety breached as a pool gradually seeps across the muddy floor.

Colm downs the rest of his pint, zips up his jacket and gets up to leave as the old fella is tipped from pub's warmth into the sobering night, to stumble his lonely, waterlogged way home.

4

Eugene takes off his muddy boots and pads to the table in his thick socks. It's been a good day. He's been out shooting with Joe and his accountant. They bagged a few birds, which are strung up by their feet in the cold pantry. He opens a bottle of whiskey and pours a glass for each of his guests and the gillies. A fire roars in the grate. Caesar and Brutus lie by the hearth, their heads on their paws, their coats steaming. Hunting prints cover the walls. There's a pair of antlers over the door and the shelves are lined with books in beige and maroon tooled leather that he rarely opens. The Polish cook has left supper laid out on the long oak table. Leek and potato soup. A crusty loaf. Veal and ham pie, plus a large stilton and a bottle of port on the silver coaster. The men cut chunks of bread and cheese and sip their whiskeys in companionable silence as the logs crackle. Their skin is glowing from the rain and wind and their limbs ache from the tramp over the moors. They discuss the shoot, business and Eugene's plans for Bolus Head. In this company there's no need to explain himself.

The room smells of dogs, wet tweed and cigars and the drinking goes on till the early hours. After his guests leave Eugene flings on his wax jacket and takes Caesar and Brutus out. Their black silhouettes bound across the wet lawn towards the beach in the moonlight. A wind is blowing in off the sea. Warmed by whiskey he stands watching as they chase across the dark sands before calling them to head back up to the house.

Siobhán is away in Dublin so he can look forward to a restful night.

5

It's late. The stove is lit and the curtains drawn against the rain. Brendan's books are spread all over the floor. Martha has been trying to sort them into piles. Those she'll keep. Those she will give away. There are gallery catalogues from long-forgotten exhibitions and glossy books on the Euston Road School and The Art of Italy. Others are on the flora, fauna and sacred sites of Ireland. So this is it. This is her life. Her husband gone. Her child gone and nothing but remnants. Open in front of her is a leather-bound *Black's General Atlas of the World,* published in Edinburgh and Dublin in the early 19th century that Brendan must have bought at some antiquarian book fair. Each plate has been engraved on steel. There are sixty-one maps from the 'latest and most authentic sources'. All coloured by hand and divided with thin sheets of yellowing tissue paper. A chart of isothermal lines gives the mean annual temperatures in different parts of the world. Another shows the comparative lengths of America's rivers. They straggle down the page like capillaries in an anatomical diagram. The long threads of the Mississippi and Amazon, the bulbous St Lawrence with its lakes like cancerous growths, its stubby, womb-shaped inlet at the mouth. On the opposite page are the world's mountain ranges grouped like the flaps of a Victorian children's theatre. The blue and brown hills of the British Isles. The ranges of Europe and Africa that fade away into the white peaks of Asia and what's called Oceania. She's always been fascinated by maps. It was something she and Bruno shared. He'd spread them on the floor, then find the most remote island and ask how long it would take to get there. Whether she thought it was inhabited and what sort of animals might live there. What was this dream of being separate, far from any continent, with the chance to begin anew? This concept of a new utopia gave desert islands their meaning. Shakespeare understood that in *The Tempest*. So did the monks who went out to the Skelligs to build a Christian refuge on those virgin crags. An uncontaminated haven in a contaminated world.

WEDNESDAY

1

Eugene is sitting over his morning coffee going through the architects' plans ready for his afternoon meeting. He likes the firm's positive attitude, the proposed use of light and space, and unusual materials. The mixture of tradition and innovation, boldness and understatement. He knows that it will be sensitive building a spa up on the headland. But people will get used to it. He wants to make it a landmark building. Something that will be talked about as an example of good design. He'll be using local stone and wants to frame the Skelligs in the big plate glass window. He's been looking at pictures of Tate St Ives with its views over Porthmeor Beach. That's the effect he wants to achieve. He may not be building an art gallery but it will be a gallery of sorts. To the body and relaxation. And, as he told Martha, the place will provide new jobs. Of course, they'll mostly be for cleaners and groundsmen. The masseurs and therapists will have to be brought in. But they'll still need to rent local places, drink in the pub. That's how prosperity works.

He's just heard from one of his men about the accident. That yesterday Paddy was airlifted to Kerry General. What the hell was he doing trying to get a heifer out of a ditch on his own? He's an experienced stockman. He must have known he couldn't pull her out by himself. There was no need for him to end up in hospital. Donald was only supposed to let the cows out of the field so Paddy would waste his morning chasing them over the mountain and have the frustration of rounding them up. All Eugene wanted was to wear him down a bit. Make him think twice about continuing to farm on his own up there. No one was supposed to get hurt. That hadn't been on the agenda. He hopes that Donald did it in the dark so no one saw him. People know he does odd jobs for Eugene. They might put two and two together. But it's impossible to get any sense out of him so there's no real need to worry. He'd better take Paddy over a bottle of whiskey. Now he's laid up, he might see the wisdom of settling for a quiet life. If he wasn't so stubborn, then none of this would have happened. What's he hanging on for anyway? He must be close to retirement and has no children. He won't be able to go on running the place much longer anyway. Apparently it was Colm who found him and called the emergency services. God knows what he was doing up on the mountain.

Eugene takes out his pen and underlines some points with thick black lines that he needs to take up with the architects. In the margin he absentmindedly draws a house with four windows and a sloping roof with smoke coming out of the chimney. He puts down his pen to admire his doodle. Then adds a dog by the front door. He must have another word with Martha. She still hasn't got back to him about her strip of land. He wonders whether he should ask her out to dinner. Woo her a bit. She must be lonely. If he plays his cards right they could come to some amicable arrangement that might just suit them both.

2

It's raining heavily. The light is fading. Perhaps he isn't going to come. Martha is sitting by the window watching the rickety headlights of a tractor bump up and down over the muddy potholes as it returns from dropping off fodder to the cows in the high field. After it's disappeared the lane is completely dark.

He offered to come by and look at her stove when she'd texted to say that it was belching out thick black smoke. A BIRD, MAY B, he answered. WLL TRY 2 GET OVER WHEN FINISHED LOT 2 DO. She sits listening to the wind lifting the corrugated roof on the outhouse. Outside the steep cliffs fall away into the sea. Behind the cottage there's nothing except damp fields leading up onto the windswept moor, a fox sleeping deep in its earth, and a huddle of sheep sheltering by a gatepost bound with baler twine. In a ditch a stoat follows the movements of a small vole, waiting for its chance.

She's decorated the windowsill with pebbles from the beach adding them to Brendan's collection, gathering driftwood and shells as if she was still a child. When she wakes before dawn she makes tea in the small blue pot, then pulls on an old sweater over her nightdress, before getting down to work on his papers. At lunch time she heats up some soup or walks the mile down to Cable O'Leary's for a cheese and pickle sandwich. Midweek the place is usually empty. Just a couple of old fellows sitting in the corner with their pints or the bloke from the garage playing on the fruit machine.

3

When Colm visits Paddy in hospital he looks old and frail. There are purple bruises under his eyes and an orthopaedic collar round his neck. The doctors say he's going to be alright but he's taken quite a kicking. He has a couple of broken ribs and needs time to recuperate. It's played on Colm's mind all day. What will the old fellow do? What will happen to his land and the cottage? There was some talk from the social worker of a nursing home. But Paddy was so distressed at the suggestion that the hospital agreed to give his sister a call. Nora, is coming over from Cork to look after him till he's back on his feet. At least that way he can go back home.

Colm spends the afternoon trying to catch up. There's a gig to organise in Waterville and they've been booked for a wedding next weekend for which they'll be well paid. There'll be folks from all over and it's a good opportunity for him and Niall to get better-known. And he needs to get down to the corn merchant to pick up some pellets. There's been little time in the last couple of days to think about his poems or Martha's comments. Life has got in the way. After he finishes work he gets in his van and drives up past Bolus Head to check on Paddy's place. He promised he would keep an eye. A few of the other farmers on the hill are helping care for his stock. So everything's covered for the moment. A full moon is hanging over the cottage, casting lily pads of light across the bay. Paddy's washing flaps on the line in the starlight. Colm unpegs his pyjamas, overalls and socks, takes them inside and folds them in a neat pile on the kitchen table. Then he goes to check the turf reek and fasten the banging lean-to door.

As he drives back down the hill he notices the light is still on in Martha's cottage. He pulls up outside and stops the van. He'd forgotten, what with all that's been going on, that he said he'd take a look at her stove. Anyway, for some reason, he suddenly wants to see her. When he knocks, she comes to the door in her socks, wrapped in a big scarf. Standing in a ring of light on the doorstep holding a torch, he can barely see her face.

Colm. How nice to see you, she says softly. Come in. I was just about to go to bed. As you can see I was trying to make sense of this pile of Brendan's papers and not getting very far. It's freezing in here. I can't get the stove to light.

He takes off his heavy jacket and hangs it on the back of the chair, then pokes and prods around in the stove, shining his torch up the dark flue.

What I thought. There's a whole load of shite up there. It probably got dislodged by the wind. It should be okay now, he says, giving it another poke so a whole pile of soot covered debris falls onto the hearth, which he sweeps up in the dustpan and tips outside the front door. D'you have any fire lighters?

A black streak of soot runs across his brow and down the bridge of his nose like war paint.

Better have a bit of a wash, if you've got a towel?

As the stove begins to heat up a smell of coal dust fills the room. She goes to the dresser and takes out a clean towel, still stiff from the line, and places it by the kitchen sink. Colm pulls up the sleeves of his thick jersey with his teeth to avoid getting covered in soot. His white, hairless arms are sinewy and there's a small tattoo visible beneath the dirt. Turning on the taps with his elbows like a surgeon, he rubs his forearms with the transparent disc of carbolic from the cracked saucer on the draining board. She stands in the doorway watching as the water runs black, then clear, a fist closing in her stomach.

Can I get you a drink? Wine? Whiskey? I think you've earned it. It was good of you to come over so late.

He takes the offered glass in his wet hand, then sits down in the easy chair by the stove, placing it on the floor and dries his arms, his wrists, the thin webbed skin between his fingers with the towel.

Sure 'twas no bother, Martha.

Is anything wrong? She asks. If you don't mind me saying so, you look rather tired.

Wrong? Well, not exactly. But you're right I am tired. It's good to sit down for a bit. It's been a difficult couple of days. I don't know if you've heard about the accident yesterday. Paddy O'Connell, you know from the white cottage up top, was hurt on the mountain and had to go to hospital. I was the one who found him.

Hurt? How was he hurt?

Well somehow his cattle got out. If you ask me someone cut the fence. Though who'd do a feckin' stupid thing like that I've no idea. But Paddy slipped trying to pull a cow out of the ditch. She fell on him, broke his ribs, and hurt his neck. He was airlifted to hospital.

Hospital?

Yer. The cattle were all over the mountain and Paddy is such a careful man.

Something in Martha grows cold. Eugene. Surely he wouldn't stoop so low?

Have you any idea how it happened? It's probably nothing to do with anything, and I don't want to be the instigator of rumours but do you happen to know about Eugene's plans up on the headland? By the way, are you hungry? I've some homemade soup on the stove if you haven't eaten. Would you like some?

Ah that would be grand, Martha, he says stretching out his long legs and relaxing into the sofa, realising how comfortable he feels in this candle-lit book-lined room.

I'm bushed.

Outside the wind is blowing. Shadows from the stove flit across the ceiling like owls.

No, he says taking a sip of whiskey. He knows nothing about Eugene's plans. Does that mean he's trying to get rid of Paddy?

She tells him what she knows about the spa, which isn't a lot.

And he wants part of my field so he can have access.

You wouldn't, would you Martha? You wouldn't sell it to him?

Well until now I haven't really given it any thought. It had crossed my mind to be shot of it. But no, of course, I won't sell it to him and let him destroy Paddy's life and ruin this special place.

I have been thinking a good deal over the last few days. About Brendan and Bruno. About the cottage and Eugene's scheme. I want to do what I can to stop him. It may not be much, but I feel it's important. That I have a responsibility. I'm one of a generation that had so much. Free health care, free education. Jobs were easy to find and we could travel cheaply, live on very little. It didn't cost an arm and a leg to buy somewhere to live. But we got greedy. House prices rose and we felt rich, so homes became investments. People began to borrow more than they could afford and the banks encouraged them. I don't want to be a part of that. I want to leave this place as it was when I came here with Bruno and Brendan. To remember it as it was.

She gets up and takes his glass to refill it. Then as she makes her way back to the sofa stops and, without thinking, brushes a damp lock of hair behind his ear. It's a spontaneous gesture. Not weighed, not considered. Not what she really meant to do at all. She turns to move away but as she does so he reaches for her hand and pulls her towards him so suddenly his tongue is in her mouth. Was this what she intended? She doesn't think so. But she hadn't realised what a hunger she still has for touch. For something to obliterate the Bruno-shaped hole in her life. She knows that she should resist. But what harm can it do? She can smell smoke and carbolic on him as he unbuttons her thick shirt and is suddenly aware of the stretch marks on her breasts. He unzips his jeans, and, as he undresses, her finger traces the outline of the Japanese carp tattooed on his left arm. Its compact muscles, the golden scales and lashing tail. In the firelight he looks very young. His white torso like a boy's with its line of dark hair running from his navel down to his wiry tuft. She buries her face in it and feels him grow like something she's cultivated. He gets up, fetches a blanket from the back of the armchair and covers them with it. Then, as he touches her, she gasps and the peat in the stove collapses into a glowing heap. Slowly her body begins to unfold from its knife-edged creases. For the first time in months the knot inside her starts to unravel. In its place is a new quietness. As though she's being returned to herself. They lie on the rug in front of the stove, drifting in and out of sleep, until the sky whitens across the damp morning fields.

THURSDAY

1

She must have fallen into a deep sleep because when she wakes he's gone. His jacket is missing from the back of the chair and the stove is out. Did she dream that he was here? But the damp patch between her thighs tells her otherwise. She climbs from the makeshift bed, her fingers still smelling of him, folds up the old tartan rug and places it on the back of the sofa, goes to the dresser, cuts a slice of soda bread and spreads it with a thick layer of butter and marmalade, which she shovels on with the back of the spoon. Then she sticks some bacon under the grill and makes some scrambled eggs. She hasn't felt this hungry for a long time.

After her shower she tidies the cottage and spends the rest of the day quietly looking through Brendan's books and papers, uncertain what to feel or how to make sense of what's just happened. Sometimes when we meet another person there's an instinctive sense that we already know them. Not because we explain things but because there's an unspoken connection. Perhaps loneliness is simply the gulf between our inner world and how others appear to experience us. Despite her long marriage, she sometimes wonders whether Brendan really knew her at all. She'd loved him through habit and history and because he was the father of her child, but often, particularly during their final years after they'd lost Bruno, she felt a deep sense of loneliness sweep over her. When they were young and first in love they'd playfully tested each other by asking: will you still love me if I lose my looks, if I have an accident or go bankrupt? After all I'd still be the same person inside.

Yet love between adults was rarely that unconditional, was it? The only time she truly felt as though she'd give everything, was for her son.

So much emotional attachment, she thinks, is a resort against isolation. The woman who nags her husband, the man who smashes his wife's face against the table edge because he suspects that she's having an affair—all done because they 'need' each other. The other person provides the necessary escape from a self we can't bear, which would be lost if they left. But with Colm there's a rare sense that nothing needs to be explained or justified. Things just are as they are. She feels it when they talk about his poems. His openness to her criticism, the way he tacitly accepts that she understands what they're about. He may be much younger, more or less the same age as Bruno would have been if he'd lived, yet there's something wise about him, about the way he experiences the world.

What does she want from him? Nothing really. She knows that what they have is fragile, momentary. But for now, for the first time in months, she feels alive.

2

Nora is waiting for Paddy when Colm brings him home. He's no longer wearing the neck brace. Luckily he suffered nothing more than serious bruising and some broken ribs. But they are still taped up so he has to go carefully. She has built up the fire, ironed his washing and baked a fresh batch of scones and is bustling round the green-painted kitchen tidying away newspapers and straightening cushions on the old horsehair sofa. This is where she grew up. Although she's been away in Cork teaching all these years she comes back to her brother for Easter and Christmas. She's never married and this still feels like home. Everything is pretty much the same as in her mother's day when the kitchen was full of children and the dog. The flour bin, the big yellow china bowl in which she mixes the dough for the scones, the brass coal scuttle by the fire. Paddy is a clean man and takes care of himself and the cottage. She's retired now. Sure forty years a primary school teacher is enough for any woman. Though she made it to head for the last fifteen. What with the welfare and education of so many children and her two nights a week singing in the choir, she's been busy. She hates to be idle. All those morning assemblies, the annual rehearsals for the Christmas nativity—when she'd insisted on real straw for the manger and one of the shepherds would invariably lose his striped tea towel as the angel Gabriel brought glad tidings from the top of her kitchen stepladder—have left her with a need to be occupied. For years her days were regimented by parents' evenings and timetables, the school bell and lunchtime supervisions in the playground. Separating fights and patching knees, she watched over the skipping games and football that every generation of seven and eight year olds have always played. Who better, then, to look after her own brother? She'll have him back on the mend in no time. But she'd like to know how those cows got out.

She's ironing Paddy's pyjamas when Colm eases him out of his van. It's strange to see him leaning on the younger man as he comes up the path past the turf reek to his green front door. They ease him into the wing chair by the stove and she wets the tea, sets out the glass dish of jam and the warm scones on her mother's flowered plates, and passes one to her brother.

3

Once Paddy is settled Colm takes his leave. It's still only mid-morning. A clear, fragile day. The sea glycerine under the thin winter sun. As he drives down the mountain he pulls up at Martha's and jumps out of the van.

Come on, he says, as she opens the door. Get your coat. The day's too good to waste. We're going for a drive.

She hasn't seen him since he left her bed and laughs at his casual effrontery of turning up unannounced. She brushes her hair, smears on some lipstick and puts on her coat and scarf.

Okay then. I'm ready. Where are we off to?

She clambers up into the high passenger seat of his rusting van. It's a mess. Full of rope, old turf bags, Wellington boots, electric wires and loud speakers. There's a little makeshift platform covered with blankets and a mattress that serves as a bed when he's away on gigs. A battered gas ring and a fridge. But she doesn't care. She's enjoying the sense of freedom.

How's Paddy? She asks. You collected him from hospital, didn't you? That was kind.

Sure I couldn't expect your man to come back in a taxi, could I? I love that old fella. Pleased to be home, I'd say. His sister Nora's with him. Busy feeding him up with her home baking. He'll mend. He's a tough old goat. But it's good to see him back at his own fireside. You heard anything more from Eugene?

No, she says. It's gone strangely quiet. But let's not talk about him. So where are you taking me?

He doesn't answer but turns on the battered radio taped to the dashboard. An Irish music station fills the van and they turn sharp right across the boggy moor, past the peat power station, towards Waterville.

A low sun streams through the windows. They drive on towards the far mountains and up the winding coast road along the Kerry Ring towards Caherdaniel. The view of the barren mountains above and the breakers coming in over the wide empty beach below seem impossibly beautiful. Suddenly Colm slows down and pulls into a gateway. They clamber out of the van and trudge to the middle of a field to look at an ancient pillar incised with parallel lines and notches in some sort of primitive alphabet. It's an ogham stone, he tells her. No one knows what they were for. Some say they mark burial sites. Others, that they were tribal boundaries.

When they reach Daniel O'Connell's house it's closed for the winter, so they make their way down the dirt track through the pines, over the grassy dunes, to the bay. Clambering over the rocks and storm-tossed seaweed they head to the furthest shore where, beneath the ruins of a small abbey, they strip off their anoraks and thick sweaters to throw themselves on the sand in the warm January sun until a chill wind forces them back to the van.

At Inny Strand they stop off near the golf course. An Irish flag snaps above the club house. The clipped hedges and lawns look incongruous among the sand dunes and rolling breakers. They make their way down to the beach, the wind biting at their scarves and anoraks. It must be a good place to surf but there's no one about except a lone man walking his dog.

This place, Colm tells her, wrapping his arm round her shoulder against the wind, is mentioned in the Book of Invasions. Do you know about that, Martha? It's an ancient text that's supposed to contain the history of Ireland. Noah's granddaughter was said to be the leader of the first Irish invasion after she was denied admission to the Ark. I'm not sure what she'd done to piss off old Noah, but anyway, somehow she ended up in Co Cork, if you'd believe that, with fifty women and three men, including Fintan mac Bochra, whom she married. The three men, so the story goes, agreed to divvy the women out amongst them. Nice for them, not so good for the women, he smiles—as well as slicing up Ireland. They hoped to populate the place or at least have fun trying. Anyway, two of the men died and all fifty women started giving out to Fintan. So he did a runner and they all perished.

The next lot were the Partholonians, I think. They were supposed to have come from Greece. And, if I remember right, after them were the Nemedians and the one-legged, one-armed Fomorians. This is the bay where the Milesians—they're supposed to be the true Gaelic people of Ireland—are thought to have landed. Now how's that for a bit of potted history? he asks, wrapping her scarf securely round her neck in the squall as if she were a child. Anyway, he laughs, you wouldn't know if I was telling you wrong!

And, as you can see, by the name of the pub over there, this was quite a place for smuggling. There were a lot of shipwrecks. A Danish schooner on the way to McMahon's timber yard at the beginning of last century fetched up here on the rocks. Some of the crew are buried in the local church. Oh yes, and while I'm being your official tour guide, the other thing is that Fascist, Charles Lindbergh, is supposed to have flown over here on his solo flight from New York to Paris. Can't think of anything else you should know, he says running down the beach towards the sea and pulling her after him, so they have to jump back from the incoming surf to avoid getting wet. And, as he skims a flat stone across it in a triple arc across the breakers, she remembers all those years ago, Bruno trying to perfect his aim. She can see him now. Collecting smooth pebbles on the tide's edge, struggling to get them to jump the waves. As if an ability to skim stones signified the passage from boy to man.

The sea is a translucent green, framed by the brown mountains on the other side of the bay. As they head back up the beach into the little town the row of brightly-painted, old-fashioned B&Bs remind her of a 1950s English seaside resort. There are signs for ice creams and cream teas, though the whole place seems to be shut. At the Butler Arms they stop for a drink and Colm tells her this is where Charlie Chaplin and his family stayed each summer. Now the little man stands forever holding his bowler hat and bronze stick in the blustery Atlantic wind.

Back in the van they take the winding road that runs along by the sea. A cluster of megalithic stones on the brow of the hill stands silhouetted against the winter sky. The surrounding landscape is boggy. Bulrushes grow by the side of the road and there's a big digger in one of the fields.

Martha wonders if it's used for cutting peat. Other fields are dotted with ruined cottages with no windows and collapsed roofs. On the other side of the lane is a row of newly-erected bungalows.

It's such a pity to see these old places left in this state.

Emigration. It was poor here, Colm says. There wasn't the work. Just subsistence farming. Anyway the family is probably still arguing about who actually owns the land, so it can never be sold. Most likely they got a grant to build one of those swanky new bungalows. The council has a book, you know. Like Ford's ubiquitous black car you can choose any design you like so long as it's hideous.

That's sad.

Sure, there's a lot that's sad here.

The light is already going when they stop and clamber over a dry stone wall to make their way over a rough field towards a small bay.

Where are we going?

Close your eyes, Martha, and don't open them until I tell you.

She takes his hand and shambles blindly down the path behind him. Then, as they round the bend, he says: Now.

Ahead, the sky is on fire. Blood-red and golden-white, glowing behind the great jagged needle of rock.

My God Colm, that's beautiful. It almost makes you believe in God.

Well, he says, some say the sun dances on the Skelligs at Easter. That it's a sign of the Resurrection.

I can understand that. she whispers, as they stand in the wind and the sky darkens, turning to purple, then black, before the great fiery ball drops into the sea.

4

She doesn't ask him to stay the night but after they finish the bottle of wine and the embers are dying he follows her up the steep staircase to her sleeping loft. As she's been out all afternoon it's freezing and they huddle beneath the duvet in their clothes. There moon is full and the little room awash with light. As they warm up they undress bit by bit.

Brr, your feet are cold Martha.

She runs a finger over his face, tracing the contours of his nose, his unshaven cheeks and eyes, trying to imprint them on her memory. She knows she will never sleep with him again.

I've made a decision, Colm, she says, snuggling up to him. I've been thinking long and hard about this. I'm sure it's the only thing I can do. I'm going home. Back to London. If I stay here Eugene will only hassle me about the land. I'm not really strong enough to deal with him and would rather do it at a distance. If I just disappear, just go back to London without telling him, he'll have to do everything through my solicitor, and, of course, I won't agree to any of it. But he can't pressurise me with endless visits and a wad of cash for a quick sale. It's not that I'd agree but I just don't want to have the anxiety, don't want to get caught up in the local shenanigans. It's too painful, she says burrowing further into his warm armpit. And I need to move on, need to decide what I'm going to do with my life. I've a few ideas. Nothing very grand. I'd like to tutor refugees. Those from war-torn countries who need to learn English to make a new life. No, Colm don't pull that face. Oh God! Do I sound really worthy and north London?

Just a little, he laughs, kissing her nose.

But seriously, Colm, I'm a teacher. I could do that. It would be good to work with young people and keep me occupied, give me something to get up for in the morning. We all need that. Goodness knows if I'd be doing much for them, but it would certainly help me. I haven't completely decided yet, though I don't really want to go back to teaching full-time.

But I do have a suggestion and I hope you'll hear me out, she says brushing his hair out of his eyes. I've decided that I don't want to sell the cottage. Certainly not to Eugene. Nor to anyone else. If I do there's no guarantee that the buyer won't then do a deal with Eugene if he offers them enough cash and that the spa won't still go ahead. Apparently he's squared things with the council. Though, of course, I don't know what that actually means. There's only me and Paddy stopping him. I want this place to stay as it is, Colm. For Paddy, for you, for me. For the next generation. There are so few truly wild places left, places where the night sky is so dark you can see the constellations, places that look the same as they must have looked a thousand years ago. Everything's changing. So much that's authentic is being lost. I want to remember this place as it was when I came here with Bruno and Brendan, and I'll do what little I can to protect it. I know that Paddy and the other bachelors on the mountain are probably the last of their kind but I'd like to give their way of life a bit longer, if it doesn't sound too sentimental. I'm not rich but I can manage in London with my lodgers and Brendan's pension. The head has offered me early retirement on compassionate grounds. I don't really need the money from this place. So what I'd like to suggest, she says, taking his face in her hands, if you'll agree—and you'd be doing me a favour, honestly you would because I have been worrying about this—is, that if you'd like to, you become my caretaker. That you have the cottage to write in for as long as you need it. I don't want any rent but if you could look after it, mend anything that needs mending, roof tiles that come off in the storms, that sort of thing, it would be the perfect solution. I'd love you to finish your collection and get it published. You can dedicate it to me, she says half-joking. And to Bruno.

Thank you Martha, he says taking her in his arms.

Thanks a million. It's a deal. The book is yours.

5

They are up with the first light. She cooks him breakfast. Eggs and bacon and a pot of strong tea. When they finish she puts the dishes in the sink and he gets his jacket. They don't say goodbye but stand hugging each other by the door of his van in the fine morning rain. She still in her pyjamas. Then he zips up his jacket, pulls down his blue hat and swings himself into the driver's seat, before winding down the window and blowing her a kiss.

Take care Martha. God speed to you.

And with that his red van turns and he drives off down the hill.

6

She goes back inside, gets dressed and packs, putting all the box files with Brendan's papers in the boot of the car with her case and walking boots. She'll leave the rest of the books for Colm. It's too problematic to take them home and she's already sent a load of the more valuable ones back to London. Anyway she wants the cottage to stay as it is now she's made the decision not to sell it, even if she is unlikely to come here any time soon. But she needs to get going while it's still early. She hasn't got a place booked on the ferry. Though at this time of year there shouldn't be a problem getting a crossing. She wants to be sure that she gets away before she runs into Eugene. She'll write to him from London. No, better still, she'll get her solicitor to write. She's not certain if not having her land will prevent him from going ahead with his plans, but it just might. It's all she can do.

She goes to the cupboard under the stairs and turns off the immersion heater and electricity, cleans out the ashes from the stove, scattering them into the wind. Then washes up the breakfast things, dries everything and puts it tidily back in the cupboards, mops the kitchen floor and empties the fridge.

Upstairs she checks in the bedroom. Then, standing in the middle of the living room, takes one last look around. So much of her life is here. So much of Brendan and Bruno. She goes to the bookcase and takes out Brendan's schoolboy Bible and, from the desk, his sketch books and the photo of Bruno. Then she locks the door, hangs the key back on the rusty nail under the eaves, and climbs into the car to head for the ferry.

21st June 2009

1

Martha hasn't told Colm she's here. Though they do stay in touch, mostly by email. There's no need to see him or anyone else. She won't be staying long. She has only come to do one thing. Arriving by taxi from Farranfore airport she books into the first B&B she finds with a vacancy in Ballinskelligs. The hall smells of air freshener and the glass cabinet in the breakfast room houses a collection of china horses and plaster leprechauns all dressed in green. Photographs of the Galway races cover the walls. Jockeys in striped vests holding up large silver cups beside their mounts and trainers. She is the only person in the dining room and tucks into her breakfast of fried eggs and bacon, the rack of white toast, which she washes down with strong tea. She won't be eating again for a while so might as well make the most of it. She woke early, with a sense of urgency, unable to sleep on the nylon sheets in the very floral room with its colour-coordinated Kleenex and dishes of pot pourri. After breakfast she goes upstairs to clean her teeth, puts on her waterproof and walking boots, and then checks her rucksack to make sure she has everything she needs. The weather hasn't been good and she's not certain if the boat will be running. Yesterday, the first thing she did when she arrived was to walk down to the pier and speak to the skipper of the Flying

Horse. It was raining but he told her that the forecast for today was more promising and that she should come back this morning.

The boat leaves at 8.00. And the round trip costs €40. She should wear sturdy shoes. Bring rain gear and maybe some sandwiches as they won't be back till gone 4.00.

When she arrives there's already a small crowd gathered on the quay dressed in weatherproofs, standing among the rusty chains and plastic fish boxes. Germans with backpacks, a clutch of Japanese tourists with cameras slung round their necks. The tide is out and the boat lies low in the water so they have to climb down a steep metal ladder fixed to the side of the wet harbour wall to get to the deck. The skipper takes their money and jokes that if anyone feels seasick then they should puke downwind. The Japanese laugh nervously. Then the engine starts and the boat judders into life, circles the little harbour and heads out to sea, chugging past Horse Island with its white cottage nestled beside a single tree growing just above the shingle.

As they pull out of the bay it begins to rain. Soft, insistent rain that seeps through her anorak. She stands in the stern and watches the stretch of grey sea grow between the boat and the mainland as the other passengers hunker down inside their waterproofs and take shelter under the awning behind the skipper's cabin. High on the cliff she can see Brendan's cottage and the clutch of other abandoned cottages dotted along Bolus Head. How precarious they look clinging to the brown mountain three hundred feet above the sea. Like a row of doll's houses. Again she wonders why they built in such a harsh place. She images a woman bent against the mizzle hurrying between cottages, a couple of warm eggs wrapped in her apron. An old man, the smell of carbolic on him, lying cold in his best jacket and boots, between guttering candles as his family keeps vigil by the coffin.

A ribbon of smoke coils from the chimney. She wonders if Colm is up there writing or on the ridge with his mother's cows. She knows that his collection is due out any day from a poetry press in Dublin. He's invited her to the launch. But she's unlikely to go. It's his success and he doesn't need her there, though she is delighted for him and pleased to have been able to play some small part in his success. Recently he repeated his promise to dedicate the collection to her and Bruno. And there is, he tells her, a girl. A young artist he met last summer while she was painting on the beach. Apparently she has a small exhibition coming up in Cork and, after that, he wrote, if it's alright, she might come down for a bit and join him in the cottage. If Martha isn't comfortable with the arrangement, he'll quite understand, but it would be good to have some company.

She wrote back immediately. She is happy for him. Glad of course that the cottage is being lived in and used. She asks about the girl. What's her name?

Imogen, he writes back.

So she's not Irish then?

No he says. English and she's fallen in love with this place.

And Paddy? How is Paddy?

Sure Paddy is grand. Still up on the mountain in all weathers. But Nora's with him now full time and I give him a hand when I can.

2

It's getting choppy as they head past the jetty to Eugene's private beach. Gulls glide on the thermals. How oddly things turn out. How haphazard life is. Over the last few years the Irish economy had expanded rapidly and the country changed beyond all recognition to the place she knew when she first came here more than twenty years ago. But just as suddenly, it seems, that credit has become increasingly hard to come by. Irish banks are being squeezed by what, some predict, will be a global financial crisis. Many of the small-time builders around Kerry have, she's heard from Colm, already gone bust. They borrowed on a three-month rollover basis to fund holiday homes and housing projects that are unlikely to be sold for years. If at all. Recession is in the air. It's rumoured that even major developers such as Liam Carroll have fallen behind on their repayments. The Tiger's teeth have been pulled.

Just before Christmas Eugene had an uncomfortable meeting with the bank about the feasibility of the loan for the Skellig Spa. Borrowing on the international market, the manager explained, tetchily, as he cleaned his rimless glasses behind the fort of his reproduction antique desk, had provided what seemed to have been an endless flow of cash. This, as Eugene well knew, had led to a massive increase in Irish property prices. But with the freezing up of world currency markets no new money meant no new loans and that meant no new property deals. He was sorry but his hands were tied.

This wasn't what Eugene was used to and he was in a foul mood as he drove to dinner with his solicitor in Killorgan to break the news.

It was a lively evening. They debated interest rates and poured over balance sheets. Eugene was unwilling to let his project drop and became very animated railing about the small minded bureaucrats who were standing in his way. There was port, brandy and cigars, and he left rather later than intended in an agitated state. The weather was atrocious, the roads treacherous and his 4x4 hit an unlit tractor parked by a ditch. He was, almost certainly, driving too fast.

Martha thinks of all those angry letters he sent her in London. The threats. The cajoling and emotional blackmail. And what had it all been for? So much aggravation, so much animosity. That would be his legacy. How he would be remembered by the locals. As the man who tried to push Paddy O'Connell off his farm. The old rectory, Colm tells her, has gone to Rory. He's studying agriculture in Limerick and is more interested in trees than spas.

3

A grey outline, like a ghostly Gothic castle, looms out of the mist. No wonder those sixth century monks, making this same journey in their open boat, thought they were heading towards the edge of the world. A cloud of squawking sea birds swirls overhead, their cries piercing the mist like lost souls. Ahead the rock is completely white. Not only from the huddled bodies of gannets gathered on the narrow ledges but from the piles of guano. As the skipper draws near the Japanese scramble to the port side, cameras at the ready. The boat lists and they giggle anxiously.

It's still another twenty minutes out to the great Skellig. When they arrive Martha is drenched. They pull in alongside the small pier but the waves are so high it's hard to clamber onto the slippery concrete. The little party makes its way up the path below the under-cliff where the ground is littered with feathers and bird droppings and she can smell the stink of the nesting gulls. The rock is bigger than she expected. More like a craggy island. A small group has already gathered at the start of the precipitous steps to snap a puffin. With its clown-like beak it's sitting in the scrub with the insouciance of a celebrity posing for the paparazzi.

The climb is so steep that she's not sure she'll make it. She's afraid of heights and worried that if she looks down she'll freeze and be unable to go on or climb back. She doesn't want to make a spectacle of herself. When she was pregnant with Bruno she'd gone to St Ives with Brendan and they'd walked along the coastal path where, on that hot summer day, they lost the track and she found herself clinging to a rocky outcrop with a sheer drop down to the glittering turquoise bay. She couldn't move and Brendan, who was none too good with heights himself, had to coax each footstep from her, until her lumbering frame was returned to flat ground. But this time she's determined to make it to the top. That's why she's come. Bruno always wanted to make this trip, had sat restlessly in the cottage that last summer, fed up with the bad weather, staring out of the window to see if the mist was lifting.

Of course we'll try and go, she promised. On the next fine day but you'll have to be up early.

But it didn't stop raining. He sat on the floor in front of the stove drawing and cutting out pictures from old magazines. And as they packed up the car to head back to London for his camping trip with the scouts, she promised that they would definitely go the following year. That the trip would be a priority.

We never know, she thinks, as she begins to climb the steep stone steps, if what begins with daylight will give way to grief. What would it be like to have him with her now, her son? A young man, healthy and tall, in his walking boots and anorak. Surely she'd be less apprehensive with him at her side. She wonders what he would have been. An archaeologist, or a historian? It wasn't only the Skelligs that interested him. They'd spent many a wet Sunday afternoon at the British Museum among the Egyptian mummies. Or looking at Roman coins found buried in the mud along the Thames. But who knows how he'd have turned out. The boy he was at ten and the young man he would have been now might have had little connection. But whatever he was, he would always be her one, her only, boy. She hopes he'd have been proud of her doing this climb. Happy that she's finally made it for them both.

She follows the walkers, trying to keep her gaze on the next stone ahead and not look down at the swell. Terns swoop overhead. A young man in a blue waterproof offers to walk on the outside and gives her his hand to steady her. She's grateful for this small act of kindness. As she scrambles up the steps she thinks of the pilgrims who climbed barefoot. The sharp stones piercing their flesh so the pain would bring them closer to seeing the Virgin, or some other sign that might bolster their belief.

She's amazed how each flat slab has been slipped into the side of the cliff and packed underneath with rubble to render it stable. What labour it must have involved to chip and hack each rock by hand. She looks up and there's still a vertical flight ahead, that seems to disappear into the low clouds so that as she climbs, she feels like an angel ascending a celestial ladder in a medieval painting. The last part is the most precipitous. She has to turn her back to the sea so she can't see the drop hundreds of feet below, then feel her way, inch by inch, cheek and palms flat against the rock face, across the narrow shelf. The stone is wet and cold against her skin. She leans in against the granite wall, her heart racing. How strange that something once molten, which came hot and bubbling from the centre of the earth, should have formed this obdurate mass that she's clinging to for dear life. Then, suddenly, the path widens out onto flatter ground.

A low stone wall marks out the tiny plot where the monks once planted cabbages and kale to accompany their meagre diet of fish and sea birds. Fasting was an intrinsic part of their life. Some of the Irish monastic regimes were so extreme that monks died of starvation. There are no springs on the rock. Rain water was collected in cisterns. And there was little bread. For where would they have got the wheat? Bitter herbs added variety to their monotonous diet. Abundance was anathema. It was thought to trigger sexual arousal and they were bound by abstinence. But the lack of nourishment took its toll on their wasted bodies. They had visions and hallucinations as they sat for hours in the wind and rain and occasional burst of blazing sun on their rocky terraces, meditating on the mercy of God, the sea booming below.

She turns a corner and suddenly the beehive huts come into view. They look like stone igloos. She clambers inside one. It's completely dark except for a ray of light that spills from a narrow slit onto the wet cobbles. The largest hut was used for cooking. There's a stone step inserted in the outside wall where the monks climbed to remove the uppermost flagstone and let out the smoke. What did they burn? There's nothing here for fuel. She tries to imagine living for months, sometimes years, in such a constrained space, a space that constituted their whole world.

She knows that further up on the South Peak, between the eighth and thirteen centuries, the monks built an even more secluded hermitage. To reach those three terraces requires real rock-climbing skills. You have to negotiate a natural stone chimney, the Needle's Eye, then climb along a narrow ledge with its drop straight down to the sea, before making your way up the foot and handholds cut into the cliff face. What superhuman zeal lay behind the desire for such solitude? What tenacity led them to build this eyrie on the edge of space, where at any moment they might have been swept to their death? Devotional submissiveness or simply the stunning views of the Atlantic? Or did they believe that here, on the rock's highest peak, they would finally come face-to-face with God?

She wonders if human beings have really changed that much in the last eight-hundred years. She's been reading about mediaeval Irish society. How children from all walks of life were separated from their parents at infancy. Girls till they were fourteen, boys till seventeen. Vast numbers were placed in religious houses under the care of monks and nuns. Some, inevitably, never returned to secular life. Were people's emotions and allegiances so very different then, that parents could give away their offspring without regret? Was the emotion invested in a child so much less than it is now? What traumas did they suffer? What nightmares did they have? Many didn't survive. Leprosy was rife. Even the common cold or an infection from a small cut could go septic and become fatal. She thinks how this religious incarceration continued on into modern times. The young men shut away in seminaries. Girls sent to the Magdalene Laundries for the slightest misdemeanour that might label them fast or loose. The only real promise of happiness the afterlife. Maybe the monks weren't fleeing, as we moderns would believe, from the pressures of life. Not taking refuge from persecution or searching for peace. Rather their purpose was to look on the countenance of Christ. They were impatient for death. But death was not in their hands. It could only be granted in God's good time. Not at a moment of their own choosing. To seek it was blasphemy. To be purified and worthy of heavenly union, was their greatest desire.

The mist has begun to lift and in the distance she can see the jagged outline of the little Skellig. She came out here in drizzling rain but, slowly, it's cleared to reveal fragile ferns and flowers growing in the crevices. The rock is surprisingly green. There are tussocks of thrift and campion, sea pinks and white alpine flowers. She'd expected it to be more barren.

She follows the narrow path up behind one of the beehive shelters, on beyond the large weathered stone cross covered with green lichen, to the chapel. Here, during the long, cold nights the monks gathered to sing the Book of Psalms as they waited for the sun to rise. A symbol both of the Resurrection and the second coming. All through the dark hours, as the world slept and sinned, they kept vigil, observing the offices: nocturns, lauds, terce, sext, none, vespers, compline. During nocturns in the small hours after midnight, they prostrated themselves on the cold, wet stones in the shape of a cross. They believed that at the centre of this cloistered life there was a deep void. That only when the self was finally annihilated would they be created anew in the divine image. Yet despite all the physical and mental hardship, there was no guarantee of spiritual fulfilment. No assurance other than faith and their blind trust in God.

Centuries after the monks came here, the lighthouse keepers followed. Two lighthouses were built in the 19th century. Though the higher one was soon abandoned, having been built too far up for ships to be able to see it in the mist. Some years ago the lower one finally became automatic, removing the need for any permanent residents on the rock. The lighthouse keepers and their families were the last people to live on the Great Skellig. Now puffins and fulmars share its slopes with rabbits. At one time there were up to four families living here and working in shifts. The position of lighthouse keeper was handed down from father to son. Most were Protestants. Few of the names, here began with O'. Thirty children were born on the rock and a teacher sent over from the mainland to educate them. It must have been a harsh life. Storms and endless gales, always wet and cold, vulnerable to the ravages of illness and disease. She walks over to the tiny graveyard. A cluster of wind-blasted headstones stand around a flat slab.

To the memory of Patrick Callaghan who departed this life on 3rd December 1895 aged 2 years and 9 months. Also his beloved brother William who departed this life on 17th March 1899 aged 4 years and 9 months. May they rest in peace.

She imagines losing first one child and then the other to diphtheria or whooping cough. The last time she'd visited Paddy, after he'd come out of hospital, she'd stopped on her way down the mountain and climbed into the high field to explore the small stony area half-hidden in the grass. She'd read that this was a *Ceallúnaigh*. A children's burial ground. In medieval times babies and young children had been interred in separate plots, reflecting the Church's refusal to allow unbaptised infants to be laid to rest in consecrated ground. As she'd stumbled through the bog and reeds, she'd noticed the graves marked by low slabs without any decoration or inscription. In the dead of night, the male members of the family had carried their forlorn little bundles wrapped in sacking, to bury them without ceremony in this lonely sodden spot. The dead child hadn't been mourned or waked. Though a flowered china bowl or an earthenware dish was placed beside them in the grave. After the burial no one spoke of what had happened as the men trudged silently back up the hill in the moonless rain.

Most lives vanish into oblivion, don't they? The architect has his buildings, the composer his musical scores. The poet a few slim volumes gathering dust in the furthest reaches of some library. But for most what is there? An album of yellowing photographs. A swimming certificate or a silver cup. A stem of dried lavender caught between the pages of some favourite book. And, if we're lucky, a small space in someone's heart. She remembers a wildlife programme on TV. An elephant was mourning the loss of her calf fallen to a poacher's poison dart. Nothing was left but the skeleton. A mound of bones picked clean by jackals and vultures. The mother elephant circled slowly around and around the remains, running her trunk tenderly across their surface, as if breathing in the last of her offspring.

To live well is to pay attention to each moment. Here. Now. On this windswept needle of rock in the middle of the Atlantic. She listens to the call of the kittiwakes and the pounding waves on the rocks below.

Disappointment is linked to wanting things to be different, isn't it? Trying to change what can't be changed. But on this remote rock, high among the clouds, boundaries dissolve. She can feel the world breathing.

The tide echoing inside her. *In out, in out…* Who said: every story has a beginning, a middle and an end, just not necessarily in that order?

Mum, where do the stars go at night?

Nowhere, darling, they're always there, it's just that we can't see them when it's light.

4

She waits until no one's around, then unzips her rucksack. Surely the parents of those buried here wouldn't mind, would understand her need to lay her child to rest with theirs. What better place for Bruno to repose than on this holy island that so caught his imagination, in the company of other children, the puffins and shearwaters?

She places the photo from Brendan's desk on the flat stone. She's put it in a plastic envelope, which she weighs down with boulders so it has a fair chance of not being blown away by the wind, and thinks of the Jewish custom of placing stones on a grave as a sign of mourning. Then closing her eyes, she breathes in the salt wind and lets the silence of this wild place sink into her.

There. It's done. She has kept her promise. Today is the longest day of the year. Slowly she begins the difficult descent back down the steps to the pier and the waiting boat. She is the last to arrive. As she clambers on board the engine splutters into life and the boat pulls out to sea. Then, as she turns to take one last look at the strange rock, the sun breaks through the heavy bank of cloud, painting a silver pathway beneath the old sky.

I have relied on the voices of those born and bred in Ireland to express opinions about their own country and am grateful to the following sources:

Magnum Ireland, Brigitte Lardinois and Val Williams (editors), Thames & Hudson, 2005.

The Life of Riley, Anthony Cronin, Alfred A. Knopf, 1964.

Dead as Doornails, Anthony Cronin, Caldar and Boyars, 1976.

Tides of Change: Memories of a Kerry Childhood, John Curran, Curran Publishing, 2004.

Voices of Kerry—Conversations with Men and Women of Kerry, Jimmy Woulfe, Blackwater Press, 1994.

Puck Fair: History and Traditions, Michael Houlihan, Treaty Press, 1999.

Celtic Music: Third Ear—The Essential Listening Companion, Kenny Mathieson (ed.), Backbeat Books, 2001.

Lifetimes—Folklore from Kerry, Doghouse Books, 2007.

'Irishness is for other people', Terry Eagleton, *London Review of Books*, Vol. 34, No. 14, 19 July, 2012.

Sun Dancing: A Medieval Vision, Geoffrey Moorhouse, Phoenix, 1998.

The Laugh of Lost Men: An Irish Journey, Brian Lalor, Mainstream Publishing, 1997.

Why Not? Building a Better Ireland, Joe Mulholland (ed.), Joe Mulholland, 2003.

Acknowledgements

Thanks are due to Linda Rose Parkes, Jules Smith, Marianne Lewin, Judy Annan and Annie Wilson for their advice and suggestions. To Chris and Sarah Dyson for making available their lovely Suffolk cottage to work on the final draft and to Noelle Campbell Sharpe for inviting me on a number of residencies in Cill Rialaig, Kerry, which provided the background.

The lines of Colm's poem are from my poem: 'The Idea of Islands' from *The Forgetting and Remembering of Air* (Salt, 2013)